SECRETS OF THE DEADLY DOZEN

PETER BERRY

www.bloodhoundbooks.com

Print ISBN: 978-1-917705-29-5

For the Dreamers, wherever you may be.

1

'I now pronounce you, man and wife. You may kiss the bride.'
The elderly groom, stooped and wearing an oversized grey suit which slightly engulfed him, leant forwards gingerly and planted a tender kiss on his new wife's cheek.

Monica Lodhia, seated nearest the central aisle in the second pew on the right-hand side of the Harrow church, reached for the hand of her lover, Thomas Quinn, and gave it an enthusiastic squeeze. 'They make such a sweet couple,' she whispered as spontaneous applause erupted around the nave, echoing across the high beams and filling the chapels.

'Our turn next,' said Thomas, his words equal parts statement and question. He lifted Monica's left hand and gently kissed the ring with its pale-green beryl jewel which he had given her around a month earlier on the anniversary of their first October meeting just over a year before. She had decided to wear it on her engagement finger although both of them had been clear with each other that there was no pressing necessity to rush these things. That they were together for the long term was plainly obvious. Monica had quoted Joni Mitchell's line that they had no need of a piece of paper from the city hall to keep them tied and true. Of course, she had then been required to play Joni's *Blue* album to Thomas in full as he had inexplicably never heard it during his sixty-nine relatively sheltered years.

Monica clasped his face and kissed him lightly on the mouth. 'Next year,' she purred, gazing lovingly into his eyes. 'Assuming we get the time. Our schedule is... annoyingly prone to unexpected changes.' She turned and smiled broadly at the other guests along the pew and behind, the other ten disparate individuals comprising the secret group known as The Twelve whose role, whose duty even, was to assassinate London's criminals without detection. The Twelve were their friends. Their gang.

Just ahead in the front pew, half a dozen members of Mehmet Durak's immediate circle had managed to fly over from Turkey to be with him on his special day; his younger brother, Altan, and his wife, Basak, plus a couple of their grown-up children. In addition, there were two friends from Mehmet's time in the Turkish police force, both in their seventies and both visiting London for the first time.

Further back on the right-hand side of the church was a small but lively contingent from the local Bulgarian community whom Mehmet had befriended following his activities during one of The Twelve's cases the previous winter, plus a smattering of people he had met at a chess club which he had joined during the summer. This underpopulated side of the church contained perhaps thirty people at most.

The left-hand side, conversely, was packed to the rafters with Doreen Archer's extended family and friends, including her eight children and nineteen grandchildren, two of whom were babies. Neither of the babies had cried during the wedding ceremony, to everyone's relief, although one of them did exclaim, 'BAAAA!' at the top of her voice at the precise moment that the vicar asked whether anyone knew of any just impediment why Mehmet and Doreen should not be wed. The priest, a jovial man in his sixties, had taken this untimely exclamation in good humour. 'You wish to make a statement of objection, young lady?' He had said with a smile, peering towards the infant over his half-moon spectacles. The baby beamed back and giggled. 'I thought not. Then with your approval, we may continue.'

'You're coming to the reception?' Mehmet asked Monica as he shuffled his way slowly down the aisle, arm in arm with the new Mrs Durak, who was resplendent in a light-blue dress and matching hat. Monica confirmed that everyone would be there. Everyone except Lexington Smith, the octogenarian former leader of The Twelve who was still in a private hospital recovering from a variety of medical mishaps over the previous few weeks which were delaying his return home, much to the old man's obvious irritation. 'Excellent,' Mehmet replied. 'We're taking a car but it's only ten minutes' walk for you spritely young folk.' Mehmet winked and continued on his unsteady way towards the church entrance with his glowing bride.

'I guess we're walking,' said retired pathologist, Anna Hopley. 'I'm glad I didn't wear heels.'

'I bloody did.' Former TV presenter Veronica Madison frowned miserably. 'They were a sixtieth birthday present and I assumed I wouldn't get the opportunity to give them a proper showing until spring but then this wedding came up suddenly and I thought why not? Martin, any chance of a lift in the taxi please?' The cabbie smiled and said that he could happily accommodate four for the short journey to the hotel where

Mehmet and Doreen's reception would be held, complete with a half-hour set by a traditional Turkish band based in Pinner.

Veronica, along with Anna, former journalist Catherine Daniels and retired surgeon Chris Tinker piled into the cab and set sail in the direction of the reception. The remaining seven – Monica and Thomas as well as plumber David Latham, locksmith Terry Wilson, former police chief Graham Best and his partner Owen Pook, ex-intelligence officer, and linguist Belinda Olorenshaw – began the short journey on foot.

'May we walk with you please?' asked one of the Bulgarian guests, a young woman whom Monica recognised as Mirela, the first member of the Balkan community that The Twelve had encountered earlier in the year while they were formulating a plan to catch a serial killer on the London Underground. After an inauspicious start, the Bulgarians had been instrumental in the ultimate success of the operation.

'Of course,' said Belinda, giving her a warm hug and turning to embrace Nikola, a tall, imposing man who had been the second Bulgarian to make their acquaintance. 'A light stroll will do us good and at least it's not raining.' She opened a palm just to check that an ominous dark cloud wasn't about to unleash an apocalyptic deluge upon them. 'And it's quite mild for the end of November. Anyway, how have you both been since March? Your English has improved enormously, Mirela.'

As they slowly descended the hill away from the church, Monica and Thomas hand in hand as the others formed a haphazard cortège of twos side by side, the young woman explained that following their adventures the previous winter, and after one of her community was stabbed, luckily not fatally by a serial killer target of The Twelve, she had taken stock of her life and decided to pivot away from begging on the London Underground and into something a bit less legally dubious. With Nikola's help, she had enrolled in an intensive

English course and now worked as a receptionist at a local gym.

'I am always happy to assist with the hopes and dreams of my people,' announced Nikola proudly to the group. 'Plus I get free gym membership so is all good. By the way,' he wiped a threatening reconnaissance raindrop from his forehead, 'we all have umbrellas if we need them. You'd be surprised how many of the things you can pick up on the Underground. People are so forgetful.'

Monica and Thomas exchanged a look.

'Also,' said Mirela, 'I am living in Mehmet's house with Dimo and Ivo.' She pointed to the two brothers who waved enthusiastically from a few metres behind. 'Mehmet is basically living at Mrs Archer's... sorry, at his wife's house now, so there is plenty of space. Don't worry. We are keeping it very tidy. We have even made friends with the neighbours. I sometimes babysit for a couple of the families in our road. We told Lexington and he gave his blessing. Is he any better, by the way?'

Thomas explained that their former leader had had a bit of a run of bad luck health-wise but that he was hoping to be back at home for the new year or thereabouts. 'So if you've been living in Mehmet's house,' he mused, 'then you must know all the juicy details about his courtship of Doreen. All we really know is that we all got an invite to this wedding about three weeks ago and here we are.'

Mirela beamed so broadly that her entire face illuminated. It had apparently been very sudden and actually very sweet. Doreen had been on her own for a few years and had attempted the dating apps without success. Being in her mid-seventies, the men to whom she was chatting didn't really measure up with regards to the romance she required. Mehmet, on the other hand, was an old-school gentleman who was kind and interesting and simply needed a bit of looking after. He wasn't into any hanky-panky, as she called it. He just wanted a cuddle and some home cooking, two essentials which she was more than happy to provide.

By June, they were meeting up and chatting daily. By September he had pretty much taken up residence in her house. Then, on Halloween, he asked her to marry him. Doreen knew the local vicar, so she called him to ask when the church might be free and, by chance, it was the end of November.

'Pretty spontaneous.' Monica grinned, lightly squeezing Thomas's bottom as the reception venue came into view and everyone broke into a light canter as the quantity of raindrops increased steadily. 'I like that.'

The walking party was just crossing the threshold into the hotel when the heavens opened.

2

'I'm absolutely flipping stuffed,' announced Terry, attempting with futility to rein in his stomach with his hands. In addition to his ninja locksmith skills, Terry also doubled as The Twelve's resident kitchen genius, his cakes and biscuits regularly fuelling the group's planning meetings whenever an assassination case was in progress. 'I never knew Turkish food could be so delicious. I'll definitely be trying out a few of these recipes over the holidays, I can tell you. I've already befriended the catering people.'

He was seated at a large round table in the corner of what the hotel had named The Cannon Suite alongside ex-plumber David Latham, who was equally sated, and Veronica whose feet were suffering discomfort after too much dancing in unbroken-in shoes which she was now sensibly carrying. 'That squid dish, the kalamar or something,' Terry continued. 'That was incredible. So soft yet crispy at the same time. Amazing. And the spiced flatbreads, my goodness.' He licked his lips, took a sip of water followed by a generous swig of fruity red wine and slumped back into his seat, finally surrendering in the battle with his belly.

Mehmet's and Doreen's wedding reception had been exquisite, particularly considering that it had been somewhat cobbled together in a matter of weeks. The Turkish band, Super Baglama, had proven to be extremely popular and had, for £500 in cash which Nikola had spontaneously donated as a wedding gift, agreed to play a much longer set than their allocated half hour because the guests loved their music so much. Even Mehmet had managed to wave his arms around to a couple of songs, supported on each side by Doreen and Chris.

'I'm exhausted,' breathed Owen as he staggered over to the table arm in arm with Graham. Catherine, who had been dancing with them for most of the evening, collapsed into a chair, exhilarated yet weary. 'But such great music. It reminds me of a holiday I had back in the nineties in a little resort near Bodrum.' He kissed Graham and then turned to Catherine and kissed her too. 'Shall we carry on this party later at our house?' The ex-journalist grinned approvingly.

'Funny being in a church again,' mused Terry. 'I can't remember the last time I was in a church. Irene's funeral, I suppose. That'll be over ten years ago. Blimey. And me, a certified celebrant.'

'You're joking. Really?' said David in surprise. 'Since when?'

'About ten years. After my wife died, I read a thing in the paper about how there was a shortage of qualified celebrants and I thought it might be an interesting thing to do, so I did a course and got a licence. Then, of course, I got the call from Lexington to join The Twelve and so I put it on the back burner but I still keep the registration updated because you never know what's going to happen.'

Veronica bent down and rubbed an aching foot. 'I'm quite fond of a church,' she said, grimacing slightly. 'We used to visit quite a few when Lauren, my partner, was alive. Not because either of us had any particular firm beliefs or anything but more because they're beautiful buildings. Very peaceful just to sit in one and reflect from time to time. You don't have to believe in God to enjoy a bit of tranquil reflection in a place of worship.'

'Unless they're full of tourists,' grumbled Owen. 'Are you at all religious, David?'

The ex-plumber reached for his glass of wine and took a long sip. 'No,' he stated succinctly. 'I used to be. In my younger years. I studied the Bible extensively when I was a child back in Trinidad. But when you lose your young wife and daughter in childbirth, I think you can go one of two ways. Either you can accept that the Lord works in a mysterious way and that somehow concentrates your faith. Or you can go in the opposite direction because you can't understand why a loving God would allow such a terrible thing to happen. I trod the latter path.'

'I'm so sorry,' said Veronica, a tear making its gentle way down her nose. She had learnt much about David's life story, along with everyone else's, since joining The Twelve back in May, but it still managed to affect her.

'What are we talking about?' asked Martin who had stumbled gracefully off of the dance floor with Belinda, Monica and Thomas. The four of them had been learning a simple Bulgarian folk dance with Mirela as their makeshift teacher. Those who had met her before all agreed that the transformation from sullen, professional beggar into radiant, confident young woman was something of a revelation.

'Religion,' said Terry, disconsolately. 'My fault. I started it.'

'Keeping it light then,' said Monica, smiling. 'What have you all concluded so far?'

'My opinion, for what it's worth,' said Owen wryly, 'echoes the view of St Augustine of Hippo, who said, "Lord, give me chastity and temperance. But not yet". Personally, I've always found the restrictive nature of religion off-putting.' He glanced knowingly at first Graham and then Catherine. 'I know Catherine agrees, even though she's the only actual semi-regular churchgoer among us.'

The former journalist drained her glass of wine purposefully and explained that she simply found solace in the peaceful community of the local church near her home in Barnes. Her priest, Father Matthew, was in his fifties and had been a good friend for over twenty years. He had been a particular comfort when her long-term boyfriend, a war photographer, had been killed in the Middle East in 2003. 'Additionally,' she said, 'he's not one of these judgemental types, so when I go into the confessional box with him after we've killed someone, we talk and he understands. Then he performs absolution and we pray together and afterwards we can have a good natter. It's a friendship thing for me more than anything, as well as helping my mental health. Mrs Mendoza finds it fascinating.'

'You confess after we've killed someone?' asked Veronica with a degree of mild alarm.

The journalist nodded. 'Uh-huh. He's not exactly going to tell anyone. It's confidential, the confessional box. Secrets stay secret. It's the best way,' she said with a wink. 'As we all know.'

'Will you feel the need to confess tomorrow after you've spent a devilish night at our place?' asked Owen with a casual wink of his own. Catherine laughed and revealed that it had only been a couple of months since her last confession following the assassination at the end of the last case, and that Father Matthew didn't necessarily need to be aware of *every* sin she committed. She didn't want to overload the poor man with her myriad transgressions.

Chris and Anna finally dragged themselves away from the dancing and plonked themselves onto the remaining chairs around the table, Anna leaning on the surgeon's uninjured shoulder. Chris looked around at the eleven intense faces. 'This looks oddly familiar,' he said. 'We could have a meeting if we had a case to discuss.'

'We're on religion,' explained Veronica. 'It's enlightening.'

Chris sighed and placed his head in his hands, lowering them onto the table.

'Personally,' said Monica, 'I don't think there's anything wrong with a bit of religion in your life. For a lot of people, it's absolutely crucial for their well-being. Most religions have the same basic messages of peace and community and doing good things, and that's an excellent way to live your life. I think all of us around this table would slip fairly seamlessly into the perfect ideal image of a "good" Christian or a "good" Muslim whether we believe or not.'

'Apart from the sporadic and meticulously planned assassinating,' muttered Chris through his hands.

'Yes, obviously,' said Monica with mild exasperation. 'But where I have a problem is with the small, noisy minority in most religions who seem to think that it's their sworn duty to interpret their chosen holy book in a certain way that causes harm to others. Live and let live as far as I'm concerned. As long as you're not hurting anyone else and in those cases I tend to subscribe to the McCartney doctrine.'

'Live and let die,' sang Anna, waving her free arm in the air.

'I've never met a Muslim that I didn't like,' agreed David. 'It's a religion of peace with beautiful and welcoming people.'

'Completely,' said Monica. 'And yet you get a tiny number who pick and choose a few verses and use them to justify all sorts of atrocities. You get the same in Christianity.'

'Unless you repent,' quoted Chris, lifting his head ominously from the table, 'you will all likewise perish.'

'Luke, chapter thirteen, verse three,' said David.

'Precisely,' said Chris grimly.

Thomas suddenly gave a wave to a couple of Doreen's children whom he had befriended and who were leaving the party to get home at a reasonable hour. 'What about Hinduism?' he asked, curious. He knew that Monica had a very selective relationship with her own religion.

'Also based on peace and spirituality, charity and generosity,' said Monica. 'But don't get me started on Hindu nationalism because, again, it's using religious messaging for entirely the wrong reasons. You just end up with greed and aggression and fear and that's not right.'

'Blessed are those who hunger and thirst for righteousness,' said Chris, 'for they shall be satisfied.'

'Matthew, chapter five, verse six,' said David.

Catherine gazed, open-mouthed at the two men. 'How on earth do you know the scripture so well? It's incredible if slightly creepy.'

'Taught by nuns,' said David nonchalantly, finishing his glass of wine.

'Same,' said Chris, who reached across the table to fist-bump the ex-plumber. 'But very much lapsed from the path of faith and righteousness.'

'Any particular reason for the lapse?' asked Catherine after she too had drained a glass.

Chris sighed. 'There's a long answer involving a turbulent priest but the shorter and simpler answer is science. As you know, I'm not merely a man of medicine. I have more than a passing interest in geology, astronomy, palaeontology, genetics, chemistry and physics. There's little room for the illogical superstitions of organised religion I'm afraid. Nonetheless, I consider myself a pro-faith atheist. That's to say, I'm all for people believing what they want as long as it doesn't negatively impact anyone else.'

'Anyone fancy another quick drink before we leave?' asked

Terry. 'It looks like this is drawing very slowly to a close. Even the Bulgarians are looking like packing it in.' Across the room, Nikola and Mirela were ostentatiously hugging the happy couple while Ivo and Dimo were gathering up the umbrellas as the rain had become progressively harder throughout the evening judging by the noise on the roof of the hall.

A smattering of hands went up. 'I'll grab another bottle between the twelve of us,' said the locksmith. 'And then we can seamlessly move on to politics.'

A few miles to the south, in the candlelight of his bedroom, Catherine's priest, Father Matthew, was in turmoil, his finger hovering over Catherine's number in his phone, uncertain what horror might be unleashed if he made the call.

3

M onica placed a fresh cappuccino on a coaster and opened her laptop the following morning with a slightly fuzzy head. Amongst the usual light blizzard of marketing emails from companies helpfully reminding her once again that Christmas was approaching at dizzying speed, there were four which looked interesting, unusual for a Sunday.

The first was from Bobby City, The Twelve's mildly terrifying but miraculously efficient administrative fixer. She had outlined in a few short, compact paragraphs that Monica's secret donation to save a children's hospice in Kent from closure had been finalised. Bobby had also attached a link to a story in the local newspaper which featured a photograph of delighted staff and children celebrating with cake and lemonade. According to the manager, Hannah Frost, the mystery donation would not only fund the hospice for the next ten years at least but would also allow them to complete some much-needed refurbishment to several of the family rooms and also fit some new equipment to assist some of the more poorly residents with day-to-day activities. *It's a Christmas miracle*, read Hannah's quote in the article.

Whoever has done this wonderful thing is truly going to heaven.

Monica smiled to herself and glanced over at her cello which was leaning against the wall in the darkest corner of the room away from direct sunlight. *Perhaps some Brahms later*, she thought. *Take it for a leisurely spin around Johannes' first sonata.*

Bobby's email ended with a reminder that she still needed to book in a first meeting with the banking and investment manager, Mr Wheeler. Monica had been meaning to arrange a face-to-face chat since ascending to the role of leader back in May but had failed to do so. Bobby suggested that it might be prudent to rectify this sooner rather than later as The Twelve's annual bonuses were due to be finalised before Christmas. She floated a couple of dates, both in the following two weeks. Monica replied, thanking Bobby for all of her help and confirming that either date would be acceptable.

Terry's email, sent at 6.07am that morning, was simply an update on a couple of potential Twelve recruits whom he was monitoring. All of The Twelve apart from Veronica were casually observing one or more people with a view to a handful of them ultimately joining the group as and when vacancies arose. Terry was watching an IT security expert who was shaping up to be a reasonably good option for The Twelve on her retirement a couple of years in the future. In addition, the locksmith had been keeping an eye on a musician who had had a mittenful of hit singles in the 1980s but had been relatively inactive since. The email relayed news that the musician was planning to emigrate to Canada after the new year and marry a thirty-five-year-old woman he'd met on a dating site. On many levels, this would somewhat put the kibosh on his chances of joining The Twelve as Terry's message suggested.

There were two emails remaining, twinkling in the semi-darkness like sunrise planets. Monica rose from her desk and padded quietly over to the corridor leading to her bedroom to see whether Thomas was stirring. He wasn't. He often slept later than she did, particularly as the depths of winter approached. Perhaps he had been a hibernating creature in a previous life, she mused, as she walked back to the remaining messages, one of which she was deliberately stalling until last.

The subject of Suzanne Green's email was simply *This Week*. The Metropolitan Police Commissioner was using email more often these days as her workload had increased considerably since the summer. *Dearest Monica*, it read. *I was going to call this email Don't Panic but then I knew that such a title would doubtless have the opposite effect so... anyway, just to let you know that a news story will break in the* Sunday Times *tomorrow (today, probably by the time you read this) claiming that I'm for the chop. Apparently there is a group of right wing Tories who are putting growing pressure on the Home Secretary to replace me with one of their favoured 'hard men' (sic). They're suggesting that the recent scandals and mishaps have resulted in a general lack of confidence in my leadership and that I should either step down or be forced out.*

Needless to say that I've been through this crap (technical term!) before and I'm in constant touch with the Home Secretary who maintains full confidence in me, or so he says. Nonetheless, it's a slightly worrying time and I shall need to keep fully focused until it blows over. Luckily there is no current Twelve case, as far as I'm aware, on which we need to devote time. If there is, or if one crops up any day soon, I might have to be a bit less hands-on than usual. I hope you understand.

I remain here for The Twelve as you have been there for me. I'm sure this storm in a teacup will be behind us before long. If I get a whiff of it becoming more troublesome, I will of course let you know. As ever, Suzanne x

That's a worry, thought Monica. Suzanne had been hugely

supportive of The Twelve's work and the last thing they needed was a change at the top of the Met, particularly if it was going to be someone more challenging to work with. The term 'hard men' didn't exactly fill The Twelve's leader with confidence. Monica responded with a brief, supportive email and suggested that if Suzanne ever required a friendly ear or a safe place to have a drink and a chat, she knew where to find it.

She drained her coffee and pondered whether to make another before opening the final email, knowing that by doing so Monica was simply procrastinating. *Grasp the nettle*, she thought. *It can't be that bad.*

The email was from Clare Lashone-Brown, a member of The Twelve in New York with whom Monica had enjoyed a long night of surprisingly enjoyable passion in September 2016 on one of the very occasional visits that members of Twelve NYC made to London. The subject box contained simply the portentous word, *News.*

Emails from Clare were uncommon, on average appearing once or twice a year, if that. They were always friendly but equally they always subtly reminded Monica of the intensity of that night they spent together. Just seeing Clare's name gave her involuntary goosebumps. The previous email had been in May on Monica's elevation to the top of The Twelve. It had been full of congratulations and love. Monica responded with a long and informative message touching on the Burrows case as well as her blossoming relationship with Thomas.

She clicked on the new email with trepidation.

Girlfriend, it read, shouting its contents from across the ocean. *How are you doing? How's Thomas? Great, I hope. And the rest of your crazy crew. Is Lexington OK? I hear he's still out of action. He keeps me updated but I don't think he tells me everything, you know? And tell me about that last case. It sounds*

17

explosive. This line was followed by three flame emojis for added effect.

Anyway, just a quick note to give you the joyful news that I am now the proud leader of Twelve NYC. Joshua decided to quit suddenly last week as he had to go into hospital for a hip replacement and he didn't feel up to all the Twelve activity especially as his likely recovery time is about nine months. He suggested I take the reins and everyone else agreed. A bloodless coup on the banks of the Hudson. Now how about that?

So, we got two girls running The Twelve now. It's about time. Are you working on anything right now? We had to abandon a case a few months back because the subject disappeared up to Canada and I ain't following nobody up there, especially at this time of year. It's cold enough in Manhattan. But since last month we've been working on a project with a guy that's defrauding charities out of millions of dollars and that'll reach its natural conclusion in mid-January, if you know what I mean. The axe will fall. Not literally. Too darn messy.

We should Zoom soon. Can we do that? It would be great to see your pretty face. Love you. Clare x.

Monica stared at the screen, goosebumps multiplying. Was the heating off or something? Clearly Canada was the place to be, she thought distractedly.

Thomas ambled sleepily into the living room, wandered over to Monica and kissed the top of her head. 'Everything okay?' he asked, not looking at her computer screen.

'Everything's fine,' Monica replied unconvincingly. 'I could probably do with another coffee though.'

4

Across the city to the east, Owen returned to the master bedroom just after 11am with a tray of three decaf coffees to find Graham and Catherine partially under the covers of the king-size bed, giggling and looking sheepish like teenagers concealing cigarettes. 'What did I miss?' he asked with a suspicious smile.

'How long have we been doing this with Catherine?' asked Graham. Owen replied that it was a couple of years that they had been indulging in occasional threesomes with the former editor and journalist, the first time after a select party to celebrate her two-year anniversary as part of The Twelve. 'I thought so. And yet somehow I've only just discovered that she's ticklish.' He disappeared under the duvet and began gently attacking Catherine's sides, eliciting more giggles and half-hearted pleas for clemency.

Owen carefully placed the tray on a window table in the couple's spacious house a short walk from Finsbury Park. 'Delighted that you were busy on important matters during my absence,' he said, removing his dressing gown and slipping back into the bed to calibrate Catherine's levels of ticklishness for himself. Five minutes later, he extracted himself from the tangle of limbs and bedding and brought the coffees nearer to the bed before they got cold.

'Interesting conversation last night,' he said, delicately sipping and then gulping a mouthful having decided its temperature was perfect. 'I very much admire your position on religion, Catherine. Balancing your faith with what I can only describe as an entirely sensible and occasionally hedonistic attitude to life.'

The former editor reached over Graham, kissing him en route, and picked up her own mug while he took the opportunity to give her bottom a playful slap. 'I think you can be non-religious and be a good person, like you both, and then equally you can be a devout believer and be an absolute monster.' She drank half of her coffee and squeezed Owen's thigh. 'I suppose I'm lucky to have a priest like Father Matthew who isn't too judgemental. He's a rarity in this day and age.'

'Why do you call him by his Christian name?' asked Owen. 'In my day, which admittedly was the sixties, it was always Father O'Reilly and Canon Griffiths.'

'He prefers Father Matthew,' replied Catherine, and then paused, uncertain whether to reveal further detail. 'His surname is Christmas so, you see...'

Graham almost spat out his mouthful of coffee. 'You are kidding! His surname is Christmas and he became a priest? That's fantastic.'

'I know,' said Catherine, defensively, 'but you can see why he prefers Father Matthew. And he's a lovely man, so I won't hear a bad word said about him. Anyway, what time do you want to chuck me out?'

Graham replied that she was welcome to stay as long as she liked as they had no urgent plans. In fact, he suggested, as they were all getting a second, caffeinated wind, it wouldn't be a bad idea to continue their activities from the previous night before maybe having a nap together, after which he could drive her back to her home in Barnes.

———

Just before three in the afternoon, they were awoken by Catherine's mobile. 'I'll pass it to you,' mumbled Owen drowsily. He glanced at the screen as he picked it up. 'It's Father Christmas,' he said, stifling a laugh. 'Sorry, I mean Father Matthew.' The phone stopped ringing.

'That's unusual,' said Catherine. 'He hardly ever rings me. He must have heard us talking about him.' Her phone pinged to indicate that the man of the cloth had left a message which was short but requested Catherine to please call him back on a matter of urgency. 'Have you got a dressing gown I can borrow?' she asked. 'It somehow doesn't seem appropriate to be naked when talking to a priest, even if it is by phone.' Graham lent her his black towelling robe and she wandered to an armchair by the window table to make the call.

Father Matthew picked up almost immediately and apologised for disturbing whatever Catherine had been doing. Her eyes drifted towards the two naked men kissing in the bed on the other side of the room and explained to the priest that she wasn't doing anything that couldn't wait. 'I wouldn't normally call,' he said, anxiously, 'but as you know, I'm aware of your secret life, as it were, from our delightful conversations in the confessional box, and I wondered whether I might request your help. I don't want it to end in an assassination, particularly. I suspect the good Lord would take a dim view of such a grisly outcome. And yet I've been wrestling with a problem for a few weeks now and I fear that something will need to be done.'

Catherine listened intently for around ten minutes before

arranging to meet with Father Matthew the following morning at the Church of the Immaculate Virgin in Barnes.

'Everything all right?' asked Owen. Catherine remained seated and outlined the bones of her conversation. There had been two murders in his parish since the end of the summer, apparently unconnected. The police had been seemingly investigating both but progress had been slow and they had so far made no arrests. The first victim had been an openly gay librarian named Liam Tucker who had been attacked with a knife on his way home from an evening event. The morning after the murder Father Matthew had found a Bible open on his altar with a verse underlined in red. He had thought nothing of it at the time. Then, the previous Wednesday many weeks after the Tucker murder, a local prostitute, Kathy De Souza, had been found dead from knife wounds in a flat in Mortlake which had been set alight in a partially successful attempt to destroy evidence.

Again, the priest had found a Bible open on his altar with a passage underlined. The text, from the gospel according to Matthew, read, *His winnowing fork is in his hand and he will clear his threshing floor and gather his wheat into the barn, but the chaff he will burn with unquenchable fire.*

Father Matthew had then spent two days trying to locate the Bible from the first attack, finally locating it in one of the rear pews of the church. The text underlined on this occasion had been from Paul's letter to the Romans and it read, *And the men likewise gave up natural relations with women and were consumed with passion for one another, men committing shameless acts with men and receiving in themselves the due penalty for their error.* Reading this had sent a chill through the priest which had led him to consider contacting Catherine.

'I rather fear,' the priest had concluded, 'that the killer may be hiding amongst my own flock.'

5

While Thomas was navigating the coffee machine, Monica responded as warmly as she felt necessary to the email from New York. Her message updated Clare on the previous case, covered the basics of Lexington's health issues and promised to set up a Zoom before Christmas, although Monica knew full well that in reality the first twenty-four days of December would rattle past at an unusually high velocity even though there was mercifully no Twelve case pending.

'Fancy coming to see the bank manager with me on Thursday?' she asked as Thomas gently placed a fresh cappuccino on her desk.

'Sounds good,' he replied. 'Should I wear a suit?' Thomas wasn't entirely sure of the last time he wore a suit to anything other than weddings and funerals but there was sure to be an appropriately businesslike tie back at his own house in Notting Hill and, even if there wasn't, he could probably borrow one from another member of the group. Monica reassured him that the meeting was almost certainly informal and was really just to introduce herself in person to Mr Wheeler and finalise the traditional Christmas bonus payments. 'We can talk to

Lexington about it when we see him this afternoon. He might have some insights. Which bank is it, by the way? Any of the ones I'd have heard of?'

Monica swigged the cappuccino thirstily. 'It's called Toast,' she replied. 'The bank. It's quite boutique.' *Of course it is*, thought Thomas. *Why would a secret organisation of elderly assassins have financial dealings with anyone run-of-the-mill like NatWest or Midland or whatever that was called these days?*

The two of them showered together, as had become their norm, and spent a leisurely morning reading the papers before they were due to visit Lexington. The news story which Suzanne had mentioned in her email was indeed fairly damaging and the situation was not helped by one of a new breed of populist government ministers, mostly but not exclusively male, who had written a scathing and mildly misogynist comment article about her leadership for a right wing online news site. *Poor Suzanne,* thought Monica. *After all she's given to the force over the years.* It felt like the political hyenas were circling a wounded lioness, patiently awaiting their moment.

After lunch, Monica and Thomas jumped in a taxi to the private hospital in Belgravia to find Lexington in a slightly downbeat mood. The arrival of visitors lifted him considerably, although it was clear that his continued enforced incarceration was taking its toll.

'It's one beastly thing after another,' he bemoaned. 'The urinary tract infection cleared up but then they found some polyps in my colon which apparently are a concern and there's also a heart issue which has been brewing for a little while. Chris did mention something a couple of years ago during a medical but said it shouldn't be too troublesome but now, of course, with all this inactivity, it's become more of a worry. And this blasted knee still isn't quite right.' He placed his hands on the sides of his bed and used his upper body strength to scale his way gently up the escarpment of pillows behind him. 'It's pretty much downhill after about eighty,' he mused. 'And at speed, like that winter Olympic sport; what's it called? The luge.'

There were, nonetheless, some small advantages to being in hospital. The constant procession of delightful company, organised methodically by Monica and Bobby City so that there was never a day without something to look forward to, plus a regular supply of books to read, some old favourites and some newly published – 'I hear there's a new Marian Keyes coming in March so that's exciting, although I hope I won't still be stuck here by then, of course.'

Thomas enquired about the latest news regarding Lexington's likelihood of getting home. The old man revealed that Christmas would be a bit of a stretch but that, if nothing unusual happened in the interim, then early January was a distinct possibility; a target to be aimed for. 'Clare sends her love, by the way,' said Monica as matter-of-factly as she could. 'From New York. She's the leader there now, did you hear?'

Lexington had indeed received a message from Clare as well as a series of emails from the former stateside leader, Joshua Auslander, who had taken to sharing daily updates on his own health. 'I remember Clare from her visit in, when was it, 2016 or thereabouts. Delightful woman. Extremely beautiful as I recall. Monica, didn't you end up...?' He shot a worried look in Thomas's direction. 'Never mind.'

'Don't worry,' said Thomas. 'I know about the night with Clare. Monica told me on one of our first Tube journeys this time last year. I was a bit shell-shocked back then but I've learnt to expect surprises now. Do you think she might come over again? Now she's leader?'

Monica said that although a visit wasn't on the cards, Clare had suggested a Zoom call might be appropriate. 'I'll probably set something up in the new year,' she said. 'We're unlikely to get a new case this close to Christmas so it's probably better to wait until we have some work stuff to chat about. Anyway,' Monica was scampering furiously towards a clearing where she could change the subject, 'have you seen this nonsense in the paper about Suzanne?'

As usual, Lexington had not only seen all of the relevant Sunday newspapers but had already been in text contact with the under-fire police commissioner. 'I sent her a note this morning along the lines of Don't Let The Bastards Grind You Down and she returned with the most glorious and hilarious text about how she planned to face down all this stupidness. She's a fighter, that one. I've asked Catherine to see if she can do anything to gently influence some of her old newspaper chums. She did seem rather distracted this morning but then I'm told Mehmet's wedding was a jolly affair so maybe the dear woman was simply in recovery. I was so sad to miss it.'

Monica and Thomas, knowing that Catherine had left the reception in a taxi with her two sometime male lovers, shared a glance which told Lexington everything he needed to know.

'There was a Lexington-shaped hole in the proceedings,' said Monica sadly. 'By the way, I've got a belated first meeting with Mr Wheeler later in the week. Any tips for me?'

Lexington reached for a bottle of water which was positioned on his side table. 'James Wheeler is one of the most brilliant yet unusual people I've ever met,' he said with a frown. 'And I've met a few. I hung out with Jack Kerouac for a while in the early sixties, for goodness' sake. We used to play cards with a group of friendly Cubans who had escaped to Florida. Wonderful people. Better at cards than poor old Jack. All I'll say about James is that whatever you're expecting from a bank manager, he certainly won't be that. But send him my love.'

Monica promised that she would before giving Lexington a farewell hug. She and Thomas stepped back into the fading Belgravia light just after three while Father Matthew was simultaneously ending his call with Catherine. Usually for a Sunday afternoon, he poured himself a brandy and gave quiet thanks that there was no evening mass, certain that his nerves wouldn't be in a state to perform it.

6

The elegant colour symphony of autumn had receded into a solemn dirge of brown and yellow as Catherine made her way towards the Church of the Immaculate Virgin. It had been built in the 1850s on the site of an earlier place of worship which had been destroyed during the Reformation three centuries before. Designed in the decorated Gothic style, the building was quietly impressive and boasted stained-glass windows which were mentioned in many guides to the churches of England for their quality and craftsmanship.

Father Matthew was seated alone at the end of a mid-church pew as Catherine quietly made her way up the aisle, genuflecting to the crucifix as she reached him. A shortish man with receding dark hair and an unruly greying beard, he stood with ease and embraced her warmly. 'Thank you for coming, Catherine,' he said. 'And I'm sorry to trouble you with this unfortunate business. It simply occurred to me that you might know what to do. Because of your retirement hobby, as it were.' It was clear that the priest was overcome with anxiety.

He had not spoken of his concerns to the police, Matthew explained over a cup of tea in the vestry, because of what happened at the same church twelve years earlier. 'You may remember,' he began, 'a Father O'Driscoll who had to return to Ireland under something of a cloud when a couple of teenage boys claimed he had asked to take, how can I put this, illicit photographs of them in the graveyard.' Catherine replied that she had indeed been aware and, in fact, had secretly assisted in keeping the story out of the national papers, although a local news website had posted something at the time. Father Matthew recalled this. 'Of course,' he said. 'I had forgotten. Forgive me. Many thanks again for your help on that occasion. I suppose I didn't know you quite as well as I do now. We had fewer discussions in the confessional box under our belts back then, largely on account of you having somewhat less to confess.'

The police had briefly visited the church following the murder of Liam Tucker but only really to see whether the librarian had been a regular attendee. He hadn't. Although Father Matthew did vaguely recognise his face, possibly from the odd appearance at the Christmas Day service. 'We generally get a full house on the Lord's birthday. People enjoy the festive familiarity of the carols.'

Matthew had spent a few minutes chatting amiably with a couple of uniformed officers while the inner turmoil raged within him. 'It's about a third full generally, although slightly fuller of late. There's been an influx of energy to the congregation in recent months, you see.'

According to the priest, a young and enthusiastic American youth worker named Elijah Timothy had arrived at the church in June and had offered to help with the associated youth group which was then run by a music teacher named Robert Henderson. The two men didn't always see eye to eye regarding their approach to spreading the teachings of Jesus but they had nonetheless managed to reach some kind of détente and, Matthew believed, a mutual respect.

'In what sense do they not see eye to eye?' asked Catherine, her journalist's curiosity antenna twitching. The priest explained that while Robert, who was in his forties, preferred to attract and work with the children and grandchildren of existing parishioners, Elijah, who was in his late twenties, had been more focused on attracting local young people in care or from foster homes. He had been hugely successful in this approach with at least thirty new faces appearing in church since July, often in more colourful and casual clothes than the pressed trousers and shirts worn by the kids of the parishioners.

'They tend to sit together at the back with Robert but they're very well-behaved. And they often come up to me after service and ask questions about my sermon. Some of them only come for a few weeks and then disappear back to their lives but the majority stick around.'

'Does this Elijah chap not sit with them?' asked Catherine, intrigued. Father Matthew explained that Elijah was sadly unable to attend Sunday mass because he had to look after his sick mother. Apparently they had daily care from health visitors from Monday to Saturday but on the Lord's day, it was Elijah's duty to provide for his parent. According to Elijah, his mother had dual citizenship which meant she could qualify for NHS care, part of the reason why the two of them had relocated from the States where her medical bills were apparently spiralling.

There was a knock on the vestry door. 'Come in,' muttered Father Matthew through a gulp of tea. An extraordinary face with bright-blue eyes, a model's geometric cheekbones and spiky black hair appeared. Catherine took a double take. It was one of the most beautiful male faces she had ever seen. 'Elijah!' said the priest. 'Your ears must have been aflame. We were just talking about you. Can I introduce my dear friend, Catherine

Daniels. She used to be a top journalist but she's retired now and lives a much less exciting life.'

Catherine stood and reached out her hand to the visitor but Elijah pulled her smoothly into a hug, something she found oddly reassuring, like being welcomed into the most comfortable blanket, albeit quite a muscular one. Elijah's stubble caressed her cheek and he emitted the most alluring smell.

'Sister Catherine,' exhaled Elijah slowly and quietly, eyes sparkling like azure. 'Any friend of Matthew is a friend of mine. I'm stoked to meet you. Are you being well looked after?' Catherine reluctantly extracted herself from the hug and pointed to her cup of tea to indicate that she was indeed fully satisfied. 'I'm so sorry to trouble you both,' the young American continued, his accent somewhere between Midwest drawl and East Coast twang, 'but I wanted to show Matthew a new flyer that I've designed. I guess you'd have some good advice too, Catherine, what with your time in newspapers.' Elijah smiled broadly and Catherine was half hoping he would envelop her in another hug just for the sheer hell of it. 'I want to make it seem as though church is fun so I can attract young men and women who may think it's a bit – what's that British word? – stuffy for them.'

The flyer was A5 in size and featured photographs of some of the new teenage church attendees playing pool and laughing over bottles of low-alcohol beer. Across the top were the initials JCW with a crucifix and along the bottom was a quote from Paul's letter to the Galatians: *Carry each other's burdens, and in this way, you will fulfil the law of Christ*. There was also a plea for new members aged seventeen to twenty-two to come to an initial meeting the following Wednesday at 7pm with the promise of a warm welcome and hot dogs, vegan if necessary.

'I like it,' said Catherine, nodding her approval. 'JCW?'

'Junior Christian Walkers,' explained Father Matthew. 'It's

an offshoot from the original youth club which Elijah here has initiated since he arrived. Once the new members are settled, they can go walking with Elijah if they wish, either individually or small groups, and they discuss scripture and try to find solutions to their problems.'

Elijah gently took hold of Catherine's hand. She felt a jolt as if a small electric charge had passed into her. 'The walks are an opportunity for us to work together to delve deeper into the issues that concern them. You see, Cathcrine, these young men and women that I wish to reach out to are often very troubled,' he said, almost in a seductive whisper. 'Their start in life has not been the best, you know? Often they feel like outcasts, I guess, because of family breakdown or whatever. They feel vulnerable. They *are* vulnerable. However, it is my devout belief that with the help of our saviour, Jesus Christ, we can turn their lives around and create positive change. Jesus said, "If the world hates you, know that it has hated me before it hated you". If I can direct these young people towards the kingdom of heaven, then I will consider my life to have been worthwhile, however long or short that life may be.' Elijah's eye contact was so intense that Catherine sensed that she could still feel it even when she closed her own eyes briefly.

Father Matthew asked whether Elijah would like a quick cup of tea while he was in the vestry but the American politely declined. 'As you know, I only drink green tea, Father, and I don't believe you have any here right now. I guess I must have used the last bag on Saturday. I'll buy some to keep the vestry stocked up if that's okay with you. It's purely selfish on my part as I know you and Robert are not fans of anything that isn't coffee or English tea.'

Once he had Father Matthew's blessing for his flyer, the young man gave Catherine another enthusiastic hug, apologised once again for his intrusion and disappeared as suddenly as he had arrived.

'He's quite something,' swooned Catherine as casually as she could muster. 'And clearly a very clean-living young man. What's his story, Father?'

What the priest knew of Elijah's life was that he had grown up in Kentucky where he had been an active member of his local church. When he was twenty, the church was hit by a tornado, killing seven people including Elijah's father. Elijah had helped to rebuild the church but, in doing so, had claimed to have seen a vision in which an angel told him that he was needed in the big cities of the world to spread the word of the gospels. He had moved to New York with his mother, who was starting cancer treatment, and began working in Brooklyn with a Christian youth group. When his mother's savings began to dwindle, and after researching whether she met the requirements for treatment in Britain, the two of them moved to London and set up home in Hammersmith just across the river.

'He's certainly a force to be reckoned with,' said Catherine. 'Do you think that he has anything to do with these murders?'

Matthew frowned and shook his head, eyes closed in intense contemplation. 'I couldn't say. To everyone who encounters him, Elijah is sweetness personified,' he said. 'He's fit and strong but he won't even swat a fly if he sees one in the church.'

'What about this other chap, Robert Henderson? Is he perhaps jealous of a newcomer challenging his ideas?'

The priest was dubious. He had never had cause to believe that Robert was anything less than a good Christian. 'Perhaps it would be helpful for you to talk to him too. And maybe observe some of the young people who are new to the church. Could you come to mass at ten on Sunday, please? It's the first mass of Advent and it will be a good opportunity for you to get a feel for the congregation. You're much more qualified than I when it comes to this sort of business.'

Catherine gratefully accepted the invitation. 'May I bring a friend or two?' she asked, putting on her coat.

The priest took both of her hands in his. 'You may bring eleven friends if you so desire,' he said with a stoic smile.

Following the conversation at Mehmet's wedding, Catherine was fairly sure that persuading everyone to attend church would be challenging. She was also harbouring a faint suspicion that the church, and maybe even Father Matthew, wasn't all that it appeared.

7

The Twelve's bank was situated behind a bright-red door down a narrow and secluded alleyway in the City of London which looked like it led nowhere but was actually an ancient cut-through between two major thoroughfares. Monica and Thomas had shared an umbrella from Bank station as an early December sky of bruises had pummelled the City pavements with heavyweight raindrops. The alleyway was, helpfully, so slim that the angled downpour had little hope of reaching ground level. Thomas harboured the suspicion that in Dickensian London, this would have been the perfect location for skulduggery.

Monica had been requested to ring the bell marked *TOAST* and wait for the door to be opened. After around ten seconds it did, pulled from the inside by a small, middle-aged woman with long peroxide-blonde hair tied in a ponytail and wearing red-tinted glasses.

'Monica,' said the woman, with elongated vowels, while extending a hand, 'and Thomas too. How delicious. My name is Damaris Cash. I work with James. Let's get you in out of this rain.'

Thomas was struck both by the firmness of Damaris's handshake as well as the appropriateness of her surname. He decided not to mention it, assuming, correctly, that the poor woman would be bored of people making the obvious connection.

'He's been hugely looking forward to meeting you after all this time. He's waiting in the drawing room.'

A bank that has a drawing room? thought Thomas. Clearly this was on a different level to his local Lloyds.

Damaris guided the visitors down a long corridor decorated with fine art which Thomas didn't recognise but which reminded him of some of The Twelve's meeting locations. At the end of the corridor was a lift to the fourth floor which opened out into a spacious room with large windows and south-facing views across the City towards the winter river. A large wall clock overwhelmed the space to the right and the wooden floor was adorned with a huge and colourful rug. A festive aroma of cloves and orange was filling the room, its origin a scented candle flickering softly on a side table beside a fully-stocked bookcase.

James Wheeler rose from his high-backed ornate chair behind his seventeenth-century desk on which sat two large computers and a small pile of papers poking out of a neat black folder. He was, as Lexington had intimated, not what they were expecting, in fact he was as distant from Thomas's mental image of their banker as he thought possible. The most striking thing about James Wheeler was that despite being in his mid-fifties, he looked extremely fit and had very short, bright-pink hair.

The second most striking thing about him was that he was dressed not in the usual banker attire of suit and tie but instead wore slim-fit blue jeans, Converse trainers and a Madonna 1990 Tour T-shirt. James's only concession to traditional banker-wear was a pinstriped jacket. He looked, if anything, like a mid-seventies punk guitarist still clinging to his heyday fashion. Thomas briefly scanned the room for errant safety pins.

'Good morning, Monica,' said James excitedly as he bounded over energetically to greet the new arrivals, 'and Thomas. Such a magnificent pleasure. Tea? Coffee? Something stronger?' The banker winked. Monica looked at the wall clock and decided that two in the afternoon was probably more tea time than anything else. They also had a Twelve meeting to attend, initiated by Catherine, straight after this one so alcohol was probably unwise. James, having checked that simple English Breakfast would suffice, pressed a button on his desk and requested four teas. 'Damaris will be joining us for this meeting as she works across your account almost as much as I do.'

'And such a joy it is,' said Damaris, ushering everyone to take a seat, 'considering some of the other clients we have to deal with.'

'Do you have many other clients?' asked Thomas innocently. He had never had a face-to-face high-level meeting with a financial expert before, particularly not two that looked like these. Damaris explained that personal data security forbade her from disclosing information about any other clients which they may or may not have. However, the two of them should be assured that The Twelve account was by far the most pleasurable to work on, as well as one of the least time-consuming.

'There's nobody dodgy, you understand,' explained Damaris, 'mostly charities, NGOs and organisations much like yourselves working under the radar as far as possible. Because of our investment know-how, we're in the fortunate position of being able to reject approaches from the more unsavoury businesses, if you catch my drift.' Thomas didn't but decided not to pursue the subject for fear of wandering out of his depth, something which had been all too common in recent months.

After a few moments of small talk and the arrival of a tea trolley which also contained a variety of sweet delicacies from a nearby boutique cake shop, James Wheeler shifted smoothly into business gear. 'Firstly, I just wanted to say what a pleasure it was to deal with the Kent hospice donation. It was very much in the spirit of The Twelve and quite straightforward to complete. Any time you wish to save a Kent hospice, or any other kind for that matter, we're totally down for that.' Monica asked whether The Twelve's funds allowed for more acts of random generosity. In response, James tapped some keys on one of his computers to bring up the total funds instantly available. It was an extremely large number. 'You could probably make a decent offer to the county council to actually buy Kent,' he said nonchalantly. 'I wouldn't recommend it though. Most councils are massively in debt and their social care bills are only going to increase over the coming years as we all age. No offence. We don't take on councils as clients for obvious reasons.'

Monica expressed her delight that there was leeway to do more good. Thanks in part to Bobby, she had been keeping a reasonably well-organised spreadsheet of charities she wanted to support in one way or another. 'On a related issue,' added James, 'I'm sure Bobby has kept you up to date with your kind offer to Tiffany and Paul Storey to allow them to live rent-free in the Woronzow Road property from the beginning of January.' Monica nodded. Her desire to help the innocent victims of The Twelve's summer case to rebuild their lives was high on her list of priorities. 'Everything is now ready for them to move in. The Kandinsky paintings have had to be moved into secure, temporary storage pending a decision on their longer term future and the place has been cleared of anything incriminating.

Bobby will assist mother and son to move in at the appropriate time.'

The next matter for discussion was agreement on the Christmas bonuses for each member of The Twelve. 'As you have been relatively busy this year,' said the banker, 'might I suggest this figure for everyone and half of this figure for Mrs Mendoza.' He scribbled another large number on a piece of lined paper and pushed it gently across his desk for his guests to peruse. Thomas, munching a mini chocolate caramel sponge, noted that it was almost double the previous year's bonus but also enquired why Mrs Mendoza was entitled to less. 'She simply doesn't need it,' replied James. 'Lexington would always offer more but she always politely refused. Her expenses are minimal. She has neither a mortgage nor close relatives apart from some cousins in Brazil. On the sad day that she leaves us, whenever that may be, everything in her estate will return to The Twelve anyway. So you could say we're simply saving paperwork down the line. Unless she's immortal, which is a distinct possibility.'

The final piece of business involved The Twelve's long-term investments. As rain whipped musically against the huge window and Monica pondered whether she should text Martin to see if he could pick them up to transport them to the Twelve meeting just down the road in Hogarth Court, James explained that Lexington had always ensured that their wealth was not used for what he described as "unsavoury purposes".

'For example,' he began, 'for the last fifteen years, none of The Twelve's extensive fortune has even been invested in anything to do with arms sales, petrochemicals, crypto,' James rolled his eyes at this point, 'or in the banking system of any country with a dubious human rights record. I'm sure you wish to continue this ethical style of financial management, and yet I felt it was only appropriate to show you the comparable profits over the last fifteen years if you had indeed taken a more morally laissez-faire attitude to your funds.' He pushed two pieces of paper across the desk and pointed at each in turn, stating that the smaller of the two, albeit not insignificant, represented the return on investment they had actually seen while the larger represented the equivalent sum if invested less nobly. Thomas stared out of the window. It had begun to sleet.

I'd like to stick with our current policy please,' announced Monica. 'We're good people, apart from the obvious. I don't want our wealth to benefit dictatorships or indirectly cause harm to innocent people. I couldn't live with myself. And I'm far from sure I know what crypto is.'

'Understood,' said James. 'And I agree wholeheartedly. You *are* good people.'

'Did you see her in 1990?' asked Thomas, staring at the T-shirt with curiosity. 'Madonna.' The banker confirmed that he had indeed been in the audience at the pop star's Wembley show as part of her Blond Ambition Tour. His hair had been longer and coloured vibrant orange at the time and he had just started working on the trading floor at one of the big American banks in London.

'I've never been your standard finance guy,' he said, grinning. 'But then neither has Damaris.' He looked over at the peroxide woman who saluted ostentatiously. 'We voluntarily left Citibank together in 2010 after the crash and we set up this. I knew Bobby City through friends and she thought that Lexington might be interested in placing The Twelve's money somewhere a bit more personal than the place you had before. He was never disappointed in our investment portfolio and my hope and belief is that you'll feel the same way. We look different because we are different. We treat clients differently to other banks. That's why we can be selective with whom we accept. We don't chase business, it comes to us; and we decide whether or not to take it on. Now, may we arrange a car to deliver you to your next destination? It's all part of our service.'

I won't have to bother Martin, thought Monica and gratefully accepted. The banker tapped out a brief text on his mobile. 'A limo will be at the end of the alleyway in ten minutes. Left out of the door. Not the way you came in. It's the quieter end. You won't miss it.'

Just before they left, Thomas bravely asked a further question which had been bothering him since they'd arrived. 'Why Toast?'

In response, the banker had questions of his own. 'Do you like toast, Thomas?' Thomas nodded. 'Does Monica like toast?' Monica's eyes sparkled as Thomas confirmed that she did. 'So do you know anyone who doesn't like toast?'

Despite sifting as many people as he could think of through his mind, Thomas couldn't think of anyone who didn't like toast. 'I think we have our answer. We nearly called ourselves VEIN for Very Exclusive Investment Network but the connotations of bloodletting were... challenging. Hence, Toast.'

James Wheeler was right. A pink limousine with the word *TOAST* written on the side could be seen waiting for them as they skipped down the alley avoiding puddles. 'Where to, ladies?' asked the driver in a deep, sensual voice. They were a stunning drag queen wearing a lime-green minidress and fake fur stole.

'Hogarth Court please,' said Monica, 'or as close as you can get.' She turned to Thomas and, smiling, clasped his hand. 'Lexington was right. Certainly different,' she said.

8

The first time that he had been at this venue, thought Thomas as Monica keyed in the entrance code, was during the Burrows case just over a year before. Dennis Burrows, the former chief of the London Transport Police had been there. It had been their initial meeting with him. Thomas wondered briefly what had happened to Dennis after the conclusion to that case and resolved to ask Suzanne whenever the moment was more appropriate.

The commissioner had also attended that earlier meeting. Both Monica and Thomas had been keeping a close eye on the news and while it seemed that Suzanne had managed to ride out the weekend media clamour for her head, the storm was far from over, rumbling angrily away in the background. Catherine, who had tried her best to mollify the furore using her senior contacts, conceded that certain editors, despite their personal admiration for Suzanne and the work she had done over the years, felt that one more embarrassment within the Met and her position would sadly become untenable. 'The nature of the beast,' as one newspaper veteran had termed it.

The rest of The Twelve were already mostly settled into

Hogarth Court's comfortable chairs and were enjoying Terry's fresh offering of home-made Hobnobs, 'Although we probably can't call them that for legal reasons,' muttered the locksmith, 'so we'll call them Nobhobs and see how McVitie's feel about that. Do we have the necessary funds if they decide to sue me?' Monica stated that they certainly did but that she would personally rather The Twelve's finances were used for more altruistic purposes than legal action against a multinational biscuit company.

Anna and Veronica extracted themselves reluctantly from the location's extensive bookshelves which were stuffed with first editions of classic novels dating back well into the nineteenth century. Veronica was enthralled as she had never visited Hogarth Court before. 'I know an antiques expert from one of my programmes,' she announced, 'who would actually faint if he was in this room. He would probably have to be forcibly dragged out screaming. There's a signed copy of *The Old Curiosity Shop*, for goodness' sake!'

'How was the bank manager?' asked Chris, nursing a mug of strong tea and debating the wisdom of dunking a Nobhob for fear of it collapsing into a sludge.

'Intriguing,' replied Monica as she and Thomas settled into a two-seater. 'In more ways than you'd expect. But to keep it simple, the Christmas bonus will be generous. I know Martin has his eye on a sports car to whizz Joanne round the country lanes following our summer excursions to the Malvern Hills.' The cabbie closed his eyes and a beatific grin spread serenely across his face at the idea of day trips with his new-ish girlfriend.

'Before we get to the main focus of the meeting, just two quick things to mention. Mehmet called and asked me to pass on his thanks to everyone for attending his wedding and also for the kind gifts which everyone gave. Secondly, you'll doubtless have seen the unwelcome media attention on our friend Suzanne. She's currently in occasional text communication and seems to be okay for the time being. I've let her know that if there's anything we can practically do, over and above what Catherine is already doing, then we will. She may not be able to easily attend any of our meetings for a while but we'll just have to adapt as best we can and hope that everything resolves itself sooner rather than later.'

'I wish we could assassinate some of these right-wing pillocks attacking her,' growled Martin. Monica admitted that in principle she was in broad agreement but that The Twelve simply couldn't go around bumping people off because of their political views or because they didn't like them as that would signify the thin end of a rather dangerous and authoritarian wedge.

'Anyway, moving on, Catherine has initiated this meeting.' Monica glanced over at the ex-journalist. 'Would you like to take the floor? I understand this might be a new case.'

Catherine was mid-Nobhob but managed to swallow it with a swig of tea and began to outline her conversation with Father Matthew. Most of the regular congregation were elderly and so unlikely to engage in murderous pursuits, she stated with an ironic wink. There were a couple of families with young children but the priest had no reason to suspect they could be involved. However, Matthew's gut instinct was that there was some link to his church. She touched on her brief encounter with Elijah Timothy, his slightly fractious relationship with fellow youth worker, Robert Henderson, and the young people involved in Junior Christian Walkers.

Of course, she concluded, there was always the possibility that Matthew was mistaken and that the murderer or murderers had no direct connection with the Church of the Immaculate Virgin. He or she could have simply vandalised the

Bibles to draw the police off the scent. 'It's worth investigation though. Plus, this young American I mentioned is extremely dishy.'

'How old did you say he was?' asked Owen. Catherine guessed at late twenties, maybe thirty. 'Too young, even for you,' mused the ex-surveillance expert.

'Not necessarily,' said Catherine defiantly. 'If I were a man and he was a woman, nobody would bat an eyelid.'

Monica sighed. 'Regardless of this man's apparent attractiveness, he might be a suspect so I would advise against anyone,' she glanced between Catherine and Owen with a playful sternness, 'and I mean *anyone* considering an inappropriate frisson with him.'

'But he's so sweet and kind,' groaned Catherine, 'and so pretty. And he helps underprivileged young people. And he only drinks green tea!'

'No,' said Monica sternly. 'If you want to befriend him for the purposes of the investigation, that's fine. Anything else, absolutely not fine.'

Catherine pretended to sulk. 'He's quite devout anyway,' she said. 'So I think he'd frown on anything sexual.'

David set his mug carefully on the floor. '"But now I am writing to you",' he said, '"not to associate with anyone who bears the name of brother if he is guilty of sexual immorality or greed".'

'Paul's letter to the misbehaving Corinthians, chapter five, verse eleven,' added Chris, grimly.

'Well, it looks like we're going to church for a while,' said Monica. 'Initially to see if we can gather some intelligence about the parishioners, in particular this Henderson fellow and the young people in the JCW youth group. We probably shouldn't all go to mass en masse on Sunday, so maybe Catherine could enrol a small group of, say, four in the first instance and we'll see how that goes over the next few weeks. Through Christmas and into the new year, I'm thinking.'

The former journalist was not short of volunteers but eventually chose Owen along with Anna and Chris, largely because of the ex-surgeon's apparently encyclopaedic knowledge of the New Testament. 'We'll keep the nature of our relationship quiet,' said Owen. 'The murderer's targets appear to be people whose lifestyles veer away from the traditional family unit. So we'll just be friends, for the purposes of making some headway.' Anna and Chris agreed.

The four of them made a plan to all stay at Catherine's on Saturday night so they could be at the church to meet Father Matthew at nine before mass. 'Elijah won't be there, sadly,' said Catherine dreamily. 'He has to look after his sick mother on Sundays. But we'll doubtless find an opportunity to catch up with him in the week.'

'I'm sure *you* will,' said Monica with a smile. 'In the meantime, I'll text Suzanne to see whether we can get an update on the police investigation. I'm trying not to bother her too much at the moment but I'm sure she won't mind. I'll let you know what she says as soon as I get an update.'

9

Even though Catherine's house had three spare rooms, only one of them had been required, a double for Anna and Chris. Since formerly becoming a couple in the summer, they had been spending almost every night at either the pathologist's house in Kensal Green or his place near Victoria Park so it seemed senseless to take up any more of Catherine's space than was required.

Owen, of course, shared Catherine's bed. 'You don't suppose Graham will be jealous?' enquired Anna over breakfast. Owen assured her that, first of all Graham wasn't remotely the jealous type, and secondly he and Catherine would thoroughly spoil him the next time the three of them were alone together.

Just before nine, they strolled the short distance to the Church of the Immaculate Virgin. It was a bright yet chilly December day, and there was a stiff breeze from the direction of the common which balletically drove fallen leaves skittering across both road and pavement.

Father Matthew was in the vestibule to greet them and, after introductions, he led the group into the vestry to outline what was going to happen during mass. For Catherine, there were naturally no surprises. For Anna and Owen, the experience was largely educational. However, the experience of attending mass for the first time in decades inspired in Chris a reaction that he could only describe as "challenging". Even the space of the building, a wilderness of dust and stale perfumed air, felt oppressive.

The priest ran through the list of hymns and also the gospel readings, one from the book of Luke calling upon the faithful to be aware of the second coming of Jesus and another from the book of Mark which did much the same. 'I know the chapter,' said Chris, mournfully. '"But in those days, after that tribulation, the sun will be darkened and the moon will not give its light and the stars will be falling from heaven, and the powers in the heavens will be shaken". It's truly festive, Father.'

'I understand your atheist sarcasm,' said Matthew, charitably. 'And I agree that the traditional Advent readings can sometimes be a funny old mixture. But they're designed to prepare the congregation to think about the imminent celebration of the birth of our Lord and also to have in mind the fact that He will come again. They can be a bit fire and brimstone, I'll admit. I try to use my sermon to inject a bit of levity and perspective.'

Chris nodded and said he would look forward to that, what with levity and perspective being noticeably lacking in his own religious education.

'We'll sit at the back in pairs,' said Catherine, 'and see if we can start up conversations with some of these new, younger parishioners. Will Robert Henderson be here, Father?'

'It's rare that he isn't,' replied Father Matthew. 'And he's usually early. He doesn't have much else in his life, I'm afraid, apart from the church. If we go and stand near the altar in about twenty minutes, I can point him out to you. Now, does anyone

48

need the toilet? Mass can be about an hour which can occasionally be a bit brutal on the old bladder.'

After everyone had made themselves comfortable, the group made their way into the south transept to watch the congregation arrive. The slightly stuffy atmosphere was thick with the aroma of frankincense from the multitude of candles spaced throughout the church. At around twenty to ten, the first half dozen elderly parishioners arrived and made their way to the front pews, smiling and nodding to Father Matthew as they delicately seated themselves. 'Hard of hearing,' whispered the priest, 'so they like to be as close to the ambo as possible.'

'Sorry, ambo?' asked Owen.

Matthew explained that that was what they called the pulpit from where he would give the sermon. 'You're most welcome to take communion, by the way, but it's not compulsory.'

'I'll forgo the body of Christ if it's all right with you,' said Chris, patting his tummy. 'Catherine provided a hearty breakfast.'

The priest nodded in understanding although he began to wonder whether the ex-surgeon, with his softly belligerent attitude towards the church, was quite the right person to be attending mass. He let it go.

Suddenly, Matthew placed a hand on Catherine's shoulder and leant in. 'There's Robert,' he said, gesturing towards a middle-aged man who had just entered alone and was genuflecting from near the back of the nave. He was, Owen thought, possibly the greyest person he'd ever seen, dressed in a grey jacket with a marginally lighter grey shirt and a cloud-coloured tie. Robert's short hair was grey and even his skin had acquired a rather monochrome pallor. He spotted the priest and skipped up the aisle, stopping briefly to greet the elderly in the front pew, all of whom knew him by name.

'Good morning, Father,' he said, smiling. 'And good morning to all of you.' He gazed around the assembled group, settling on Catherine. 'Hello. I've seen you before but we've never been formally introduced. Robert Henderson.' He held out a limp hand which Catherine shook.

'Catherine is an old friend,' explained Father Matthew, 'and she has brought some new friends into our church for a while. This is Chris, Anna and Owen.' The former surveillance expert decided that Robert's was amongst the most insipid handshakes he had ever experienced. Chris barely felt his handshake. It was like being greeted by a moist tissue.

'Anna, did you say?' The ex-pathologist smiled sympathetically. A wistful look came across the grey face. 'Luke, chapter two. "And there was a prophetess, Anna, the daughter of Phanuel, of the tribe of Asher. She was advanced in years, having lived with her husband seven years from when she was a virgin and then as a widow until she was eighty-four".'

Anna frowned slightly and looked at Chris who winked knowingly. 'Well, Robert,' she said hesitantly, 'I may be advanced in years but eighty-four remains a little way off. We understand you work with some of the young people in the parish. We'd love to meet some after the service if that's at all possible.'

Robert's face suddenly came alive. 'Yes, absolutely!' He beamed. 'I expect we'll have around sixteen or so today. I'll gladly introduce you to as many as I can. Will you come and sit at the back with us? I can try to engage some of them before mass if you like. They'll mostly drift in late, though, so we'll have to see how it goes.'

'He's a strange fish,' whispered Chris to Anna as they moved slowly to the rear of the nave. The church was now filling up to almost half capacity and many of the congregation were observing the new arrivals with interest bordering on suspicion.

'Doesn't make him a murderer, of course, but he does seem to know his gospels. Even I didn't know that bit from Luke.'

Robert had already positioned himself in the back row when the four friends arrived. 'The boys and girls prefer this row,' he said, 'so if you wouldn't mind sitting in the one in front, I can do the intros whenever it's feasible.' An organist began playing a prelude and just before ten the doors opened and a group of people, mostly in their late teens and early twenties, entered the church.

There were four girls and ten boys, all quiet although Owen noticed that some of them smelt of cigarette smoke. Clearly they had been waiting outside until the last possible moment. They wore mostly puffer jackets and hoodies in bright hues and trainers of varying degrees of quality. Robert nodded awkwardly to each of them as they shuffled along the pew, some of them frowning at the unusual appearance of four strangers directly in front of them. The greyness of Robert made him somehow stand out amidst the primary colours, like a brown Quality Street amongst the more vibrant flavours. Unusually for late teenagers, none of them were scrolling through mobile phones. One of the younger boys, perhaps eighteen and wearing a white puffer, was seated at the end of the pew slightly apart from the rest of the group.

Catherine turned round and smiled at one of the girls, a thin, curious-eyed youth with hair that had been dyed red a few weeks ago and now required urgent attention. The girl smiled back, her entire face lifting. *A bridge of mediation has begun construction*, thought the ex-journalist.

'Lucky the Bible doesn't mention tobacco,' whispered Anna.

'Nothing suspicious about a smoker, though,' replied Chris under his breath, 'however medically unwise the habit may be.'

10

M onica's Thursday text to Suzanne had elicited a brief response that evening saying that she would get an update on the status of the Barnes murders investigation and respond more fully when she had done so. On Sunday morning, this promised text arrived with profuse apologies for its lateness and with a brief explanation that she had been in almost constant communication with the Met's publicity team and with various newspaper editors.

Thankfully there had been no follow-up in that Sunday morning's papers and the worst of the headlines appeared to be over as the news agenda had conveniently moved on to a prominent soap star's multiple indiscretions involving drugs and prostitutes. However, there were still a few unfortunate memes of Suzanne dotted around social media and she was more conscious than ever that her job depended on good fortune more than actual quality of performance. *One dodgy uniformed copper filmed doing something stupid on a smartphone and it'll be muggins that takes the rap as usual*, she had written.

Anyway, the text continued, *on these Barnes murders. Currently minimal progress. No obvious link between victims.*

DNA picked up at both murder scenes doesn't match anything on our database. Also, the DNA at each scene doesn't match so two different killers. Both male. There's a detective inspector going through CCTV for the second murder at the moment. CCTV for the first murder is inconclusive but there's a possible suspect who is moving at speed away from the common towards and then over Hammersmith Bridge before disappearing in the warren of streets south of the flyover. Have asked for regular updates from the investigation team and will pass these on as they come through. Keep me updated too please. Hopefully meet soon. Merry Christmas if we don't manage a face-to-face. Sx.

Moving at speed, thought Monica. That would appear to rule out older members of the congregation. She forwarded the text to the group with an additional message suggesting another meeting the following day, perhaps in The Twelve's Shepherd's Bush house as it was closest to the scene of the action.

Monica's text arrived midway through the Lord's Prayer just as the majority of the congregation were exhorting God to forgive their trespasses. Everyone's phones were on silent mode but nonetheless the simultaneous low vibrations from the same pew caused a couple of the young parishioners seated behind to share suspicious glances. A couple of the girls suppressed giggles. Chris removed his phone from his pocket, saw that the message was from Monica and decided to read it at the next convenient opportunity.

'Let us offer each other the sign of peace,' said Father Matthew from the ambo. The members of The Twelve all shook hands and then turned to greet the young men and women in the pew behind.

Chris shook hands with three of the young men, he guessed in their very late teens, two of them with cornrow hair and the third with a long fringe swept forwards. 'Nice iPhone, bruv,' whispered one of the cornrows as he released his grip. Chris smiled and nodded, secretly hoping that the comment was merely one of admiration rather than of criminal intent. 'But you should turn it off in church, please, yeah?' *Okay*, thought Chris, the comment was actually gentle admonishment for his own poor behaviour.

He looked at Anna and made a face. 'That's told me,' he mouthed, shielding with his hand. While the majority of the congregation, including the back row, took Holy Communion, the four quickly took in the information, positioning their phones on their laps to avoid being overseen, and individually thought the same thing. One, possibly two, younger assailants. Potentially, although far from definitely, seated behind them.

'Let's split into twos and try to talk to as many as we can,' whispered Catherine. 'Owen and I will take the girls seeing as you've already made friends with the boys, Chris.' She wagged a reprimanding finger. Chris looked more irritated than contrite.

After mass, the four members of The Twelve made a beeline for the exit in the hope of engaging with the young worshippers as they left the church. The breeze had subsided slightly but now there was more than a suggestion of rain in the air. Robert emerged from the vestibule followed by three of the girls who all looked with sullen disinterest towards Catherine and Owen. 'I've managed to persuade three of our newest members of the flock to say a quick hello,' he said with a degree of discomfort. 'This is Shayna, Letitia and Riley. I'd like you to meet Catherine and, ummmm, sorry my memory these days, Ewan was it?' Owen corrected him politely and he and Catherine shook hands with the three girls, one of whom, Riley, was the partially red-haired one who had smiled at Catherine earlier.

'You just visiting?' asked Shayna, a slim girl with long eyelashes and blue painted nails. 'Or you finally found Jesus at this late stage of life?' Riley and Letitia burst into hysterics inspiring a disdainful look from Robert who apologised for what he regarded as their rudeness.

Catherine smiled demurely. 'I've been coming here on and off for a few years,' she said. 'I'm friends with Father Matthew. Owen here…' she hesitated slightly, measuring her options, 'he's exploring his spirituality.' Owen frowned momentarily, then composed himself and nodded in agreement.

'And what about them other two?' Shayna was smiling but the conversation was beginning to feel like an interrogation. She was gesturing towards Chris and Anna who had managed to engage in a chat with three of the young men. 'The naughty one with his phone on in church and his boo.'

'Much the same,' said Catherine before skilfully turning the interview on its head. According to Shayna, the three of them, all nineteen, were friends from the council estate nearer the river. Each of their mothers, all single, had tried to keep them out of trouble with varying degrees of success – Riley had almost gone to a young offenders' institute for shoplifting.

One day in late August, they had been drinking at a pub on the river, enjoying the sunset at an outside table, when they were approached by a man who turned out to be Elijah. Under normal circumstances, they would have quickly given him the brush-off, but Letitia fancied him so they let him chat for an hour. Elijah persuaded them to come to his church youth club the following Wednesday. 'It's actually really fun,' piped up Letitia, 'and Elijah is fit, man, but I don't fancy him anymore. I've got a boyfriend.' She waved over to one of the boys who was talking to Chris and Anna. The boy struck a cross-armed pose in response and grinned back.

'Didn't you think he was too old for you anyway?' Catherine was keen to keep the girls talking as they seemed to be getting somewhere. 'Elijah, I mean.'

Riley laughed. 'Nah. Not too old for Letitia. She fucked a forty-year-old in her time.'

'I did not!' protested Letitia. 'He was thirty-six. And I didn't fuck him, I just blew him for a twenty. And don't fucking swear in church, bitch.'

'I'm not *in* fucking church. I'm *outside* fucking church. It don't count.' The two girls started play-fighting, giggling wildly.

'I don't think Elijah likes girls anyways,' said Shayna, quietly. 'His favourites are always the boys.' Catherine raised an eyebrow. She felt sure the American had been flirting with her earlier in the week but maybe she had been mistaken. 'He loves Devante at the moment. He'd do anything for dat boy.'

11

While many of the young men had left the church, immediately lit up cigarettes, checked their phones and wandered off in ones and twos through the churchyard, Anna had managed to politely ask one of them to stay behind and this number had expanded to three as they were all friends.

Harrison, the boy who had reprimanded Chris about his mobile, turned out to be Letitia's boyfriend. His friends, Caden and Nathan, were sufficiently intrigued by Chris and Anna to join the conversation, particularly as Chris was attempting to look cool by leaning on a gravestone. 'Don't dis the dead, bro,' Harrison had joked. 'After what you did with your phone, I reckon you going to hell, innit. Sooner rather than later if you get me. I'm gonna have to keep my eye on you.'

Robert Henderson was now loitering hawkishly on the outskirts of this group, partly to keep an eye on the boys and partly to overhear what was being discussed. These older people were friends of Father Matthew; at least, one of them was. Yet, Robert couldn't help suspecting that their motives for suddenly arriving in church on that December Sunday weren't entirely innocent.

'So, what drew you young gentlemen to the church?' asked Anna, trying to sound casual.

'Policing,' replied Harrison.

'You were in trouble with the police?'

'Nah, fam. We have to police the church to make sure old folks ain't using their phones, is it.' The group all burst into laughter and started punching each other gently.

'Gentlemen,' said Robert, stepping forwards awkwardly to intervene, 'less boisterous in the graveyard please.'

The three apologised and rolled their shoulders. Caden explained that they had met Elijah at another youth club back in October and he had invited them to try his group.

'That other club was vanilla, man,' he said. 'You couldn't drink or smoke or nuffink. With Elijah, there's just a vibe, man. And he doesn't mind what you do as long as he gets to talk to you about the Bible, which is sick. And I'm actually learning some major stuff. I didn't learn shit in that other place. Except how to roll a spliff.'

Chris mused that he too needed to 'learn stuff'. Like what most of these words meant in the strange context Caden was using them. He wondered whether there might be something like a Baedeker for inner city phrases which could guide him through this strange, new linguistic landscape.

'What are you learning?' asked Anna, aware of the cautious eyes of Robert Henderson a short distance off to her left.

Caden drew himself up to his full height of about five foot ten as if preparing to enter stage left. He cleared his throat. '"The angels will come out and separate the evil from the righteous and throw them into the fiery furnace".' Nathan and Harrison applauded.

'Matthew, chapter thirteen,' whispered Chris to himself. 'What does that mean to you, Caden?'

The young man scratched his chin. 'I dunno, bruv. But it

sounds sick. Like Samuel Jackson in *Pulp Fiction*, innit.' He pointed an imaginary gun at Chris and pretended to shoot. 'Pop, pop!'

'It means that God knows if you're doing bad stuff,' said Nathan, 'and on the judgement day, if you've been naughty like using your phone in church, then you're in trouble, innit.' The three boys convulsed yet again into hysterics.

'I'm just starting out though,' said Caden. 'Devante's the expert.'

'Who's Devante?' asked Anna, eager to find out as much as she could without the conversation turning into too much of an interview.

Harrison reached into the pocket of his jacket and retrieved a packet of ten cigarettes with eight remaining. 'He gone already.' The young man pointed in the direction of the church gate. 'He'll be halfway home by now. He started coming to the club in September. Originally, he just wanted to meet new bitches, sorry, I mean girls. But he got really into it and now he's always walking.'

'Walking?'

'With Elijah. The two of them go off walking the streets and talking about God. It's Junior Christian Walkers after all, innit.' He lit up a cigarette after offering the pack round to the rest of the group including Anna and Chris who politely declined. 'Anyway, we'd better go. Elijah got us tickets to the Arsenal this afternoon, is it. Laters.'

Chris held out his hand to shake but the young men all preferred fist bumps. The ex-surgeon adapted with trepidation.

'They seem sweet,' Anna said and she moved back under the cover of the vestibule with Chris and Robert as a light drizzle had begun to moisten the graveyard. Robert agreed and admitted that he had initially been uncomfortable about Elijah's intention to attract more young people from the poorer areas of south-west London. He still felt that some of the unintended consequences could have been handled better – a couple of middle-class parents had removed their boys from the club after they had been caught smoking weed in their bedrooms.

However, there was no denying the positive changes in the young people whom Elijah was attracting. 'Some of them don't stay for more than a few weeks,' said Robert wistfully. 'There was a lovely young man named Tyrone who started in the summer and was learning so much. Then, one day about a month ago, he just stopped coming for no reason. Overall, though, I think it's been positive.'

Father Matthew had by now managed to bid farewell to all of his flock and had joined the group in the vestibule along with Owen and Catherine. 'Robert, could you bear to deal with the hassocks please? The front three pews are in particular need of care. Bless you.' The ashen music teacher shook hands weakly with the four friends and stumbled off to tackle the unruly pile of knee cushions.

'Any progress?' asked the priest, conspiratorially lowering his voice.

Catherine said that they had begun to form an early bond with the three girls, although there was no suggestion that any of them had even the remotest involvement in a murder. 'We had a similar experience with the three boys,' said Chris, 'although the way Robert was staring at us was a little unnerving. We'll need to keep an eye on him.'

'Which one was Devante?' asked Anna. Owen chipped in that the girls had mentioned him too.

'The boy with the white puffer coat,' said Matthew. 'A lovely young man, although he has been a bit quiet of late. He's eighteen and I believe he's been shunted around quite a few foster homes during his short life, bless him. Maybe he's going through a difficult time. I'll ask Elijah whether there's anything I can do to help. He'll be here in the morning. Maybe you should all attend the youth club on Wednesday. I'll ask Robert if that would be okay. Now, if you'll excuse me, I must go and count the collection plate in the hope that our brethren have already been imbued with the spirit of Christmas generosity. Last week the takings amounted to £97.20 and a blue button. Delightful though that is, it won't go far to help fix the desperate situation with the roof on the south transept.'

'Maybe they give in secret,' suggested Chris. 'As Matthew's gospel says, "Thus when you give to the needy, sound no trumpet before you as the hypocrites do in the synagogues and in the streets".'

A pained expression drifted over the face of Father Matthew. 'They don't, I'm afraid,' he said, a note of resignation in his voice. 'And as this church was built in the mid-nineteenth century, Christopher, not a year goes by without some part of it requiring the attention of a local tradesman or two. Anyway, peace be with you all.' He made the sign of the cross four times and wandered back into the church.

'And also with you, Father,' muttered Chris under his breath. 'And also with you.'

12

'This is one of the places I *had* earmarked for renting out to deserving key workers, for example,' announced Monica as the group settled into the spacious living area of a Victorian villa in Shepherd's Bush, bright in winter sunshine with plenty of two- and three-seater sofas in tasteful, pastel colours. The Twelve's leader had, back in the summer, expressed her desire to do more good for society over and above ridding it of criminals. To this end, Monica had decided, with everyone's approval, to rent out a handful of the group's lesser used properties for little or no return. 'It would make a lovely home for someone but I suspect I'll have to wait until after this case. We've not used it for a while but it'll be the most convenient for us on this occasion. I might even decorate it for Christmas. Nothing major. Maybe just a small tree and some tinsel.'

The house had an extensive garden which, Monica had learnt via Bobby City, required regular upkeep. Just as all of the Twelve houses had sporadic visits from a specialist cleaning company to keep everything shipshape and avoid a build-up of dust and cobwebs, so the Shepherd's Bush house was additionally attended with loving care by a local gardener,

Charlie Turkington and his son Jonty, the former edging serenely towards retirement.

Apparently The Twelve's regular fee to the gardener was enough to keep their small business afloat even during fallow periods when they had no other work. Monica made the executive decision that any future tenants would need to agree to keep the arrangement with the Turkingtons, paid for by The Twelve, as part of any occupancy contract. She would also stipulate in the contract that the gardener and his son must be furnished with cups of tea as required and permitted to use the downstairs bathroom as necessary.

The house had been bequeathed by Ian Bamford, a widowed pharmacist who had joined The Twelve soon after his retirement in 1972. Bamford had been one of the most prolific assassins ever to be part of the group, having a key involvement in fourteen successful cases between 1973 and 1980 when he regretfully decided that enough was enough and retired for the second time. Monica had spent many hours during the autumn poring over The Twelve's case studies which were kept in a locked room in their Baker Street property. She had developed a great admiration and fascination for Bamford, often returning home to Thomas with extraordinary tales of how he had sometimes developed his own unique poisons to successfully conclude a tricky case.

Both of Bamford's children had made their own fortunes by the time of his terminal cancer diagnosis in 1983 and so they had no issues with him leaving the house to his favourite charity, the West London Canine Trust, on his death a year later. This organisation was, naturally, a cover for The Twelve although the leader at the time, Frank Davis, had to live in the house and pretend to look after stray dogs for a few years just in case either of the Bamford children made an unexpected visit to check on their father's bestowal.

In 2010, with all dogs rehomed, Margaret Wilmot, then leader of The Twelve, felt that enough time had passed and arranged for the necessary paperwork to be completed confirming ownership. This also allowed her to transfer some Frank Auerbach charcoal portraits from the attic in Minera Mews and finally put them on display in W12. 'These are gorgeous,' said Veronica, studying them closely with Thomas and Martin. 'I'd guess about 1950 or maybe a little later.' Martin said they reminded him of the 1989 production of 'Singin' In The Rain' although he refused to elaborate.

Once everyone had gathered and once Terry had furnished the group with tea, coffee and chocolate chip shortbread which he'd made in bulk so that there was enough to see Mrs Mendoza through the week, Catherine gave an overview of their initial Sunday mass encounter. Her opinion of Robert Henderson, that he was definitely a suspect, was politely challenged by Anna.

'Just because he's a bit strange and has a handshake like a sickly flannel, that doesn't make him a killer. Martin's a bit strange and he's not... oh, wait...'

'Cheers,' grumbled the cabbie, raising a mug of strong Earl Grey. 'I love you too.'

'I also don't think you should dismiss this Elijah character just because you fancy him,' continued Anna.

Catherine was adamant that she was doing no such thing but simply wanted to make it clear that, in her view, Robert was more likely to be the one to watch. 'We're going to attend the youth club on Wednesday evening,' she said. 'I think it should probably stay as just the four of us for now and we'll bring in reinforcements as required. We've made some initial progress with the young members of the congregation but I suspect that if we bombard them with more new faces then that could get quite challenging for them. Besides,' she took a sideways glance at Anna, 'not everyone has had the opportunity to gaze upon the delicious Elijah yet.'

Anna rolled her eyes.

Monica was keen to learn more about the young people, conscious that the police investigation was focusing, as much as it reasonably could, on that line of inquiry.

'We met six of them,' reported Owen. 'Three boys and three girls. Nice kids. One of them told Chris off for using his phone in church.'

'You didn't!' exclaimed Monica in horror.

'Your text arrived,' protested Chris, his voice rising an octave. 'I thought it might be urgent.'

Monica made a mental note not to use the group chat on Sunday mornings in future. At least not while certain members of the group were attending mass.

Owen's further update on the young people suggested that they had made a good start in developing a relationship with at least a few of the JCW attendees. He was optimistic that they could make further inroads when the four of them visited the youth club on Wednesday evening. 'We'll be careful as I suspect it'll take time to win their trust. That's even if they know anything useful, which they might not. There's a young man named Devante who looks to be worth approaching if we can. We'll probably need Elijah's help to begin with. Catherine's asked Father Matthew to let him know we're coming on Wednesday, just to observe. The cover story is that we're thinking of setting up a similar youth group in north London where Graham and I live, although we won't go into details of our living arrangements, naturally.' He grasped Graham's hand and gave it a romantic squeeze.

'We might need a bit of money for new fashion items,' suggested Chris. 'To get in with the kids. Puffer jackets, trainers. Owen could do with a hoodie from Uniqlo.'

'No,' said Monica firmly. 'If you want to start being a septuagenarian style guru, there will be plenty in your Christmas bonuses to cover that. Anyway, that's a decent start. We'll have a quick catch-up at yoga on Thursday after your evening at the youth club.'

She concluded the meeting with two updates, one from Lexington who remained on schedule to be allowed to go home in early to mid-January and one regarding Paul Storey, the young man whom The Twelve had saved from probable death by malnutrition back in August. 'Tiffany, Paul's mum, says that although he had a slight setback last month, he's been responding so well to treatment that he'll be home by Christmas, which is great news. According to James Wheeler, everything will be ready for them to move into the Regent's Park house in the new year and Paul can start his apprenticeship at the zoo whenever he feels up to it.'

'That deserves a toast,' said Terry, raising a mug.

Monica asked whether anyone had anything else to discuss and Chris announced that his grandchild's due date was March 15th so if it would be possible to avoid anything dramatic around that week, he would be most grateful.

'Beware,' said Martin, wagging a doom-laden finger.

Chris nodded. 'The Ides of March. I know. But there's nothing I can do about that and most first babies are late anyway so I'm not going to lose any sleep. I'll leave that pleasure to the new parents after the arrival.'

13

'I 'm conscious that I haven't done one yet. An assassination.' Thomas was lying wide-eyed in bed in the St John's Wood apartment with Monica, more relaxed in a post-lovemaking glow, on his chest. It was early afternoon the following day and some brittle winter sunshine was peeping suggestively through the clouds and casting hesitant beams onto their rumpled duvet. Monica had an inkling that this was going to turn into a longer, more intense chat which may require coffee but, for now, she was content to remain in position and listen to how these anxieties might play out.

'With Burrows,' he continued, referring to his first case with The Twelve, 'obviously I helped a fair bit and I was there when he died but I didn't pull the metaphorical trigger. And with McMullan, I didn't even go to the Malverns. At all. I went shopping.'

'For this gorgeous ring,' purred Monica, waving her bejewelled finger.

'Exactly.' He kissed the finger before returning it, along with the rest of Monica's hand, to his chest. 'But, do you know what I mean? If this turns into a case, as it looks like it might, then it'll be my third in just over a year. I suppose I just feel that I haven't played my full part yet.' Monica shuffled reluctantly in preparation for having to go to the kitchen. 'Don't get me wrong, I'm not saying that I have an urgent and desperate lust for blood or anything. I just...' He rolled a nagging thought around momentarily to see whether it would settle. 'I just feel that I could be doing more.'

Monica swung her legs out of bed and tiptoed over to the door to fetch her dressing gown. Part of her was mildly irritated at having to relinquish the comfortable position on Thomas's chest but, at the same time, she knew that if something was troubling him, the best course of action would be to talk it through. There was also the strong possibility that, if she could assuage his doubts, Monica could find herself back in the same blissful position within the hour, potentially after a second, more sedate round of passion.

'Decaf?' she asked, slowly tying up the gown. 'Or do we need something more energising?'

Thomas suggested the latter. He listened to her pad barefoot down the short corridor to the living area before hearing the sounds of Monica choosing a CD and then putting it on while waiting for the coffee machine to complete its statutory duties. A year ago, Thomas would not have recognised the soft, piano-heavy jazz as Thelonious Monk but he had recently learnt so much from this remarkable woman, especially about music and culture. He sank into the pillows and smiled, revelling in his good fortune, temporarily forgetting his confidence issues.

Returning to bed with two mugs which she placed carefully on each side table, Monica kissed Thomas warmly on the lips and settled into a seated position with pillows resting on the headboard. 'Now, you delicious man,' she said lovingly, 'where's all this unnecessary anxiety come from?' It crossed Monica's mind that her tales of Ian Bamford's fertility when it came to assassinations may have somehow given her lover a feeling of inadequacy. Perhaps he was envious of a long-dead pharmacist.

Thomas pushed himself up so that he too was less slumped and more straight-backed. He admitted that he'd had a niggling feeling since the late summer, he supposed after his lack of involvement in the McMullan business. The sense of inactivity had been heightened by the fact that he hadn't been chosen for the church excursion and so there was a worry that he would be taking something of a back seat on this case too.

Monica enquired whether he knew much about religion. Thomas's mother had been a churchgoer but never pressured her son to join her, except at Christmas when, he assumed, she had hoped the carols and the nativity stories would inspire him. His dominant father hadn't had any inclination and so Thomas had experienced a generally secular upbringing.

'Then you'd probably be completely useless,' exclaimed Monica with no sense of malice. 'And I mean that in a positive way.'

Thomas frowned. Clearly there was more work to do. 'Okay,' began Monica, 'short history lesson coming up. Brace yourself.'

Thomas reached over to test his coffee. It was too hot. He placed it back down again, rolled towards Monica and wrapped his arm around her, twiddling the end of her dressing-gown belt with his fingers.

'None of the current members of the group actually killed anyone on their first case. It's not as if it's a rule. It's just how it's happened. I know Lexington was always keen to let new recruits go at their own pace and I feel the same way. Veronica's key involvement in the McMullan case was welcome because her television background allowed us a cover story to get to him, but she didn't pull the trigger, as you put it.

McMullan pulled that himself, after I'd loaded the gun, as it were.

'In fact, now I come to think of it, the only person currently in the group who actually did the deed as early as even their third outing was me. Everybody else was fourth or fifth, I think. Belinda's was, hang on...' She started counting on her fingers. 'Belinda hasn't actually personally killed *anyone* yet but then the reason for bringing her into the group in 2017 was because we had had a couple of cases where we needed to communicate with people for whom English wasn't their first language.

'Belinda may *never* actually kill anyone but that doesn't matter. She's a valued and vital member of the team and she always plays her part. She's never *asked* for a more active role in the sharp end of proceedings and I would certainly never pressurise her into feeling that she should.'

Monica extracted herself from Thomas's arm and grabbed her coffee. It too was still steaming but she made a start on it anyway.

'Tell me again about your first one,' said Thomas, ignoring his coffee as he knew from painful experience that Monica's palate was less sensitive to heat compared to his own. He vaguely remembered hearing the story on one of the couple's many Underground journeys into the suburbs during the Burrows case a year before. 'Someone called Heath, wasn't it?'

Monica congratulated him on his powers of recall and started swigging the coffee which was now merely searing as opposed to blisteringly hot. Dylan Heath had been a London property developer working predominantly on South American projects and managing them remotely. His company, Heath Construction Management, had been responsible for ensuring the safety and robustness of a series of apartment buildings in Brazil and Uruguay.

Through Mrs Mendoza, who had distant relatives in Brazil,

it came to The Twelve's notice that two of the apartment buildings, one in the Uruguayan town of Rocha and the other in Porto Alegre, Brazil, both built and owned by Heath, had collapsed during the space of six months in 2013 with the loss of twenty-four lives including four children. Martin, who had joined The Twelve in 2012, was particularly upset by the deaths of two cats and a dog named Arturo.

An in-depth glance through Heath's personal emails had revealed that he had deliberately used substandard building materials on all of the apartments with a view to increasing profits for the management company. In one of the emails, sent in response to valid concerns from a surveyor in Montevideo, Heath had written that he *wouldn't have a problem if they all fell down because they're insured up the kazoo and we'll still get our money.*

Lexington had asked Monica to work on a suitable way to dispatch the odious Heath and, knowing that the property developer was addicted to painkillers following a skiing accident, she had formulated some fatally high-strength Percodan tablets to replace the low-dose codeine that he was already taking on an almost hourly basis. It was Lexington himself who swapped over the packets during a lunch at La Stella, ostensibly to agree a new multi-apartment deal based in Guyana. On that occasion, Monica had further assisted by lacing Heath's drink with strong diuretics, ensuring that he needed frequent visits to the toilet.

'You're amazing,' said Thomas, finally, tentatively beginning his coffee.

'He was dead within half an hour,' Monica reminisced. 'We dragged him out the back of La Stella and plonked him in Martin's cab. We didn't have the acid bath in 2014 so we took him back to his own apartment in Battersea, broke in using his own key because we hadn't acquired Terry at that point either, laid him on his bed and made it look like an accidental overdose. I think Anna might have done the tox report, even though she hadn't yet joined The Twelve. She was friends with Lexington so she knew what was what.' She rubbed her hands together as if dusting off flour or sawdust. 'Job done. Anyway, please don't worry about your involvement or lack of. Your time will come. It might be this case or the next one or the next one. But there's really no need to panic. It's not a competition.'

She finished her coffee, placed the empty mug on the side table and returned to her original position on his chest. 'Did I help?' she murmured contentedly.

'You always help,' said Thomas as he gently stroked her hair. 'You always have. Ever since my tears in the hotel bar all those months ago. And that's just one of the many reasons why I love you.' Monica snuggled closer and, in her mind this time, dusted off her hands for the second time in as many minutes.

14

Junior Christian Walkers congregated in a relatively newly-built hall around fifty yards from the church, a welcome addition to the parish during the 1960s when parishioners were apparently more generous with their donations. It had become a well-used space over the decades with Cub and Brownie meetings, coffee mornings for young mothers and, according to the under-crowded noticeboard in the foyer, a popular whist drive on a Tuesday afternoon. A Christmas bazaar had been held recently, its faded poster, designed by Martha aged seven, now clinging precariously to the noticeboard using a couple of brightly coloured tacks.

On Wednesdays from 7pm until nine, the hall transformed into the venue for JCW. Robert had explained that, until the arrival of Elijah, the club had been called Young Believers and had organised activities including advice talks for younger children about to experience communion and confession for the first time, as well as Bible readings and movie nights for older teenagers.

Elijah's quiet but swift revolution had seen an end to the club's work with anyone younger than sixteen – Father

Matthew had either integrated those events into regular church business or, in the case of the pre-communion children, simply moved their slot to Mondays. Instead, a new, more streetwise and slightly older clientele was populating the hall which was furnished with four tables adorned with handheld video game machines and surrounded by plastic chairs in various shades of beige. A pool table had been installed at one end of the hall and the word *Faith* had been graffitied onto one wall like a tag although what the Tuesday whist players made of such decoration was unclear.

'A handful of the pre-Elijah kids remain,' bemoaned Robert wearily. 'The better-behaved ones. Most of the parents that we used to see back in the spring decided to take their children elsewhere.' The music teacher sighed with regret. 'I don't really blame them. On the positive side, we do tend to be more full. And more rowdy.' As if to prove his point, a group of girls who were playing on a Nintendo in a corner started cheering wildly, inspiring a couple of boys to run over to see who had managed to achieve victory.

Elijah had greeted the four visitors with huge hugs which caused Anna to remark that although she couldn't condone Catherine's attraction to the young American, she could at least partially understand it. His hugs felt like being enveloped in an extraordinarily protective cocoon within which nothing bad could ever happen.

'I am so delighted to see you again, Catherine. And your beautiful friends, oh my gosh. You're all so welcome.' Elijah apologised that he would need to spend most of the evening busy with the young people in his care, but promised that he would ensure that he made some inter-generational introductions as time allowed. 'I let them find their own way for the first hour or so. You'll probably see me going round everyone and gently checking in on their lives and what's been going on since they were last here. Yo, Raheem! Brother!' He held a hand up for a passing young man to slap. 'High-five, my man.' Raheem obliged then sauntered off in search of a drink while Elijah continued outlining his mission. 'Sometimes, I might find out about someone's problem and they'll want to go for a walk and talk it through. That happens a lot. Many of these young people have nobody else to share their anxieties with, and you can solve a bunch of stuff through simply talking and using the word of God for guidance.' His eyes widened to exaggerate the point. 'Then, in the last hour, we'll do some group discussion about Jesus's teachings and how we can integrate His example into our own lives.'

Catherine and her group watched as Elijah spent the next half hour or so patiently moving from person to person, always greeting them with his trademark hug. Riley and Shayna came over for a brief chat. Nathan and Caden largely ignored the visitors except to say 'Yo' as they went to get some low-alcohol beer from the kitchen. Harrison and Letitia kept trying to leave the hall to snog in the graveyard but as Robert had positioned himself custodially by the exit, their romantic plans were frequently thwarted.

'Devante's over there,' said Chris, spotting the young man sitting alone at a table and scrolling through his phone. 'I'll see if I can start up a conversation with him.' He and Anna zigzagged through various small, chattering groups and stood a short distance from the teenager. 'Um, excuse me,' said Chris. The boy looked up, his face one of intense curiosity as if he wasn't used to being approached in a friendly way by adults. 'It's Devante, right? We met some of your friends on Sunday after mass. Did they tell you?'

Devante bit his lip and looked back at his phone. 'Ain't got no friends,' he said, more a statement of pride than of sadness. 'Except him. He's my true friend.'

Anna and Chris wheeled round just as Elijah clapped them both on the shoulder. 'Here's my main man,' the American said, beaming. 'What's up, D? You met our visitors, Anna and Chris?'

Reluctantly, and still seated, Devante offered a handshake and nodded half-heartedly. 'All right?' he mumbled.

'We were hoping to have a brief chat with you, Devante,' said Anna softly.

Elijah bristled protectively. 'Maybe another time,' said the American. 'I just need to catch up with him first, if that's okay.' He shouted to Caden and another young man who were swigging their drinks nearby. 'Hey, Caden. T-Dog. Come talk with these good people for a while. I need to get the lowdown on what's vexing D here.' Caden and T-Dog, whose real name was later revealed to be Toussaint, dutifully ambled over and fist-bumped first Chris and then Anna. 'Give us ten minutes, yeah?'

The ex-surgeon and retired pathologist were ushered slowly but purposefully in the direction of the kitchen. When they turned back to where Devante had been sitting, both he and Elijah were nowhere to be seen. Anna glanced at her phone to check the time. A quarter past seven. *We'll wait ten minutes and then try again*, she thought.

It wasn't until after eight that Elijah reappeared, alone and full of apologies. 'Devante had to get home. I thought it would be a quick ten-minute chat but he's had some real problems lately that he wanted to talk through. We had to walk all the way to the river and then I wanted to make sure he got back safely so I walked him to the bus stop and waited until his bus arrived. He lives over towards Sheen at the moment but things are not good in that young man's home. Anyway,' a beatific smile spread across the American's face, 'I'm back just in time to start the group talk.'

'What sort of problems?' asked Chris. They had spent well

over an hour keeping an eye on the door awaiting Devante's return while Robert had patiently brought a variety of young people with the full spectrum of religious engagement into their orbit while simultaneously shepherding Harrison and Letitia away from temptations of the flesh.

Elijah smiled broadly. 'I don't want to get too personal because these are difficult challenges that the young man is facing. And I'm sorry that you didn't get the chance to speak with him on this occasion but I hope you can understand that he's at a very fragile point in his life having just turned eighteen with all that that entails. The adult world can be scary. New connections may not be good for him. Let's just say that because of his time in care and foster homes, he finds it hard to comprehend that he is loved. By everyone in this room. But we talked and we prayed together and I reminded him of the words of St Mark: '"Whatever you ask for in prayer, believe that you have received it and it is yours. And whenever you stand praying, forgive, if you have anything against anyone, so that your Father also who is in heaven may forgive you your trespasses".' He's in a much better place now. Anyway, if you'll excuse me. The Lord's work cannot wait.'

He made his way to the front of the hall and clapped his hands. 'Okay, ladies and gentlemen,' he began. 'If I could have your full attention please. I'd like to speak a little bit about Paul's letter to the Romans which I was rereading over the weekend so get yourselves a fresh drink if you need one and let's talk.' The last word was shouted triumphantly and was greeted with wild cheers.

The thirty or so young people speedily extracted themselves from whatever they were doing and pulled some plastic chairs into a haphazard triangle facing Elijah, some of them after a quick visit to the kitchen for refreshments. For the next twenty minutes, the group were held spellbound by the oratory which focused on the apostle's letter but also drew inspiration from prominent rappers and influencers to make the words more accessible, before Elijah opened the floor for discussion which flowed enthusiastically.

'He's very impressive,' whispered Anna as they watched attentively from the back of the hall.

'Indeed,' replied Chris, 'but turn carefully to your right. By the door.'

Anna slowly moved her head until the corner of her eye settled on a solitary grey figure, his envious face etched with fury.

15

M onica's phone pinged with furious delight and gratitude for about five minutes as the various members of The Twelve excitedly checked their swollen bank balances on Thursday morning. *You can thank me properly at yoga later,* she messaged back. *But you all deserve it.* Veronica texted to say that she couldn't remember such a large number arriving in her bank account all in one go, even at the height of her TV fame. Martin messaged to ask whether he could please take Joanne to New York for ten days over the holidays. There were some new and returning shows on Broadway that they were both desperate to see. Monica briefly pondered the likelihood of Martin and his taxi being urgently required on the current case in the immediate future and decided that she'd take the risk. Martin's response consisted of three emojis: a red heart, a bag of dollars and the Statue of Liberty.

'After yoga,' Monica began as Thomas emerged from her bedroom towelling his hair dry, 'do you fancy a quick shopping trip for our Christmas Day guests?' The two of them had oscillated between two festive options: a quiet Christmas Day celebrating not only the birth of Jesus but also the first anniversary of Monica's seduction of Thomas on her sofa, and the alternative 'family' Christmas with Thomas's daughter Emily and her nine-year old twin girls, Flora and Lucy, plus his son, Simon, and his fiancée, Akiko.

After much discussion, and largely at Monica's persuasion, they had decided on the latter. 'When was the last time you all got together for Christmas Day?' she had asked, and Thomas had calculated that although he and his children had been physically 'together' on Christmas Day 2014, on that unhappy occasion it had involved Pret a Manger festive sandwiches and vending machine coffee around the hospice bedside of his wife, Alice.

The last time they had actually sat down together for a traditional Christmas lunch with all the trimmings had probably been a decade ago, before the twins had been born.

'I've actually already got most of the presents,' he admitted sheepishly. 'I tend to start early and I'm usually done by the end of October. Last year was a bit unusual because I wanted to get something for you so I did a quick, last minute Selfridges dash and bought a few extra bits.' Monica was impressed by his uncharacteristic organisation. 'But we can mooch around the shops if you like and if we see anything we like, we can get it. Especially with all this money sloshing around in our accounts.'

Monica thought for a moment. She hadn't really needed to do much gift shopping over the last few years, apart from a few candles for friends and hampers for the other members of The Twelve. 'Have you bought my present?' she asked, intrigued. Thomas confirmed that a number of gifts with her name on were safely stowed in his own house. 'How on earth do you know what I want? I haven't got yours yet. I've got a few vague ideas but I was secretly hoping to get inspiration today. Either that or you could just tell me what you'd like.'

Once Thomas had revealed that he had been covertly

storing up gift ideas since June, listening out for conversational clues as to what Monica might enjoy unwrapping on Christmas morning, she walked over and grabbed his face in both hands before kissing him wildly. 'You are the sweetest human being,' she said, breathlessly. 'If we didn't have yoga in an hour, we would be going straight back to bed.' She checked the time on her phone. 'But let's hold this thought until we get back from shopping.'

Anna, who taught yoga, was already in position when the two of them arrived at the makeshift studio in a house in Euston, closely followed by Belinda and David who had come straight from visiting Lexington. 'He's got a release date,' revealed Belinda. 'January 3rd if all goes to plan and there aren't any backward steps. He's delighted, as you can imagine. He says he wants to have everyone round for lunch at the end of January to say thank you for being such good friends.'

The news of Lexington's discharge from hospital brought a joyous energy to the session even though Anna made it quite challenging. Her excuse was that, as it was the second-to-last yoga class before Christmas, the group needed to prepare their bodies for the orgy of greed ahead. Chris secretly suspected it was to give herself and Graham increased strength before their regular skiing trip after Christmas.

'Shall we have a very quick catch-up on the Barnes case?' asked Monica after everyone had given themselves a restorative shake following namaste. 'Just so we can begin to formulate a plan for the next few weeks.'

'We didn't get much of a chance to talk with Devante,' said Anna, as she pulled up one of the chairs which had been moved against the wall to create more space, 'which is a shame. But we're going again next week so we'll have another try. We're building a good connection with some of the other young people but there's a lot more work to do. We haven't talked at length to any of the kids that were there before Elijah turned up. There aren't that many of them, to be honest. Three or four.'

'And how is this Elijah?' asked Monica.

Catherine pretended to swoon. 'Dreamy,' she said.

Anna was more objective. 'He's certainly charismatic,' she said. 'He'd make a decent dictator if he ever decided to go into politics. You can see how he manages to persuade the young people to join his group and, once they get there, how he inspires them to stay.'

'Most of them,' said Chris, leaning forwards on one of the chairs, a small towel dangling from his neck. 'Robert said that some of them drift away after a few weeks. Boredom probably. God ain't everyone's cup of tea.'

'Right,' said Anna. 'But the young people we saw are completely bewitched. A bit like Catherine.' The former journalist stuck out her tongue. 'And he's very good at getting them to really think about the Christian message. You saw how they all stopped what they were doing when the group chat started. They're in the palm of his hand.'

Belinda asked whether they could try to get a photograph of Elijah, 'Just so that Catherine doesn't have the monopoly on worshipping him.'

Monica agreed that this would be a good idea. 'Not,' she explained, 'for the purposes of salivating but simply because we might need it. In case anything happens to him. Talking of which, I understand this Robert might be a person of interest.' Chris outlined to the group that Robert was the polar opposite of Elijah. Uninspiring, monotone and possibly harbouring some suppressed anger towards the American.

'But no obvious motive for killing random people,' said

Terry, 'and didn't you say there were two different killers and they're probably young?' Monica agreed that Suzanne's assertion that the suspects were moving at speed towards Hammersmith Bridge probably ruled out the music teacher, but suggested they try to get a photograph of Robert too. Perhaps a group selfie before Christmas if that could be achieved without arousing too much suspicion.

'I'll attend mass on Christmas Day too,' said Catherine. 'I don't need company unless anyone really wants to.' Both Owen and Graham said that they had no objections to a few carols and a bit of angel on shepherd action, after which the three of them could indulge in some festive frivolity of their own.

Monica sighed. 'Just don't give anything away in the church, please,' she warned gently. 'And certainly no physical affection. You don't want to unwittingly become targets. Focus on the animals in the stable rather than fondling in the pew.'

'There are no animals mentioned in the Bible during the nativity,' corrected Chris wearily. 'Yet another misrepresentation.'

16

The following Wednesday evening, the four who had been most closely involved with the case arrived at the church hall to find Elijah engaged in a mildly competitive game of pool with a boy they'd never seen before. 'This is Kris,' he said as the boy looked up from the table, cue posed and seeming disinterested, while Elijah bestowed his customary hugs upon the visitors. 'Like you, Chris, but with a K. He's just starting today. I've been chatting to him on and off at his residential kids' home in Mortlake. Say hi, Kris.'

The boy, whom Anna estimated to be about seventeen or eighteen, barely nodded and returned to focus on his shot. Chris with a Ch scanned the room. 'No Devante today?' he asked when he was reasonably certain of the boy's absence.

Elijah sighed. 'Regrettably not,' he said, mimicking a sad clown face and rubbing away imaginary tears. 'More problems at his foster home, with the mum mostly, but I'm working with him privately so that his journey towards the light continues. Sometimes it's better that I take a one-to-one approach to help these guys through their most challenging times. But you can talk to Kris if you like.' A benign grin crossed the American's face. Kris angrily potted a stripe ball and looked around the four elderly faces with an expression which suggested he would prefer to run across a busy motorway barefoot than speak to any pensioners.

Catherine excused Kris from the ordeal by saying that they didn't want to interrupt the game and would instead talk to Robert who was, as usual, floating uncomfortably and aimlessly like a discarded crisp packet on the fringes of a group of boys who were engaged in a vibrant game of PlayStation football. 'Robert,' she said, slightly startling the music teacher, 'how's tricks?'

Robert reached out a hand and limply shook with each of the four visitors, stooping forwards so that his body proximity to them was as distant as possible, before speaking. He had experienced a difficult week, soul-searching about whether he was still of any value to the youth club which had been his life for so long, and wondering whether the new year might be a suitable time to ask Father Matthew to let him do something else within the parish; something a little less stressful.

'It's a shame,' he said, 'because I used to feel I was making a real difference. These days, I'm much more uncertain than I've ever been about my own abilities when it comes to changing lives through the teachings of Jesus. I've asked Him for guidance,' Robert's eyes turned briefly heavenwards, 'but I'm experiencing challenging feelings that I've never had before.' Anna reached out for the man's shoulder to offer comfort but he drew away, eyes lowered this time towards the other place. 'The seven deadly sins are a terrible thing, two of them in particular,' he muttered cryptically before pausing and regaining some spiritual equilibrium. 'Come and say hello to William and Archie,' he said brightly. 'I don't think you met them last week. They're "originals", as I like to call them. Here before...' Robert drew in a long, exasperated breath, 'the changes.'

He guided them to a table where two young men with storm-cloud fringes were deep in conversation with Nathan. 'Hey, guys,' said Robert with an undertone of resignation. 'What are you chatting about?'

'Football,' said Nathan, smiling. 'These are tryin' to tell me that Arsenal are going to win the League. I'm like, shut up. Arsenal always bottle it at the end. City all the way.'

'Do you support City?' asked Anna, uncertain of which City was being name-checked but simply reaching for a conversational foothold. Nathan made a face. It transpired that he hated City, who turned out to be from Manchester, because he personally supported United, also from Manchester. He also quite liked Fulham but not as much. 'I'm Anna, by the way.' She shook hands with Archie and William, who had preferred to be called Will in recent months. 'I met Nathan last week. These are my friends Catherine, Owen and Chris. With a CH.'

'You met the new boy then?' Nathan grinned, glancing over to where Kris and Elijah were in the death throes of their pool battle, Kris victorious. 'My guess is that he'll be glued to Elijah for the evening, or at least until group chat. That's how it works, innit. No cap.'

Chris's interest was piqued. 'How what works exactly?'

The three young men playfully punched each other on the shoulder and almost fell into a half-hearted fight before Archie spoke. 'If you're Elijah's favourite, he spends more time with you. He's always got one. First there was Reece and then Tyrone. Recently it's been Devante but now that he's out of the picture, it's the turn of Kris.'

Robert's face assumed a glum expression of introversion, having inadvertently retreated from the conversation.

'Devante's out of the picture? What does that mean? Is he okay?' Anna tried to mask a look of shock, worried that some misfortune had befallen the young man in the white puffer.

Will decided it was his turn to add his opinion. 'He's not, like, dead. I seen him on Monday. He was sitting in the churchyard talking to Elijah. But I'm not sure he'll be at the club again. Once Elijah thinks they've become the CEO, like, he moves on. It's like they become a beige flag, man.'

Chris momentarily considered referring to a notebook in which he'd written down various translations of street speak, but felt confident that beige flag wasn't yet one of the phrases he had included. Perhaps they needed Belinda's help with interpreting what the young people were saying, although it was probable that even the linguist might struggle. 'Sorry,' he said, 'I'm seventy years old. Forgive me for not being au fait with the lingo. Beige flag?'

'Easy,' replied Will. 'It just means he's no longer interesting. It's like Elijah gives someone all the attention but when he thinks they're ready, he just lets them go and moves on. Like the supermarket checkout, innit.'

Robert, who had been sitting listening carefully a short distance away while keeping half an envious eye on the pool game, suddenly got up and left the hall. 'That guy is sus, man,' said Nathan, clicking his fingers. *Sus*, thought Chris, mentally scrolling his notebook. *Suspicious*.

'Nah,' said Archie, 'he's actually all right. I known him for a while. Since, like, before you started coming here. He's just salty. Elijah is the main character now. He probably feels out of place. Like United's manager. Under pressure and awaiting the chop.' Nathan took this comment as the opportunity to jovially wrestle Archie to the ground.

Anna suggested that she go and talk with Robert outside while the remaining three continued the conversation with the boys as it seemed some form of progress was being made. She slipped quietly out of the door of the hall and into the cold winter air where she found Robert slumped disconsolately on one of the wooden benches by the side of the north transept. 'May I sit down?' Robert nodded solemnly. 'We don't have to talk. I just wanted to check you were okay.' Anna made the decision not to reach out a comforting hand again, mindful of the reaction to her previous attempt.

They sat in silence for a few minutes, Anna grateful that she had chosen to wear her warmer coat. A light breeze from a curdled night sky whistled through the trees and gravestones. Somewhere in the distance to the north, a police car siren rose and fell. Finally, Robert exhaled and turned to the ex-pathologist. 'You mentioned that you might be starting a new youth club elsewhere in London?' Anna nodded. 'My time here is done. Would you consider employing a middle-aged, reclusive homosexual? I've had all the police checks done and I've never been in any trouble.'

Anna laughed. She reassured the music teacher that his sexuality was absolutely none of her business and that neither that nor his age and certainly not his introversion should exclude him from working in youth clubs, especially those that only existed theoretically for the purposes of a Twelve case. 'I think you're needed here, though, Robert,' she said kindly. 'From the little I know, Elijah seems the sort who gets bored easily. He probably won't be here this time next year. He may even be gone by Easter. Father Matthew will require a steadying influence. So will these youngsters. I can think of nobody better than you to provide that for them.'

Robert considered this for a moment before emitting a long sigh. 'Maybe you're right. It just feels like it's all spiralling away from me. Do you understand?' Anna confirmed that she knew exactly what he meant. She suggested a cup of tea in the vestry and the music teacher eagerly agreed.

As the conversation began to flow fitfully while the kettle boiled, Anna became increasingly convinced that Robert was nothing more than a good man, if slightly unusual and insular. She texted the group to let them know where she was and within minutes Chris had joined the impromptu counselling session.

After three cups of tea and a visit to the toilet for each of them, Anna looked at her phone and saw that it was almost nine. 'We'll just catch the end of the group chat,' said Robert who had become slightly more animated and open during the previous hour, 'but I'm not sorry to miss it tonight. This conversation has been much more enlightening. Thank you both. I think I know what needs to be done now.' Anna wondered whether he might be in the mood for a hug but Robert simply guided the two friends out of the vestry, turned off the light and locked the door behind them.

Catherine and Owen were waiting just inside the JCW hall as the three returned. 'How's it been?' asked Chris.

'Dynamic,' said Owen, pointing towards Elijah who was standing amidst the massed seats of young people with his arms outstretched and eyes ablaze as he reached the climax of his oratory.

'And remember the words of Luke's gospel when you are feeling like the world is against you. "Blessed are you when people hate you and when they exclude you and revile you and spurn your name as evil on account of the Son of Man. Rejoice in that day and leap for joy, for behold",' he stepped forwards and laid his hands on Kris's head, '"your reward is great in heaven".'

17

The last to leave, Elijah locked the hall at just after 9.40pm and strode through the graveyard adjusting his coat against the stiffening breeze, the South London pathways and pavements swollen by a sheen of dead and decaying leaves. He turned right towards the river, satisfied with the evening's achievements. The group chat had been vibrant, possibly aided by the lack of Robert's bleak presence to flatten the atmosphere. He didn't know where the music teacher had vanished to, and frankly he didn't care.

The other positive about the evening was that Elijah had begun the delicate process of nurturing a replacement for Devante because that young man's journey of enlightenment would soon be coming to an end.

As the bridge heaved into view, he was aware of someone following reasonably close behind and getting nearer. There were roadworks on the bridge – weren't there always? – but it remained open to pedestrians so Elijah quickened his pace and manoeuvred his way past the various obstacles and directional signs at the southern end of the river crossing. His pursuer, shielding their face with a grey scarf, also picked up speed as

Elijah passed the first tower, adrenaline beginning to flow into his muscles. If this was someone hoping to steal his phone or worse, the American was confident that his strength would make the assailant think again.

Almost halfway across the bridge, the cold, dark eddies swirling angrily below, Elijah turned, prepared for a confrontation. 'Oh, it's you, Robert.' He sighed, relieved. 'You kinda scared me. I thought you were a mugger or something. Are you okay? I didn't think this was your route home.'

Robert Henderson, despite being almost a foot shorter than his nemesis, grabbed Elijah by the throat and pushed him towards the edge of the bridge, taking the younger man by surprise. 'Oh my, Robert,' he said, taking care to remember to neither swear nor blaspheme despite the struggle. 'What's gotten into you? Let me go.'

The initial effort, along with the briskness of the walk up to the bridge, had sapped some of Robert's energy and he retreated momentarily, eyes burning with rage. 'I know what you are,' he spat, his words tumbling out in a staccato rhythm. 'And I'll beat you. It may take me a while but I will beat you.' Robert turned back the way he had come and began staggering uneasily off the bridge, apparently content that he had made his point.

Elijah swayed uneasily in a state of shock. 'Wait. Robert.' The older man, now just by the tower, stopped and turned back, his face still flushed with remnants of fury. 'I don't know what you mean. I'm simply trying to spread the word of God. Like you are. Are you not happy with all the new members of JCW? Can we talk it through? Please? Remember Mark's gospel. "For whoever does the will of God, he is my brother and sister and mother".' Are we not brothers you and I?'

Robert moved to the edge of the bridge and looked down into the swirling current. He felt consumed by hatred, a feeling he had never experienced before. The conversation with Anna in the vestry had somehow had the effect of clarifying certain elements in his mind which had been troubling him for weeks. 'I do not believe you are a man of God,' he half-whispered, half-hissed. 'And you are *not* my brother. You deliberately take them from me.'

A few feet closer to the centre of the bridge, Elijah scratched his head in bemusement. 'You're making no sense, Robert. Who do I take away?'

'All of them!' Robert screamed into the darkness. 'Reece. Tyrone. Now Devante. My boys. As soon as you know I like them, you start using your influence on them and they leave before I've had a chance to really get to know them. Before they've had a chance to get to know me. To them you're like an angel of some sort. To me you are the Devil.'

'Have you been drinking, Robert?' Elijah's face carried a look of profound concern as the music teacher's words suddenly began to make sense. Robert sank to the ground and he sat, knees bent on the damp, cold pavement, his back against the bridge structure, scarf hanging lank and despondent from his neck. 'Oh, Robert,' said Elijah, moving tentatively closer before he felt that the distance was appropriate and then sitting a couple of feet away from the stricken man. 'I had no idea. I'm so sorry.'

They sat together in silence, the monotonous chorus of distant traffic from the main road on the other side of the river punctuating their uncomfortable solitude. To the south, a midweek office Christmas party could be heard mutating rapidly into an evening of alcoholic regret. 'You know,' said Elijah quietly, 'I could talk to Devante for you. I know he likes you. Maybe I could set something up for after Christmas.'

Robert glanced upwards at the kind-faced American. He hadn't expected this reaction. Had he possibly made a mistake? Over the last few weeks, his mind had been whirling ominously with numerous images, possibilities and anxieties. He no longer knew what to think. 'Why would Devante like me?'

'I know him. He's like you in so many ways. That's why I've had to spend so much time talking things through with him. He's been so confused about his own sexuality with nobody to talk to. He's been denying who he is for so long but he's slowly coming to terms with it. I reckon the guidance of an older man could be just what he needs.' Elijah smiled benignly. 'I could arrange for you to spend some time together. Just the two of you. Maybe in the church when it's quiet. Just the two of you.'

Robert's mind filled with images both confusing and beautiful. He had imagined himself kissing Devante so many times, holding him, just as he'd pictured the same with other men over the years. Even just befriending him would have been enough. Naturally, Robert's crippling shyness and self-disgust had never permitted him to make any sort of approach, let alone organise anything physical. Every minute he craved the touch of another man but for his entire life this had been nothing but an unattainable dream. A wish beyond his reach.

Elijah stood and held out his hand to pull Robert gently to his feet. 'Let me see what I can do,' he said, searching for eye contact. 'No promises. And it may take a little time what with the holidays and all.' Robert nodded that he understood. 'Trust me. I'm your friend.' The American considered a conciliatory hug but, knowing that Robert reacted badly to such affection, settled for a light slap on the shoulder. Robert even recoiled from this.

'We should both get home now. My mother will be waiting and you need to get out of this British weather.' Elijah watched as the music teacher trudged steadily away from the bridge in the direction of Barnes village before disappearing from view, his greyness dissolving into the winter night. The American walked north towards Hammersmith but stopped at the end of the bridge, considering the strange events of the last few minutes. His mind settling on an idea, Elijah found a bus shelter, pulled out his phone and composed a text.

> D. Can we meet tomorrow? I've been given a
> sign and I know now what God needs you
> to do.

He pressed send and waited for Devante to reply positively before completing the short walk home to his basement flat with bars on the windows to keep out intruders.

'I'm home, Ma,' Elijah shouted joyfully as he entered the flat and locked and bolted the door behind him.

The only answer was a faint and plaintive knocking from the far end of the darkened building.

18

'He's just a bit weird,' said Anna over coffee and cake with Chris, Monica and Thomas. 'I don't think he's a killer.'

The four friends had been due to visit Lexington at 2pm but his nurse had informed them on arrival that The Twelve's former leader had recently fallen asleep and, rather than wake him unnecessarily, that they should go and find a convenient café for half an hour. This suggestion filled Chris with excitement as he had noticed a tempting French patisserie on the windy walk from the Underground. 'Having said that,' Anna continued, 'there's definitely an anger that he's suppressing. I'm sure Mrs Mendoza would have a field day with Robert Henderson. It feels like there are years of repression and self-loathing there. If he wasn't so ordinary, I might be worried.'

'The banality of evil which could manifest itself in spontaneous and random violence,' added Chris, ravaging a generous slice of tarte citron. 'But equally there are things about Elijah that concern me. I know Catherine is slightly besotted but I've got a niggling feeling that something isn't entirely right. He's obviously keeping us away from Devante and that could simply be overprotectiveness because of the boy's mental health problems but it might equally be something else. Something more sinister.'

Monica, who was sharing a mille-feuille with Thomas, believed that all they could realistically do at this point was to keep monitoring both men. 'When you spoke to Robert in the vestry, I don't suppose you mentioned either of the murders?' Anna said that she had, in passing, made a reference to the Liam Tucker killing back in the summer. Robert had immediately expressed immense sorrow as Liam had been a friend of a friend. There had been no sense of anything but genuine shock and sadness at the librarian's untimely death.

The nurse texted from hospital to say that Lexington was now awake and looking forward to their delayed visit. Chris hoovered the remains of the tarte, using a finger to tidy the sides of his mouth of pastry crumbs, and the four of them set off on the short journey to their friend.

'I feel awful,' Lexington said as they arrived in his private room with a takeaway box of tarte Tatin, 'to have been asleep when you came earlier. So rude of me. Please accept my deepest apologies. Bobby came over yesterday and it was a bit of a late night.' He winked conspiratorially at Chris who smirked in response.

Thomas was delighted to see the old man in a chair as opposed to his bed. He even stood with relative ease to lightly embrace everyone for the first time in weeks.

'That was a scare,' said Anna. 'When you said you felt awful I thought, that's not good for someone who's meant to be going home in a matter of days.'

Lexington apologised for the second time in as many minutes

and confirmed that actually he was feeling extraordinarily well, all things considered. Better than he had for many months. His knee was performing well, his blood pressure was decent and the regular visits from everyone were hugely aiding his recovery.

'I feel that I could probably go home now,' he exclaimed, more animatedly than Thomas had seen him since Monica's and Chris's joint birthday party in the summer. 'Yet I must be uncharacteristically sensible and abide by the wishes of the health professionals. However, January 3rd is D-Day, as it were. Martin and David are going to help me with the transfer back home and Bobby is going to stay with me in the flat for a while just in case I need anything. Martin's moved his return flight from the Big Apple so he can be back on the 2nd, bless him. Heavy-pencil Sunday the 23rd of January for lunch at my place. I shall confirm the week before.'

As Lexington appeared invigorated from his nap, the group filled him in on the Barnes case on the off-chance of a nugget of wisdom – 'It's certainly a strange one; but then I never did have much time for organised religion. I visited the Vatican a few times with Sophia Loren in the fifties and I always felt that the sheer opulence of the place was somewhat incompatible with the teachings of Christ. All that stuff about rich men and camels and eyes of needles and the place is dripping in stolen gold.' He was also delighted to hear that Suzanne Green's woes had temporarily abated. The two of them had been in irregular text contact and Lexington had humbly offered sage advice regarding the Home Secretary which apparently had been most useful.

'It wasn't the frilly knickers, was it?' Monica had remembered a story about the politician from Lexington's New Year's Eve party almost a year before.

The old man laughed and said that no, it was something

exceedingly more controversial which he felt should probably wait for another occasion.

Just after 4pm, the nurse popped her head around the door to ask whether anyone needed anything as well as to let Lexington know that Bobby City had arrived with the surprises. 'Christmas gifts for you all,' he said brightly as the leather-clad fixer sashayed into the room carrying four brightly-coloured bags. 'Small tokens really, of my appreciation over recent months. The others will get theirs as and when I see them over the coming days. Belinda and Terry are coming tomorrow.'

Bobby said a formal hello to everyone and passed round the gifts.

'You can open them now,' Lexington announced, 'so I can watch your reactions.'

With typical consideration, Lexington had personally chosen presents to suit each friend. Anna received a signed book by Anne Tyler, one of her favourite authors, while Chris had been given a personalised mug on which was written *World's Best Grandad* which made him laugh. An expensive miniature of whisky completed the ex-surgeon's present. Thomas opened a small, framed drawing by the artist Tracey Emin of the London 2012 Olympic stadium where many of the athletes he worked with towards the end of his career had won medals. Monica's gift was a CD by the jazz pianist Herbie Hancock. 'Look inside,' said Lexington, a cheeky grin developing across his face. Secreted inside the CD case was a small Christmas card in which Herbie himself had wished Monica and Thomas the greetings of the season.

'How?' asked Monica. 'Just how? You seem capable of performing miracles even from your sick bed.'

The old man beamed. 'Herbie and I go back a long way. We spent some time together in the early eighties during his incongruous "pop" period. I once had to appear on *Top of the*

Pops with him as one of his backing musicians. A real musician had issues with his visa and couldn't fly over. Luckily I only had to mime. We've stayed in touch on and off. Anyway, I hope you all enjoy them.'

Monica and Thomas promised to visit again on Boxing Day while Anna said she would probably next see Lexington when he was back home in Pimlico as she would be off skiing a couple of days after Christmas. Chris said he would liaise with Monica and fill any visit gaps as required. 'I look forward to that with great anticipation,' he said. 'Now, if you'll excuse me, I should probably pay some attention to Miss City here.'

He glanced towards Bobby who was loitering patiently in a corner. 'I suspect we may decide to carry on where we left off last night.'

In Barnes, meanwhile, Father Matthew was anxiously pacing the floor of his vestry, silently praying to whomever might be listening that his actions of the previous weeks hadn't somehow made matters worse.

19

'It's time you learnt the truth,' said Elijah as he and Devante sat at a bus stop in East Sheen to shelter from the rain which was pouring from a slate-grey December sky. The American had collected Devante from a nearby budget hotel where he had been staying for a few days, paid for by Elijah. Nobody from the boy's foster home had visited the church to enquire about him. To all intents and purposes, Devante had disappeared.

A bus approached, slowed. The two potential passengers made no sign of wishing to travel so it accelerated again, lightly splashing their feet under the plastic screen of the shelter which played temporary hostess to Christmas supermarket advertising. 'You and I have spoken many times about the need to live our lives according to the teachings of Jesus.' The boy nodded solemnly. 'And, of course, I have grown to love you as a brother and hopefully you feel the same way. And brothers take care of one another, right?' Devante smiled feebly. He hadn't previously experienced the care that Elijah had shown him. Over the last couple of months, he had somehow grown increasingly dependent on the inspirational American, thinking about him constantly. Not in a sexual way but simply in a devotional way, as if he had become somehow enslaved voluntarily.

'However, we've also spoken of how a great number of the people in this city are sinners. They flatly refuse to accept the love of Jesus into their hearts and repent and that makes them the worst kinda sinners in the eyes of the Lord.' Elijah was staring hard at Devante now, his piercing eyes burrowing into the side of the boy's head like an invasive parasite. 'And it is our duty as true followers of Jesus that we cleanse the streets as best we can. It is the most important work that we can do. Does not the gospel of Matthew say about this city of sin that "it will be more bearable on the day of judgement for Tyre and Sidon than for you. It will be more tolerable on the day of judgement for the land of Sodom than for you"?'

Devante looked up and met the intensity of the American's eyes. 'What do you need me to do about it?' he asked with a quiet determination and reverence.

'It will not be easy, my brother' said Elijah kindly, 'but I will work with you to ensure you succeed in the eyes of the Lord.' He paused. An ambulance passed, siren screaming. 'You know that Robert likes you? In an unclean way.' The boy gave a shocked gasp and turned away. 'And you know also Paul's words to the Corinthians when he wrote, "Do not be deceived; neither the sexually immoral, nor idolaters, nor adulterers, nor men who practise homosexuality will inherit the kingdom of God".' A resigned nod.

'Robert is a sodomite and we must join together in Jesus to end his suffering,' said Elijah, placing a hand on the boy's knee. 'After Christmas. Epiphany. You must take the next step towards righteousness.'

Devante leant forward. There was an overwhelming noise in his ear, traffic on wet tarmac as well as an internal buzzing. 'I will,' he said. 'I've been reading John's gospel as you asked of me. "The one who rejects me and does not receive my words has a judge; the word that I have spoken will judge him on the last day". I want there to be no doubt of my faith on the last day.'

Elijah beamed with a radiant glow. He was proud of this young man, possibly the best so far. The rain had eased off and an elderly woman with a shopping basket was approaching, apparently intent on joining them. Elijah eyed her with concealed fury. 'Let's walk,' he said. The two of them stood and smiled politely at the elderly woman who gratefully sat under the shelter, took off her showerproof hood and shook it, second-hand raindrops pattering softly onto Devante's trainers.

'Sorry, dear,' said the woman. 'I should have waited until you'd gone.'

'No problem,' replied the boy in a bleak monotone. 'May God be with you.'

What a nice young man, thought the woman as Elijah and Devante hastened in the direction of the hotel, the older man assuring the younger that he had been told of God's plan for the killing of Robert Henderson and that this would be revealed to Devante in the days and weeks before Epiphany.

As they arrived at the hotel, Elijah reached into his pocket and retrieved a new mobile phone. It was fairly basic but Devante recognised its purpose immediately. 'From now on, I only want you to contact me using this phone. My number is programmed into it. Nearer to Epiphany, we will need to dispose of your smartphone but you can use it for now. Just don't call me from it, okay?'

Devante said that he understood. 'You'll help me afterwards, right? You'll hide me until the day of judgement?' Elijah assured him that God's plan included salvation after a period of repentance.

The American held out his arms to the boy for one of his

consuming hugs. 'I can now tell you the true meaning of JCW,' he whispered. 'To most, the initials stand for Junior Christian Walkers. Yet, for a special few, JCW represents Jesus Christ's Warriors.' He eased his embrace and placed his hands on Devante's slim shoulders, pinioning the boy with his eyes. 'We are waging an eternal war, my brother,' he said, 'and there are always casualties in war. I'll see you tomorrow.'

A few minutes later, settled in his bleak hotel room, Devante fired up his new phone. As expected, Elijah's number was the only contact under the pseudonym 2C1114.

20

That Christmas Day was unusual for every member of The Twelve for many different reasons. As it was Belinda's first Christmas of actual widowhood, she and Veronica had decided to leave London and book a three-day spa break at a country house in Bedfordshire. The idea of total relaxation while others were hurtling about visiting relatives held a distinct appeal and both of them seemingly spent most of their time texting the group with pictures of themselves sipping a variety of cocktails or lounging by pools in towelling robes.

Anna and Chris had decided to spend the day together, just the two of them, at Chris's house in East London. They had arranged a mini tour of Chris's three daughters for Boxing Day and the following day before Anna departed for the slopes. After rising at an improbably late 10am, and following a leisurely half hour of Christmas sex, they washed, dressed, breakfasted and assessed the weather before venturing outside for an equally unhurried walk.

He was not prone to introspection but Anna had noticed Chris becoming more distracted as the year drew to a close. This, he revealed, was a result of many landmark occurrences in his life over the preceding twelve months: turning seventy; his brush with death back in March at the end of the Burrows case and the ensuing mental health anguish; and of course, the impending arrival of his first grandchild.

Since the summer, Anna had wondered often whether he was considering leaving The Twelve but, whenever the subject was broached, he had always denied such thoughts. He was enjoying himself too much, he claimed, despite the occasional dangers. Yet her concerns remained, along with the increasingly attractive notion that both of them could leave over the course of the next year and spend their remaining time together doing what normal people do. Could she subtly shepherd him towards a huge life change? Would she even want to?

In Whitechapel, Terry woke early to bake Christmas cookies, having already made three Christmas cakes earlier in December, storing them and feeding them with rum every few days. Removing the third batch of cookies from the oven as the skies finally became light just after eight, he inhaled fully and remarked to himself that his house was almost certainly the most festive-smelling place in London at that precise second. He also took a moment not just to enjoy his solitude but also to think of his wife, Irene, lost to liver cancer over a decade previously.

His quiet thoughts were interrupted by a mobile phone call from two of his seven grandchildren calling from Essex with news of their gifts. They too had been awake for hours. He would somehow manage to see all of his extensive family over the coming days.

At 10am, Terry took one of the cakes and a box of cookies down to Mrs Mendoza and stayed with her for an hour, chatting casually about everything and nothing. At eleven he returned home to collect the remaining goodies and took a cab over to Belgravia where David was already in effervescent conversation with Lexington. The old man was delighted with Terry's treats, as were the nursing staff as they knew from experience that they would become the main recipients of the former locksmith's culinary expertise as well as the largesse of their delightful patient.

Just after two, the two tradesmen retired to a half-empty pub just off Sloane Square for Christmas lunch and a couple of refreshing pints before returning to their respective homes by taxi at around five.

Later in the day, across the Atlantic, Martin awoke next to Joanne on their second morning in their hotel on West 52nd Street, a short skip from both Central Park in one direction and, crucially, the theatre district in the other. They had already taken in the revival of *Company* and a splendid production of *Waitress* and were planning to book more shows after a Christmas Day spent sightseeing. Joanne was keen to visit the Empire State Building to relive the final scene of *Sleepless in Seattle* and although Martin had never actually seen the film, he wanted this trip to be perfect.

Arriving at the building just after eleven, they realised that the queue was already so long that it would probably take about two hours to get to the top, so instead they took a yellow cab down to the World Trade Center, Martin enjoying a genial chat with a fellow cabbie who hailed from Brooklyn, and then wandered slowly around Soho and Greenwich Village for a while before taking a cab back to their hotel past the Empire State Building queue which had grown even longer.

Fresh from an afternoon snooze, the two of them ventured out again, bescarfed and mittened, to take in the lights from Times Square to the Upper East Side. Returning to Midtown and finding the queue had become more manageable, Martin and Joanne finally made it to the top of the Empire State

Building where they kissed, wonder-smitten, looking south over Manhattan Island towards the statue and the sea.

At Monica's apartment in St John's Wood, she and Thomas spent the morning prepping lunch, him mostly peeling potatoes and carrots while she cooked the turkey and arranged the table with festive serviettes, crackers and edible glitter. She had never cooked a turkey for seven before but Terry had assured her that it was basically just a big chicken and that the beauty of a turkey was that you could cook it early and leave it to rest, even for an hour or two, and it would still be delicious. The gravy is key, he had said, and had provided a foolproof recipe which Monica had made earlier in the month and frozen for ease.

For the first time in over twenty years, Monica's apartment was the essence of Christmas with a real tree, fully decorated, and the whole living area ablaze with tinsel. Hanging on her mantelpiece, as always, was the solitary bauble that remained from her second marriage, an annual reminder of Patrick who died in September 2001 at the very spot that Martin and Joanne would visit in a few hours.

Just before noon, Emily arrived with the twins and they were followed twenty minutes later by Simon and Akiko. Presents were gratefully opened and Monica was particularly thrilled with a singing bowl which Thomas had bought back in September after she had expressed a desire to own one. She had promptly forgotten about it but, in contrast, he had made a mental note and found a shop near his house which sold the finest Tibetan bowls and whose delighted owner was brimful of wise advice. Her gift to him was a long weekend away on the island of Capri to be taken whenever circumstances allowed.

Lunch was punctuated by regular texts from Veronica and Belinda which had to be explained to the guests as simply a couple of friends enthusiastically communicating their adventures. Afterwards, the twins Flora and Lucy, played in

Monica's spare room while the older generations watched the Queen's speech, Thomas and Monica, hand in hand, sharing a loving, secretive glance in memory of the moment a year earlier when she had seduced him on the same sofa.

They considered a late-afternoon walk but it had begun to rain during lunch so instead elected to play Scrabble, one of the many games that Thomas's wife Alice had enjoyed playing with the children when they were teenagers. Emily and her girls made up a team while Simon joined with Monica and Thomas with Akiko. The Simon-Monica team won with a last-minute FLUX on a triple word score.

Following a round of coffees and mince pies which Akiko found intriguing, they settled down to watch a movie, after which Flora and Lucy began to get sleepy and all the guests decided that they should probably be heading home. All seven of them agreed amidst the warmest of hugs that it was the best Christmas Day they could remember and the twins announced that it was their best one ever and demanded that every future Christmas take place at Monica's house without exception.

After clearing the Christmas detritus and polishing off the remaining four cold roast potatoes between them, Monica and Thomas settled back on their historic sofa with a glass of white wine each and some Beethoven piano sonatas in the background, both agreeing that they couldn't recall a happier Christmas.

Owen and Graham turned up at Catherine's house just after ten and the three of them set off for the church half an hour later, guided by jubilant nativity bells.

Father Matthew greeted everyone dutifully while gazing with anxiety at the clouds threatening a downpour at any moment. There was no sign of Elijah who apparently was taking care of his mother on this most joyous of birthdays. A handful of the young people were in their customary back pew although not as many as usual, perhaps eight or nine. Many of the others, according to Matthew, had probably been out drinking on Christmas Eve and were therefore still in bed. He hoped that a few more might be attracted to the noon mass on the next day, the Feast of St Stephen.

The most interesting quality about the Christmas mass was Robert's demeanour. He had worn a colourful tie, red adorned with trumpeting angels, and was positively ebullient and full of festive cheer. He greeted each member of the congregation warmly and even, unthinkably, gave Catherine and Owen a light hug; Graham, whom he hadn't met before, had to settle for a cellophane handshake. Owen commented on this uncharacteristic new bonhomie and Robert simply replied that he was in a good mood because Christ is born.

'Plus,' he said, smoothing tufts of his grey hair down at the sides, 'I have an excellent feeling about the new year. Something truly wonderful may be about to happen.'

21

Midway between Christmas and New Year's Eve, Graham and Anna left to go skiing in Austria until January 7th, an annual trip since the winter after Graham joined The Twelve in 2018. This meant that Chris was at more of a loose end than usual. Without a spontaneous New Year's Eve party at Lexington's to attend, he, Thomas and Monica spent the last day of the year visiting the former leader, demob-happy and mere days away from release from hospital, before a late-evening dinner at La Stella.

Over a tableful of indulgent antipasti including bruschetta, fritto misto and mini mozzarella in carrozza which delighted Chris as the small spheres of fried cheese vaguely resembled doughnuts, the three discussed the year gone by which had been dramatic for each of them in different ways.

Monica recalled that she had begun the year cautiously hopeful that she might become leader of The Twelve; there was also the excitement of meeting Veronica for the first time at Lexington's New Year's Eve party and then there was the conclusion to the Burrows case closely followed by the events which led to various members of the group travelling out of

London to deal with a corrupt former police detective at the sharp end of the next case. Did Monica feel settled into the role yet? asked Chris.

She rolled this thought around her mind for a moment, chewing a mouthful of tomatoey, garlicky toasted ciabatta as a catalyst for decision-making. 'I'm not sure I ever will,' she said, post swallow. 'I look at Lexington and all he's achieved in his life and all the amazing people he knows – I mean, he was on *Top of the Pops* with Herbie Hancock, for heaven's sake! – and I wonder how little old me could ever compete. And then I realise that it's not actually about competing at all. It's about being happy with what you can personally achieve and not worrying too much about what you can't. Every leader has made the role their own and put their mark on The Twelve. So I'm trying to take inspiration from some of the phenomenal women who had the post before me, like Beryl Edwards and Margaret Wilmot. Thankfully they had the feminine foresight to leave an abundance of notes and advice which I'm dipping into.'

She took a swig of Pugliese Fiano to help rinse through the remaining crumbs of the bruschetta. 'So I suppose the real answer to your question is that I'm muddling through, knowing in my heart that that's essentially what we're all doing on a daily basis. In The Twelve as well as in life. Nobody has all the answers but if we're good people and we surround ourselves with other good people whom we love, all we can do is our best. And try to leave the world in a slightly better place than it was when we arrived here. That's our duty as human beings surely?'

'Very Lexingtonian if I may say so,' Chris said, grinning. 'Does anyone want this last mozzarella doughnut thing?'

Thomas's year had been equally revolutionary. If he cast his mind back to the October before last, his life had been very much in a holding pattern with a regular schedule of shopping, bin days, visits to Emily and the twins, the very occasional walk to Alice's grave and little else. Perhaps it was because they were sitting in La Stella that the situation demanded that he contemplate all that had happened since his first meal there.

He glanced wistfully over to the corner table where he and Lexington had sat on that life-changing autumn afternoon just over fourteen months earlier. The unsmiling face of mid-career Brando still glowered from the wall above although, of course, the restaurant was busier on this particular evening than when he had been gently persuaded, cajoled into joining The Twelve. This in turn had led to his making many new friends so that his social life had become more replete than it had ever been. Furthermore, he had unexpectedly fallen in love, something as unplanned and as glorious as anything he could have conceived.

He grasped Monica's hand and kissed it, not requiring words at that moment as she knew all that he was thinking.

'And as for you,' Monica said, nodding at the former surgeon, 'your seventieth spin around the sun has been a rollercoaster if ever I saw one.'

Chris let out a snort of understatement. 'Stabbed. Traumatised. Creator of a makeshift field hospital in a spare bedroom.' He paused in momentary contemplation. 'I wouldn't have missed it for all the world.' He picked up his glass and hovered it over the table in preparation of a toast. 'But on the positive side, I too have fallen in love again and there's a grandchild on the way, so, if I may, I'd like us to raise a glass to the future. Whatever it may bring.'

It was Thomas who first noticed that Simone, the owner, wasn't quite his usual jovial self. His greeting at the beginning of the evening had been slightly subdued and throughout their starters Thomas had perceived that the restaurateur appeared uncharacteristically stressed despite La Stella being almost full of delighted customers.

As he came to clear away the main-course plates –

strozzapreti alla Norma; spaghetti vongole and beef agnolotti –
Thomas touched him gently on the arm and asked whether
everything was okay. 'Oh, Signor Thomas. I can keep no secret
from you. Something bad has happened,' said the Italian
mournfully, dispensing with the h's. 'I tell you after coffees.
When we are a little more empty. You will have coffee? And
maybe some dolce?' He turned to Chris knowingly.

'I wonder what's troubling him,' said Monica anxiously as
the owner slouched back in the direction of the kitchen. 'I hope
he's not unwell. I couldn't bear the thought of Lexington getting
fixed just as Simone suffers a health scare.'

After coffees and a shared slice of polenta cake with vanilla
cream, extra large because Simone knew that Chris would
demolish most of it, the Italian pulled up a chair, vacated from
an adjacent table, and revealed the cause of his anxiety. The
Mexican restaurant two doors down from La Stella had closed
just before Christmas and almost immediately the building had
been shrouded in scaffolding and sheeting with a discreet yet
ominous sign the only clue to what might be happening beyond.

'They're opening a new Pasta Tansa almost next door,' said
Simone, gloom overcasting his usually radiant face. 'You are
familiar with Pasta Tansa, si?'

Chris and Thomas weren't particularly well acquainted
with the London casual dining scene and so Monica had to
provide explanations. A celebrity chef named Jeremy Tansa
had, earlier in the year, launched a new chain of high-quality,
low-cost pasta restaurants with the view, he claimed, to
eventually have a Tansa in every town and city in the UK. He
had managed a low-key launch with the first restaurant in
Brighton but the reviews had been spectacular and, as a result,
Pasta Tansa had opened branches in Oxford, Bristol, Milton
Keynes, Reigate and Portsmouth at the rate of roughly one a
month and with greater fanfare.

'This will be his first in London,' said Simone. 'And, allora, it will clean up. I have friends with restaurants in Oxford and Bristol and they say that their own trade has, how do you say it, fallen from the cliff. And they don't even have cliffs in Oxford. I was not going to retire for a few years but now I wonder whether I should start planning to get out of this business sooner rather than later. Before I am pushed by this Tansa.'

Monica stood up and put a comforting arm around his shoulder. 'Simone, try not to worry. This is La Stella. You have a hugely loyal following built up over decades. Your restaurant is part of the London hospitality furniture. You'll be here long after we're all gone.'

He forced a feeble smile. 'You are always so kind to me, Signora Monica,' he said. 'But next year will be a big challenge. I can feel it in these old Italian bones. And the restaurant business is tough at the best of times. The last thing I need is competition from a household name.'

'We could burn his books in the street in protest,' said Chris. 'This Tansa fellow. I imagine he has books.'

Monica confirmed that he had published over a dozen cookery books and was constantly on television in one form or another. In addition, there was a range of Tansa tinned spaghetti shapes available in most supermarkets and even branded crockery decorated with Jeremy's face which customers could buy from the restaurants. The global empire of Jeremy Tansa was not something with which it would be easy to compete.

'Well, look,' said Monica, giving Simone a friendly kiss, 'we will always come here rather than two doors down and we will continue to tell all of our friends to come here, particularly if you keep serving food like you did today. The strozzapreti was outstanding.'

'You are too kind,' said Simone, brightening incrementally.

'You know the tale of the strozzapreti, si?' The three friends shook their heads. 'There are many variations on the story to be honest but I prefer the one where the villagers in central Italy used to invite the local priest for lunch on Sunday after mass. If the priest liked the food, he would often return again and again which was, of course, a drain on the meagre resources of the villagers. These were not rich people, you understand. So to subtly inform the priest that he had overstayed his welcome, they would serve this shape of pasta, the strozzapreti.

'Roughly translated it means priest strangler.'

22

E lijah's instructions were clear. As Devante approached the heavy wooden outer door of the church on the evening of Epiphany carrying a small rucksack, his overriding emotion was not one of fear but of clarity; a sense that his entire short life had been leading to this point.

The two morning masses celebrating the visit of the Magi to the infant Christ were long finished and the building was empty with only the lingering aroma of frankincense as a clue to the earlier gatherings. Devante sat in one of the middle pews, pulled on the tight leather gloves which Elijah had instructed him to wear, and waited.

Just before six, he could hear the methodical crunch of footsteps on the gravel path leading up to the church. These were followed by the loud creak of the door opening and the appearance of a drizzle-damp Robert, breathless and smiling in his familiar dark-grey coat and light-grey scarf. 'I dared not believe you'd be here,' exclaimed the music teacher, his voice echoing through the bones of the building. 'I assumed Elijah was having a joke at my expense. But here you are.'

The two of them gazed at each other with timid uncertainty

across the pews. 'So... um, Devante.' Robert hesitated, battling his shyness. Even in his mid-forties, this situation was entirely new to him. 'What do we do now? Do you want to sit and talk?'

Devante, in contrast had been prepared for this moment. Since the beginning of the year, he and Elijah had met daily to finesse the entire plan and seemingly every possibility. He stood and moved slowly in Robert's direction until the two men were inches from each other. Robert felt that his heart might burst through his chest with excitement. Had it ever beat so fast? And why did he have a sudden urge to urinate?

'I'm sorry, I'm a little damp from the rain,' stammered Robert, inexplicably delaying what he had been desiring desperately over the thirty repressive years since puberty. 'But I didn't realise it was...' Devante leant forwards, took Robert's face in both gloved hands and kissed him gently on the mouth, repulsed by what he was doing but knowing it was necessary to complete the task that God had ordained for him.

For a brief moment, the older man was sure he could hear angels singing in the roof timbers, a heavenly choir condoning his actions. Robert barely noticed as Devante's hands inched down and took hold of the ends of the scarf and began to pull. To tighten. It took a few seconds for him to realise what was happening but by then it was too late. 'Devante,' he gasped, 'what are you...' but the words were merely stifled syllables as Devante's face transformed into a picture of violent hatred.

Robert attempted to use his hands to break free but he was no match for the stamina of the eighteen year old. Elijah had provided him with free weights to further build his upper body strength in the days leading up to this fateful meeting.

It took just over a minute until Devante finally felt the last remaining filament of energy seep from Robert's body and he let the dead man fall to the aisle and crumple, head hanging limply, by one of the pews. Devante wiped the kiss from his mouth with a sleeve. It had been necessary but it disgusted him. It was a vile stain to be eradicated. There was an overwhelming desire to kick Robert's lifeless body but Elijah had warned against this. The police might be able to trace fibres from Devante's shoes.

As instructed, he moved silently to the front pew where Elijah had left a specific copy of the Bible, bookmarked with green ribbon for ease at the Book of Romans, chapter eight, which the American had highlighted earlier in the day. Devante took the book to the altar and lay it open at the relevant page before stumbling over the verses in a whisper.

'"For those who live according to the flesh set their minds on things of the flesh, but those who live according to the spirit set their minds on things of the spirit. For to set the mind on the flesh is death but to set the mind on the spirit is life and peace".' Devante stood silently for a moment in contemplation of his actions of the previous few minutes. 'Life and peace,' he repeated, as if in a trance. He looked down the aisle at the motionless Robert, who had slipped further onto the floor with the unlikely fluidity of the dead, and then up at the crucifix which hung watchful above the altar.

'Forgive me, Lord,' he mouthed before running from the church. Instead of taking the gravel path down to the road, Devante took the rehearsed route through the graveyard and through a gap in the hedge to an alleyway leading to a cul-de-sac of newly built houses. He followed a remembered map through smaller roads and avenues. This way, he would largely avoid cameras until reaching the main road where he headed north in the direction of the bridge.

Here, Devante found a suitable spot and reached into the rucksack to retrieve a new pair of trainers into which he changed before casting the original pair into the river where they floated silently eastwards.

He had memorised the route to Elijah's home. Although he

had never entered it, Elijah apparently concerned about waking his mother, he and the American had walked the journey a dozen times or more since Christmas, so, even in the dark, it was easy.

There were no lights on inside as he walked down the steps to Elijah's basement flat but Devante assumed this was simply because the inhabitants were in the rear of the property. He rang on the doorbell as requested, a shrill, trebly note. There was no answer. He walked up the steps just to check he hadn't made a mistake. Elijah was walking quickly towards him bearing a couple of blue, brandless carrier bags.

'You just beat me,' Elijah said in a state of high excitement. 'I had to pop out for supplies for everyone. Is it done?' Devante confirmed that Robert was dead. 'And the Bible?' Also achieved as required. Elijah placed the bags on the ground, opened his arms wide and enveloped the young man in a gigantic embrace. 'I knew you were the best,' he said in a tone of ecstasy. 'Now, are you ready to begin your period of repentance?' The teenager nodded. Elijah descended the handful of steps and opened his front door. 'Good. Reece and Tyrone have been patiently waiting for company. Let's go join them. You can go in first. Straight down.'

Elijah closed and bolted the door behind them before ushering the boy down a long corridor towards the back of the flat, stopping briefly to retrieve a sevoflurane-drenched flannel from the kitchenette.

23

Lexington's earliest days back at his Pimlico flat had also been the busiest, bringing a tsunami of visits from all members of The Twelve as well as other diverse friends from his long and exceptional life. Even Suzanne, despite her ongoing political challenges, had managed to carve out a precious hour to have a cup of tea and three of Terry's butterscotch crunch cookies at the former diplomat's home. During this hour, at least one of the commissioner's many problems had been solved by a well-placed phone call from Lexington to a friend in the civil service.

So it came to pass that Catherine was at Lexington's enjoying a delicious supper of chicken and leek pie with Veronica, Chris and Owen when the frantic call came from Father Matthew. He had entered the church around 8pm for a moment of quiet prayer to be confronted with the corpse of his friend Robert Henderson, skin now as grey as his clothing, collapsed and cold in the ornate aisle. Catherine advised the priest to try not to panic, something she immediately realised was unlikely, and told him she would be there within twenty minutes. Chris decided to join her while Veronica and Owen deliberated momentarily but then decided that on balance they would be better served staying with Lexington on account of a rhubarb tart, newly-baked by Terry, in the fridge. Besides, it didn't take four people to tend to a priest in his hour of need.

The former newspaper editor and the surgeon apologised for their hasty exit and promised to return another day soon before taking the lift to the ground floor and hailing a grateful taxi to take them south through the sparse, dark January streets to the Barnes church. There they found Father Matthew sobbing next to the body of Robert, the music teacher's unwashed-linen face emotionless and passive. Catherine comforted the priest while Chris did the necessary medical checks. 'Definitely dead,' he confirmed, 'and although this is more Anna's department than mine, I'd say he's been here for a good couple of hours. He's not completely cold but he's certainly not warm. His corneas are clouded but there's no rigor mortis yet.' The ex-surgeon lifted up an arm and let it drop limply to the floor to prove his point.

Catherine looked up with a how-do-you-know-this? kind of expression. 'Pillow talk with a forensic pathologist. Sorry. Have you called the police or an ambulance, Matthew? He's been strangled, by the way, in case you hadn't realised. Probably with this scarf although I'm not going to touch it for obvious reasons. I don't want to contaminate the body too much, even though I have a cast-iron alibi and any strangler worthy of the name would wear gloves anyway.'

The priest admitted that he felt unable to call either emergency service. This was both on account of the initial shock but also the consideration of what would happen to the church if there was another scandal. What would the papers say? What would the bishop say? Catherine redoubled her embrace as the priest began to weep again. 'We need to inform the police,' said Catherine quietly, 'as they will need to do a full forensic investigation and they'll need to question you I'm afraid.' The priest's eyes widened in fear. 'But, I think I may be able to maintain a degree of secrecy if you don't mind trusting me for a few minutes.'

The ex-journalist moved towards the front of the church and made a call to Monica, explaining the situation in brutal detail. Monica in turn called Suzanne Green who immediately texted Catherine to say that someone would be with her within the hour. Someone familiar whom they could trust.

Just before 9.30pm, the church door opened and DI Ted Black walked in, accompanied by a young woman wearing a disposable overall and gloves. 'Evening, all,' said Ted chirpily. 'I've always wanted to say that. My dad used to play me videos of *Dixon of Dock Green*. Lovely to see you both again. It's been far too long.' He turned to the young woman. This is Beth Truscoe. Forensics. Beth, meet Chris and Catherine and,' he shook hands with the priest, 'I'm surmising that you're Father Christmas. Cheers for the bike in 1980.'

'Pleased to meet you all,' said the woman as Catherine corrected that Father Matthew was preferred. The detective inspector apologised and said that he could fully understand.

'It's a shame Anna is skiing,' continued Ted. 'She and Beth would have got on like a house on fire. Never mind. Anyway, what have we here?' He turned his attention to the body in the aisle and gestured to Beth to begin her examination.

'Strangled,' said Chris. 'Around 6pm. With his own scarf, most likely.' The young crime-scene investigator nodded respectfully. 'I've not touched anything, by the way. Apart from his arm and his wrist for the obvious routine medical checks.'

'I understand that you found the deceased, Father,' said Ted with as much sympathy as he could muster. 'Do you mind if I ask you a few questions? Is there somewhere quiet we can go?' Catherine lifted the priest to his feet and the three of them eased gingerly towards the vestry where Catherine put the kettle on and made everyone cups of tea, leaving Chris to make small talk with the forensics expert who was already studying the deceased with her magnifying glass.

'I have a friend who used to be in forensics,' he offered. 'Retired now.'

Without looking up from her work, Beth Truscoe replied, 'I'm aware. Anna Hopley. An inspiration of mine. A pioneer for women in this field and one of the best of us. The commissioner told me about you. Don't worry. Your secret is safe.' Beth smiled in an attempt to convey trustworthiness. 'I'd say you're right about the time of death. And the strangulation which is fairly obvious owing to this bruising and the petechiae on his face. Two points of interest that you've missed though. Neither of them your fault because they're almost impossible to spot with the naked eye.' Chris raised an eyebrow, equally impressed that this woman was in awe of his lover and curious at what she had uncovered in such a short space of time.

Beth looked up. 'There are some tiny fibres under his fingernails where he's attempted to fight back. That might offer up some DNA depending on whether it's skin or material. And also, more likely to be useful, judging by the minor disturbance in the lip balm he was wearing, he's recently been kissed, probably by a man owing to the lack of lipstick and probably just before he died.'

Betrayed with a kiss, mused Chris, glancing momentarily at the crucifix above the altar.

24

Once Devante had regained consciousness, he realised that he was in absolute darkness apart from a couple of very small, very distant flashing red lights. He attempted to speak but something was obstructing his mouth, meaning that only a muffled consonant emerged. He tried to move but, as with speaking, that too was constricted by something heavy attached to one leg and one arm. He couldn't initially make out what it was in the blackness. The smell of human waste filled the air making him choke momentarily. He was cold. There was a noise, a monotone hum that sounded like an air filter or extractor fan.

He reached down with his left hand which seemed to be unimpeded; his left ankle appeared to be chained to something. Likewise his right wrist, and this had the effect of contorting his body unnaturally and making it a challenge to sit up.

Devante reached up to his face to see whether there was a possibility of removing the tape or whatever it was that made speech impossible. It wasn't tape though. His face was strapped into some form of tight mask which was padlocked at the side of his neck so that it couldn't be removed.

It was now that the fear took over. He remembered entering Elijah's flat and there had been some talk about Reece and Tyrone and then nothing. Devante listened. There seemed to be someone else nearby; he could just about hear laboured, uneven breathing. He made the muffled sound again; cautious, scared. From about ten feet away came a feeble, similarly muffled response followed by another, further off and from a slightly different direction.

A small square of white suddenly appeared almost ahead of him but to the right. A window, possibly high up in a door. Someone had switched on a light in an adjacent room. A few seconds later, Devante was blinded as the room abruptly illuminated as if he had been inadvertently standing next to a searchlight. It took around a minute to become accustomed to the overwhelming brightness but eventually he managed to focus and gradually blurred images formed into a view that resembled something from a horror movie.

He was chained to a wall in a bleak, sparse room of austere concrete. A short distance away was another young man whom Devante recognised as Tyrone from the JCW; the two of them had met briefly back in October before Tyrone disappeared, moved to a different part of the country to continue God's work, as Elijah had announced proudly at the time. And yet, here he was. He had lost weight over the interim months and now Tyrone's sunken eyes were filled with sorrow, resignation and defeat.

Further away, a third man, also chained, lay malnourished and half asleep in a corner. Reece, Devante presumed. Opposite this third man was a toilet which, although it had a cistern, didn't seem to have the luxury of toilet paper. A large metal trunk glowered darkly from beyond the toilet. In two corners between wall and ceiling, small cameras were blinking, observing, judging.

Even more horrifying was a solitary wooden chair by the door on which had been placed a skull with clumpy strands of long, lank hair draped over it like some ghastly, decaying curtain. Some of the teeth on the left side of the skull were missing.

Elijah's smiling face appeared at the window and, seeing that Devante was awake, he unlocked the door and stepped into the room, directing his attention first to the skull. 'Good evening again, Mother,' he said brightly. 'I just came to check that our new guest was behaving himself and settling in okay. I know that sometimes it can be a bit of a shock moving from a moment of action into a period of repentance.' He moved towards Devante who flinched reflexively. 'But Mother here watches over you to check that you're not falling into bad habits while you repent.'

Now that it was light, Devante could see that he was indeed chained to a wall with only one leg and one arm free to move. Judging by the sight of Tyrone and Reece, he was also wearing a tight leather mask with a gag and zips where the eyeholes were positioned.

'Now, before we take our medication, does anyone require the washroom?'

Devante now realised that he needed to pee but he decided to wait and see what indignities this would entail. Luckily Tyrone also put his hand up warily and Devante watched as the complex process of going to the toilet began.

Elijah moved towards the trunk and opened it with a thump as the lid hit the wall. He removed a pair of handcuffs and a longer piece of chain with a manacle at one end. He walked over to Tyrone who looked up pleadingly. 'Aaaaawwww, Tyrone,' said the American, 'don't give me that look. You know your period of repentance is not yet done. And as soon as you've pissed or shat or whatever it is you gotta do, it'll be Ritalin time and everyone will be happy again. Even Mother. And she's rarely happy these days as you well know.'

He zipped Tyrone's eyeholes so that the young man couldn't see and then carefully handcuffed him before exchanging the shorter leg chain for the longer. Then he helped Tyrone to his feet, the young man's muscles complaining from lack of use, and led him slowly to the toilet. Once there, Elijah pulled down Tyrone's jogging bottoms and underpants and sat the miserable figure on the seat.

'Now,' Elijah directed his attention back to the petrified Devante, 'in case you're wondering why Tyrone doesn't make more of an attempt to escape, it's because he knows from bitter experience that any such behaviour is frowned upon by me and by Mother, and can often result in serious injury. Take Reece for example.' Elijah gestured towards the other figure as the sound of Tyrone defecating and then urinating echoed through the room. 'Now Reece is no longer in possession of all of his fingers and that's simply because he tried to escape when it was just him. He had to be punished. As we know from Paul's letter to the Romans, "for those who are self-seeking and do not obey the truth but obey unrighteousness, there will be wrath and fury". You wouldn't want to incur wrath and fury, would you, Devante?'

The young man shook his head, tears clustering in his eyes. Then he gestured towards Tyrone who was unsteadily standing from the toilet, drips of urine falling bleakly onto the concrete floor. 'You need a little wipe?' said Elijah as if talking to a baby. He returned to the trunk and retrieved some toilet paper which he used to give Tyrone a perfunctory clean before pulling up the man's pants and joggers. 'Do you need to go too, Devante?' A nod. 'Okay, wait one sec while I get Tyrone back to his bed.'

Elijah returned Tyrone to his original position and reattached the wall chains before unzipping the eyeholes. 'Just like Bartimaeus in Mark's gospel,' he said, turning his attention to Devante. 'The gift of sight is restored. Now, your turn.'

Devante closed his eyes just before Elijah zipped the holes but just as the American was exchanging the manacle for the handcuffs, Devante used the fraction of time available to punch Elijah in what felt like the American's cheek. At the same time Devante made the loudest noise he could under the circumstances in the hope that somehow Tyrone or Reece would be able to help to incapacitate Elijah.

Instead, Devante felt himself pushed to the floor as if by a bear, his already aching head pummelled repeatedly. He tried to protect himself with his cuffed hands but he couldn't see which part of his body was being targeted and so each punch came as a surprise. After a minute, the onslaught ended as quickly as it had begun. Devante could taste blood from somewhere. 'You can't say I didn't warn you,' said Elijah calmly. 'Mother was not entertained by that little outburst. Yet God is merciful and so, as it's only your first night here with us, you will not lose a finger. However, you will not receive medication tonight and I will have to think very carefully about whether you deserve breakfast in the morning.'

The American reconnected Devante to the wall chain before standing and, after deliberately leaving the new arrival's eyeholes zipped, walked back towards the door, the smell of Tyrone's unflushed excretions lingering in the small space. 'Revelation, chapter two, verse ten,' Elijah exclaimed. '"Do not fear what you are about to suffer. Behold, the Devil is about to throw some of you in prison that you may be tested and for ten days you will have tribulation. Be faithful unto death and I will give you the crown of life".'

Devante heard the door shut and two locks being activated. Then, for the first time since he was a toddler, Devante pissed in his pants.

25

W hen Beth had completed her initial examination of both the deceased and the crime scene, and after Ted had managed to wring a few potentially useful droplets of information from the distraught Father Matthew, the corpse of Robert Henderson was placed carefully into a body bag and Chris helped Ted and Beth to carry him to their unmarked estate police car before returning to the relative warmth of the church narthex. Father Matthew, grateful that somehow all of the people currently in his church appeared to be doing their best to keep Robert's murder as low key as possible, asked what would happen next.

'I'll go back to Scotland Yard and do some more work on these possible DNA samples,' said Beth, carefully placing the Bible from the altar into a plastic bag and sealing it. 'There are no obvious fingerprints on the body apart from Dr Tinker's but there might be some on this Bible so Ted will need to take this as a piece of evidence. Naturally there are two potential problems with the Bible.'

Only two? thought Chris.

'One is that it will probably have been used by many

members of the congregation over time and secondly that this scritta paper that they use for Bibles isn't ideal from a forensic examination perspective but we'll do our best.'

'What about Robert?' asked Father Matthew. 'I'll need to perform a burial at some point. He didn't have any surviving family but I know there are members of the congregation who will wish to attend his funeral.'

Catherine explained that after a post-mortem, they would arrange for a local undertaker to look after Robert until Father Matthew could organise a funeral. The Twelve would pay for all the relevant costs including a headstone. 'What will you tell the congregation, Father?' she asked delicately. 'And particularly the young people from the Wednesday group?'

Matthew had been trying not to think about this although it had been chipping away in the back of his mind since his discovery of the body. 'I suspect that I shall need to ask the Lord for His forgiveness once more as I shall require a lie or two. I can trust the four of you, can't I?' He gazed around the faces expectantly. Catherine confirmed that he could rely on their discretion. 'Then I think that I will simply say that he died suddenly. A heart attack, or something. I found him but it was too late. Yes, that sounds credible. Catherine, could you help me please in the event that a newspaper starts asking questions?'

The ex-journalist agreed that she would do all in her power where the media was concerned but suggested that if everyone kept quiet then there would be nothing to alert any journalist to foul play. 'Nobody but us and the killer knows what really happened here, and I'm pretty sure that he or she isn't planning on issuing a press release about it.'

Ted Black chuckled and flipped a few pages back in his notebook. 'I'll need to have a chat with this Elijah Timothy that you mentioned, Father,' he said. 'Do you have a home address for him at all?'

The priest looked awkwardly towards Catherine and then to the heavens. 'I'm not sure that I do,' he replied. 'I know that he lives with his sick mother somewhere over the other side of the bridge but as for an actual address, I don't think I've ever had one. He's an unpaid volunteer so I just invited him in.'

The detective inspector scowled at the priest's naivety. 'No DBS check for working with kids?' Matthew shook his head anxiously. 'Hm, I'm afraid that's a criminal offence, Father, but under the circumstances I'll see what I can do. I have to say that I am brushing so much stuff under the carpet on this one that someone is going to trip over the bumps sooner or later. And you're sure you've never been to his house?' Again, a negative response. Ted sighed in exasperation. 'Okay, well, do you know when Elijah might be in the church again?'

Father Matthew suddenly perked up. 'Yes! That I can help with. Tomorrow. I'm sure he'd be delighted to talk to you then.'

Ted scowled again. He had been enrolled on a course the following day and couldn't realistically miss it without incurring the wrath of his tetchy superintendent. 'I'll send a DC down to take a statement,' he said. 'Catherine, please may I ask you to be my contact here? I can text you the details of the detective constable coming to do the interview.'

Catherine agreed that she would be in the church at the appropriate time and also mentioned that it might be best if she also attended the interview with Elijah as she had begun to feel that she and the American were becoming friends and that he trusted her. Chris gave her a knowing nudge causing her to blush.

'Okay,' said Ted, 'I think we're done here. Catherine, if I may have a quick word.' He ushered the former journalist outside while Beth wandered in the direction of their makeshift hearse and Chris followed the priest back to the vestry to help wash up some cups and teaspoons.

'Everything all right?' asked Catherine as the two of them sheltered from the cold next to an imposing family tomb.

'More or less,' he replied. 'I'll talk to Suzanne about all this tomorrow and we'll obviously feed back when we've got the forensics and after speaking with Elijah. She'll probably want to get more involved if she has the bandwidth.' Catherine said that she understood. 'Just one thing for you to be aware of for the time being.

'Matthew doesn't have a decent alibi.'

26

Catherine and Chris ambled sombrely the short distance back to her house and, after settling on a sofa with a gin and a whisky, Facetimed Monica who was in St John's Wood with Thomas, waiting patiently for an update. 'Highly unlikely that Robert has anything to do with the earlier murders then,' she surmised wryly. 'And from what you tell me, and despite his lack of alibi, Father Matthew is probably uninvolved, apart from being the unfortunate one who finds the Bibles open at certain pages. Maybe it's someone who has something against him personally. Perhaps we should delve a little into that possibility.'

'Let's not completely lose sight of the fact that he was the one who found Robert,' said Chris, adding that the person who finds a body is rarely completely in the clear. In the ex-surgeon's mind, there was something about the priest that didn't entirely add up, although putting his finger on precisely what was proving tricky.

And then there was Elijah with no record of an address and no relevant checks. The DNA examination from Beth and the police interview would hopefully clarify matters one way or another. Monica said that she would check in with Suzanne in the morning and then maybe everyone, including possibly the commissioner, would be in a position to meet after the weekend. With more questions than answers, the four of them said goodnight, Monica and Thomas in St John's Wood, Catherine and Chris a few miles to the south in Barnes.

'I should get going,' said Chris. 'I need to do a bit of tidying in Anna's flat before she gets home from skiing tomorrow afternoon. I've been in and out for the last week just to keep the houseplants watered. Teacups in the sink and all that. Fresh milk in the fridge.'

Catherine sleepily leant her head on his shoulder. 'You're welcome to stay,' she whispered. 'Spare room and all that.'

'You and I both know that if I stayed, the spare room would not get used,' he said, kissing the side of Catherine's head. 'Tempting though it may be. I'm a one-woman man now, Catherine. Anna has tamed me.'

'Pity,' Catherine replied, finishing off her gin in a hasty swig before rising from the sofa. 'I'm envious but I get it. I'll order you a taxi. I've got a funky new app for such emergencies. They rarely appear by magic down in darkest Barnes I'm afraid. South of the river, you see. Ask Martin. Even he's rarely been this far south in all likelihood.'

Within five minutes a black cab had drawn up outside. 'Anna's a lucky woman,' said Catherine as she helped Chris on with his warm coat, the surgeon wincing slightly as his injury tugged somewhere inside the muscle.

'Says the girl with two lovers.' They kissed warmly on the lips like two good friends remembering that once upon a time, for a few short weeks, they used to be more. 'Anyway, I'm the lucky one. See you after the weekend.'

Catherine arrived at the church the following morning just before eleven to find Father Matthew sitting morosely in the pew next to where the body of Robert Henderson had lain a few hours earlier. A text had confirmed that a detective constable named Sanjeev Kumar would be with them around half past and although Elijah's timetable was fluid, Father Matthew was fairly certain that he would be at the church at some point before lunch.

Sure enough, the American bounded through the doors a few minutes later with a small bruise on the side of his face. He embraced Catherine in one of his trademark hugs before sensing from Matthew's grim expression that all was not well. 'It's Robert,' said the priest quietly. 'He's dead.'

A look of intense shock crossed Elijah's face before he collapsed into a nearby pew, face in hands and began to shake uncontrollably in disbelief. Catherine instinctively put an arm around his shoulder and Elijah crumpled into her like a wet carrier bag blown into a bare winter tree. 'He can't be,' he sobbed. 'I only saw him on Wednesday evening. When did this happen?'

Catherine had explained to Matthew that he should keep secret as much information as possible in case it jeopardised the investigation and so the priest simply feigned ignorance, noting that the list of sins for which he would need to plead forgiveness was lengthening by the hour. 'There's a police detective coming to the church to ask you a few questions.'

Elijah suddenly sat bolt upright. 'Me?' he said, his sadness instantly replaced by something angrier. He glared at Matthew with a fury so intense that the priest noticeably cowered. 'Why me?'

'There's nothing to worry about,' said Catherine calmly. 'It's standard procedure. They spoke to Matthew yesterday. It's just so that they can get a fuller picture from the people who knew Robert best. There's no indication that you're a suspect.'

The American's mood had changed dramatically and he was now frantically looking back towards the door, calculating whether the best option would be to run. His mind oscillated violently between choices before deciding that the best plan would be to remain calm. He could answer any questions they threw at him. He'd managed to outwit the police before; he could do it again.

The church door creaked open and a fresh-faced young man in a dark-blue suit entered carrying a thin portfolio. 'Good morning,' he said brightly as he walked briskly towards the small group. 'DC Kumar. I was told you would be expecting me. Father Matthew?' The priest stood and shook hands with the young detective. 'And Catherine. So pleased to meet you. And you must be Elijah, right?'

The American stood, all trace of sorrow and anger suddenly gone. It was as if the previous few minutes were a distant memory and the everyday, vibrant Elijah had been reborn. 'Come to me, Detective Kumar,' he said and enveloped the young man in a warm hug. 'I understand you'd like to talk with me about poor Robert. Well, I can't say I'll be able to help too much but let's do it!'

DC Kumar's face betrayed an element of confusion. He was clearly not used to being greeted quite so enthusiastically by potential murder witnesses but he took it in his stride. 'It's Detective Constable but I'll take Detective for now. Is there somewhere quiet we can go?' he asked. Father Matthew suggested the vestry and Catherine asked whether Elijah would like her to sit with him during the interview for moral support.

'Bless you, Catherine,' Elijah replied, 'but I think I have everything under control. I've nothing to hide after all.' He led the detective constable towards the vestry, glancing back just once to give Catherine a look that she'd never seen on Elijah's face before, somehow less anxious and more energised. Like an actor waiting in the wings, anticipating their cue.

27

Within fifteen minutes, the two men had returned, chattering like reunited old friends. 'Sanjeev has been telling me all about his parents,' said Elijah with a satisfied grin. 'His mum is a huge Bollywood fan which is why he's named after a film star. Apparently she couldn't help herself. Isn't that wonderful?'

'Did you talk about anything else?' asked Catherine, warily. 'Like Robert, for example.'

Elijah's face once again underwent a tectonic emotion shift. 'You didn't tell me he was murdered!' he half-howled, now a picture of grief. 'My poor, dear Robert. I think I'm in shock. I don't exactly know what shock feels like but this sure feels like it.'

DC Kumar explained that he had all the information that he needed and that Elijah had an alibi for his whereabouts which would be checked. 'I hope your mother is feeling a bit better when you get home,' he said as Elijah once again gave the detective a semi-reciprocated hug. 'DI Black will be in touch after the weekend with an update,' he said, turning his attention to Catherine. 'I'd better get back and write this up. Good to meet you all.'

'Thank you so much for your time, Sanjeev.' Elijah seemed to glow as the young detective constable disappeared into the vestibule before turning his attention back to Catherine and Matthew. 'He was nice.'

Catherine stared at the young man who seemed once again to have lurched emotionally into a state of placid dismissiveness. 'Are you okay?' she asked. 'Would you like a green tea? We could go to a café in the village for a change of scene. Oh,' she pointed to his bruised cheek, 'and what's with the bruise?'

The American put a strong hand on Catherine's shoulder. 'Bless you again.' He smiled, touching his face gently with his middle finger. 'I was lifting mother and she accidentally caught me with a stray hand. It's nothing. She spasms sometimes. And thank you for the offer of tea but I will have to politely decline. I have some preparation work to do for next Wednesday's talk and then, if it's all right with you, Father, I may just sit near the altar quietly and read from Luke's gospel before I get home to Mother. She's being hard work right now.' He gave them both a hug and slunk back in the direction of the vestry.

'I guess we'll see what comes back from the DNA and the alibi,' said Catherine, trying to ignore Elijah's unusual behaviour before she could process it alone. 'I'll see you on Sunday at mass, Father. I imagine you'll have to tell the parishioners about Robert.'

The priest exhaled the deepest of sighs. 'It will be the most difficult sermon I've ever had to construct,' he said sadly. 'I will pray for God's guidance to find the appropriate words.'

On Sunday, Matthew's sermon, delivered with the haunted look of a man in desperate need of sleep, took the form of an emotional eulogy. Many of the congregation, especially those older members in the front pews, were unaware of Robert's passing and there was genuine grief when the news filtered through. At the back of the church, Catherine and Owen noted that the young people were less animated than usual, Shayna explaining that Elijah had called most of them on the Saturday so that the music teacher's untimely death didn't come as a complete surprise during mass.

As usual, Elijah was nowhere to be seen and Father Matthew was occupied with a flurry of older parishioners after the service, so the two members of The Twelve were able to chat freely with Shayna, Harrison and the others outside the church. It was a cold but sunny midwinter day and the girls at least were eager to talk.

'You heard about Robert?' squeaked Shayna. 'I reckon someone wet him.'

'Nah,' said Riley, 'Kris told me he was strangled, innit.'

'Kris would know, yeah. He's got Elijah's ear, innit.'

Catherine and Owen listened intently as the rumours ebbed back and forth. 'It's gonna be weird on Wednesdays without him,' said Shayna. 'Even though he just used to loiter about most of the time, it was still nice to see him.'

'Will you be going to the funeral?' asked Owen, aware that these young people might still be their best chance of gathering information over the coming days and weeks. The boys were unenthusiastic but Shayna and her friends said that, depending on the date and time, they would probably be there.

'I got commitments, yeah?' said Riley, 'but if I can make it then I will. Not gonna lie, I ain't sure I got no black clothes, though, innit. Might have to just wear one of my mum's jackets or whatever.' Letitia commented that, as it was Robert, grey clothes might be a more suitable mark of respect.

It was when Catherine asked whether any of them had seen Devante recently that the boys began to show greater interest in the conversation. All of them had been told separately by Elijah that Devante had moved away from London to a new foster home but none of them had heard from him since before Christmas. 'I tried his mobile a few times,' said Caden, 'but he never answered. Sent him some Snapchats too. Nothing. I guess he's maybe changed his number or something. Maybe his phone got swiped.'

'It's like he just disappeared,' added Nathan softly. 'Like Tyrone.'

28

It was just before lunchtime on a crisp and breezy Tuesday before Suzanne could spare a moment to meet The Twelve, the first time she had managed to do so for almost two months. 'As you all know, I had an unusually challenging and unfestive December which slightly buggered my enjoyment of Christmas,' she admitted as she settled into an armchair at the Shepherd's Bush house, 'and although those particular storm clouds have partially evaporated, thanks in part to Lexington's timely interventions, I should make clear that the circling vultures could return at any time. I had to pull in a few favours from friends in the media so that means that the favour cupboard is looking pretty bare right now. Oh, bless you, Terry. You're a dear.'

The locksmith had brought over a fresh coffee for the commissioner along with a plate of home-made Garibaldi biscuits – 'one of my favourite Delia recipes' – which he placed conspicuously within her reach. 'I add a bit of nutmeg just for a giggle,' he announced proudly.

'Because everyone knows that nutmeg is the spice of hilarity,' joked Chris.

'Exactly, Doc,' replied Terry, grinning.

Martin had arrived at the meeting, their first of the year, wearing a new leather jacket and a bright-blue T-shirt with the word *Brooklyn* emblazoned on it. 'Joanne bought me these in NYC,' he said proudly. 'She's stealthily updating my wardrobe. What do you think?'

'Very boy band,' commented David playfully. 'Is there a bandana to go with it? Or a baseball cap?'

Martin frowned with a faint degree of embarrassment but his mood was lifted when both Veronica and Belinda said that he looked very trendy. 'If I wasn't gay,' added Veronica with a seductive wink, 'you'd certainly be on my "to-do" list.'

The news from Scotland Yard following Robert's murder was unhelpful. Elijah's alibi, that he withdrew £40 from a cashpoint in Hammersmith at 5.36pm and then visited a small supermarket before returning home, was confirmed by both CCTV and his bank. Moreover, the DNA extracted from under Robert's fingernails didn't match either the DNA from the Liam Tucker murder or from the Kathy de Souza killing.

Three different murders; three different killers; no obvious motive and the only link between them was someone's inexplicable urge to mark each death with an open Bible on a church altar.

'It's possible,' said Monica, 'that there is actually no direct connection with Father Matthew's church apart from its proximity to the killings leading to the death of Robert within the building itself. It's simply that someone is orchestrating these murders and then placing the Bibles on the altar to deflect attention away from him. We've been preoccupied with the church element but it may be a complete red herring.'

The most obvious next step, in Owen's opinion, would be to put a camera in the church. Catherine suggested that Father Matthew might be resistant to that idea but she would use her persuasive powers to make it happen. 'Then it's simply a waiting game,' said the former surveillance expert.

Chris still maintained that they needed to monitor both Elijah and Father Matthew. 'Perhaps it might be an idea for me or Catherine to get closer to Elijah. Invite him for a coffee and...'

'He only drinks green tea,' interjected Catherine.

'Of course he does.' The ex-surgeon sighed wearily. 'Okay, well, you can have a coffee and he can have a green tea or whatever. I think that if we can get him on his own and build up some trust then we might be in a position to make a breakthrough.' Catherine said that she would make the offer at the JCW the following day.

'Always happy to volunteer for a coffee date with a hot young man,' she said with a grin.

'See if you can subtly ask him whether he's been in contact with Devante and Tyrone and the other young man who disappeared,' said David. 'That's another mystery where we shouldn't lose our focus.'

Monica's phone started buzzing. 'It's Simone,' she said, sighing. 'Does anyone mind if I get this? I asked him to call me if he had any more worries about this Jeremy Tansa business.' Everyone agreed that she should take the call so the former chemist wandered into the bright conservatory which overlooked the garden, resplendent in its dormant, mulchy hibernation with only the winter jasmine unleashing grenades of yellow against the onslaught of January's palette of brown and green and grey. Monica stared at her phone and pressed Accept.

'What's the Jeremy Tansa business?' asked Suzanne back in the meeting area. 'I mean, I know who he is but I'm not a particular fan. I met him at a function about a year ago and I just thought he was a bit of an arrogant twat to be honest. That's the official police terminology.'

Thomas explained about the impending opening of a Pasta Tansa two doors down from La Stella and Simone's understandable concerns for future trade.

'Okay, Simone,' said Monica returning to the main group. 'Try not to worry. I can't get there right now but I'll send someone within half an hour. Okay? Ciao. Ciao.'

'Problem?' asked Anna with concern.

Simone was in a panic because Jeremy Tansa and his head chef had spontaneously arrived for lunch at La Stella and were hungrily working through virtually the entirety of Simone's menu. 'I can't go to him because I've got a hair appointment straight after this and, if I don't sort these roots out today, there'll be trouble.'

'I've got my Mrs Mendoza meeting in an hour and a half,' said Chris, otherwise I'd do it.

'I'll go,' said Veronica, raising a hand. 'I've met Jeremy before. Briefly. At a TV awards thing a couple of years ago. He might not remember me but you never know. Belinda, do you fancy an Italian meal on me? Dig into the Christmas bonus?' The linguist jumped at the chance and Martin agreed to drive them both to save time. Monica said that she'd fill the three of them in with any further meeting decisions by text.

'Did you like him?' asked Suzanne as the ex-TV presenter pulled on her coat.

Veronica scowled. 'Not especially,' she said. 'Like you said, he came across as a bit of an alpha male berk, if I'm honest.' Suzanne nodded in agreement. 'Just wanted to talk about himself for the whole evening and kept ogling the waitresses.'

'And did you win an award?' asked Graham. Veronica confirmed that she had, adding that Jeremy Tansa had frostily departed the ceremony early after being beaten in his nominated category by a young Caribbean street-food chef.

'Thanks, V,' said Monica and stretched for a Garibaldi. 'Oh, have the strozzapreti if it's still on the menu,' she called as the diners wandered down the hallway. 'It's outstanding.'

'Apparently it translates as priest strangler,' added Chris. 'But don't let that put you off. There might also be one that translates as celebrity chef stabber. You never know.'

29

L a Stella was typically busy, even for a Tuesday lunchtime in mid-January. As they gently pushed open the door, Veronica and Belinda were greeted by a frazzled Simone who nonetheless managed a warm smile when he set eyes on his new visitors.

The second thing Veronica saw was Jeremy Tansa seated at a far corner table away from the window next to a large, thickset man with a boxer's nose. The table in front of them was laden with plates of half-eaten pasta dishes, some Carta di Musica and an almost empty bottle of Barolo – 'Is their second bottle,' whispered Simone with a sigh. 'Is one of the most expensive on the menu so I hope they don't expect a freebie.'

The Italian shepherded Veronica and Belinda to the table next to Jeremy who glanced up, slightly the worse for wear, and registered a familiar face. 'I know you, don't I?' he slurred. 'Victoria something. From that antiques programme. *Antiques Chariot* or whatever.'

Veronica politely offered a hand. '*Antiques Caravan*. And it's Veronica but we've only met the once so it's an easy mistake. This is my friend Belinda, by the way.' The linguist waved elegantly as it was less effort than moving around her table to shake hands. Veronica made the decision not to mention the TV awards dinner in case it still held bad memories for Jeremy who partially stood to greet the two of them.

'All right, Belinda? This is Jason. He's my executive head chef.' Boxer's Nose ostentatiously waved an empty fork at the two women and carried on ploughing through a plate of crab ravioli with a saffron sauce which was one of the day's specials. Out of the corner of her eye, Veronica could see Simone hovering anxiously in the kitchen doorway as a smiling young waitress handed the two women menus. Jeremy took the opportunity to look the waitress up and down appreciatively before nudging Jason knowingly. 'She'd be good,' he whispered to his colleague. 'In more ways than one. And we could offer her more money.'

Veronica began perusing her menu. 'Anything you'd recommend?' she asked the celebrity chef, observing his plate-strewn table with a mixture of fascination and disdain. 'You appear to have sampled most of the dishes here.'

Jeremy snorted. In case they didn't know, he was opening a new restaurant virtually next door and simply wanted to check out the local competition. 'La Stella has been an institution around here for decades and,' he waved a hand in the general direction of the other diners, 'it's pretty full for a traditionally quiet month so dear old Simone must be doing something right. I've never been here before so I thought I'd better give it the old Tansa once-over.' He twirled a fork through some pappardelle with a venison ragu. 'This is incredible, by the way. As long as you're not vegetarian.'

'You're a fan of Italian food then?' enquired Belinda, bravely, she thought, as she was finding both men slightly overbearing and was glad of the obstacle of the table between them. Jeremy admitted that it wasn't his favourite cuisine but that his market research team had discovered that Italian was becoming the most popular type of food on the British high street, about to overtake Indian, and had identified a gap in the market for low-priced dishes with a celebrity name attached. 'So you won't be actually cooking in the kitchen?'

'Fucking hell, no,' said Jeremy. 'That's what Jason and his horrible mob are for. I just do the grip and grin these days.'

'And rake in the money,' Jason said through a slurp of ravioli.

Jeremy glowered. 'I can easily find another exec head chef, you little shitfuck,' he hissed. Jason quailed.

'And do either of you speak Italian?' Belinda was slowly gaining confidence.

'Si,' said Jeremy, draining the second bottle of Barolo into both glasses. 'Pomodoro. That's probably my limit, to be honest. Apart from a couple of swear words. What about you, fat boy?'

Jason shook his head. 'Buongiorno?' he offered with a strong Cockney accent.

'He's from Mile End, not Milan,' said Jeremy, laughing, noticeably pleased with himself. At that moment, Simone wandered over to take Catherine and Belinda's order. 'Simone, could I get another bottle of this Barolo, mate?'

'Certo,' replied the Italian. 'I just take the order from these young ladies and I will fetch that for you, Signor Tansa.'

'No rush, mate,' said Jeremy sarcastically, rolling his eyes and scratching his cheek with a finger. 'I'm only dying of fucking thirst but don't stress about it.'

Belinda seamlessly switched into fluent Italian to talk with La Stella's owner. 'We're not quite ready, Simone,' she said, 'so feel free to satisfy these people's dire needs first. With any luck they'll leave after their third bottle.'

'Si, signora. Perfetto. Grazie.' Simone scurried off in the direction of the wine rack.

Jason pulled a small notebook out of his jacket pocket and rooted around for a biro which had become nestled horizontally at the pocket's base and was resisting rescue. Eventually he began scribbling notes with Jeremy adding ideas. 'Venison ragu tastes like there's some juniper in there,' he said. 'This is fresh, probably red deer, but we should be able to get cheaper frozen venison and then maybe we use rosemary unless we can get the forager to rustle up some juniper.'

'What about this crab ravioli?' asked Jason, lowering his voice.

Jeremy scratched his chin pensively. 'We could recipe test it with more brown meat than white to save costs,' he said. Jason nodded. 'Maybe bulk it out with breadcrumbs from the leftovers of the previous day's service. The sort of people who come to my places won't know the bleedin' difference anyway.' Simone returned with the wine and a fresh glass. He uncorked and poured a small glug for Jeremy to try. 'Great,' he said, having swirled the Barolo showily around his mouth.

'Does he ever say please or thank you?' Belinda asked Simone in his native language.

Simone raised his eyes to heaven. 'Non ancora,' he replied. Not yet.

Veronica silently wondered whether there might be a way to tempt Jeremy to open a restaurant in the Barnes area within the current homicide catchment zone.

30

On the day of the first Junior Christian Walkers meeting since Robert's death, Catherine and Owen arrived at the Church of the Immaculate Virgin early on Wednesday evening to check on Father Matthew's welfare as well as broaching the delicate matter of installing a security camera in the nave. Elijah had also arrived early in order, he said, to refamiliarise himself on sanctified ground with a passage from Paul's letter to the Romans which he intended to use to conclude the evening's discussion.

Both Catherine and Owen noticed a perceptible change in the American's mood. Although he greeted them both with his trademark hug, the embrace was looser and somehow colder, as if trying to create distance between them, both physical and emotional. In addition, rather than chatting amiably, Elijah kept himself to himself for half an hour, mostly popping in and out of the church in silence, before the attendees of the JCW began to noisily assemble in the nearby hall. Catherine wondered whether Robert's death had hit him harder than he had anticipated. However, as the evening progressed, it became clearer that the reason for Elijah's behaviour was more complex.

She messaged Father Matthew whose return text was hugely apologetic. He had been delayed returning from a meeting of fellow clergy in Westminster and would be back in Barnes around 8pm. He would meet them at the JCW, adding that it *might be a good distraction for me to be around young people after a day with the mostly over 60s, delightful company though they are.*

While Owen spent some time assessing the best place for positioning a camera or two, Catherine sat in the pew opposite where Robert's body had lain just under a week earlier. Something deep inside inspired her to say a quiet prayer for the music teacher. 'We will find the person who took you, Robert,' she whispered softly, eyes closed. 'And they will be punished. And then I shall ask for forgiveness.' Catherine reached forwards to pick up one of the Bibles from the wooden book rack attached to the pew in front. She flipped casually through the flimsy pages and settled upon the gospel according to Matthew. 'Appropriate,' she muttered, her thoughts drifting in the direction of the priest, and began to read quietly.

'"Do not think that I have come to bring peace to the Earth. I have not come to bring peace but a sword".'

'Not exactly "love thy neighbour", is it?' said Owen who was striding down the aisle having identified several possible locations for surveillance equipment.

Catherine smiled at him and continued her reading as Owen sat beside her. '"The one who receives a righteous person because he is a righteous person will receive a righteous person's reward". Are you feeling righteous, Owen?'

'Never more so,' he replied, caressing her face and kissing her on the cheek. 'Do I get a suitably righteous reward later?'

Catherine grinned. 'We should get to the JCW,' she purred. 'But if we're both still feeling righteous afterwards, I suspect some form of reward would definitely be on the cards.'

They opened the door to the JCW hall to see Elijah, unusually, talking with a group of four girls, two of whom appeared to be new. Owen leant into Catherine, gesturing to a table near the kitchen and whispered, 'Look over there; Kris.'

Catherine followed his gaze and saw that the young man was engaged in a passionate kiss with a girl named Celeste whom they had met briefly at an earlier JCW. 'Might be why Elijah is behaving so weirdly.'

They loitered in the doorway for a few minutes, half expecting Elijah to join them but he merely glanced over and gave a subdued wave before a quick, sorrowful look towards Kris after which he returned to the girls. Shayna and Letitia, conversely, bounded over and gave the two pensioners a hug.

'I feel like I seen so much of you two that you're becoming like my grandparents,' said Letitia, beaming.

'I never had no grandparents,' said Shayna. 'At least not that I know, like. My mum's parents died and I never met my dad, let alone his parents.'

Catherine gave the young woman a second, this time sympathetic, hug. 'Kris appears to be settling in well,' she mused. The girls giggled. Letitia revealed that he and Celeste had got together at the weekend when a small group of them went out to a club in Richmond.

'I guess Elijah will just have to find another favourite,' she said with a giggle. 'Looks like Kris has got his hands full for a while.'

Just after eight, the hall door opened and Father Matthew scurried in, slightly flustered and apologetic after having had to wait for a bus from Putney for longer than seemed necessary and then requiring a quick visit to the vicarage toilet before joining them. 'I'm sure this Robert business has played havoc with my bladder,' he said anxiously. 'I do hope that's not revealing too much information.'

The three of them sat at the back of the hall as Elijah invited the thirty or so young people to gather for the evening's discussion. 'Father,' Catherine began quietly, 'how would you feel if Owen put a couple of discreet security cameras in the church? Out of the way so that only we know they're here. That way, the next time someone places an open Bible on the altar, we should have a record of it.'

The priest thought for a moment. 'Would it be permanent?' he asked anxiously. Owen confirmed that the cameras would be removed once the case had been concluded to everyone's satisfaction. 'Well, in that case I don't see any harm. When would you be able to fit them, Owen?' The former surveillance expert replied that he could easily acquire the necessary technology by the weekend and then, if he wasn't busy, Terry could help him to fit everything on Saturday.

Around forty minutes later, Elijah's lively discussion ended with a reading from Romans which he had been revising earlier in the evening. '"We rejoice in our sufferings",' the American recited, glancing occasionally towards Kris who was hand in hand with Celeste, '"knowing that suffering produces endurance and endurance produces character and character produces hope and hope does not put us to shame because God's love has been poured into our hearts through the Holy Spirit who has been given to us".'

He stared silently into the middle distance for a moment before continuing. His voice had been becoming progressively louder during the oration but now it assumed a sombre, pensive softness. 'Many of us have been suffering privately since the tragic loss of our dear friend, Robert. But if we can endure that suffering then our character will ultimately lead us to hope. As usual, if you need to walk and talk with me about how God can help us at this difficult time, then I am here for you. May God be with you.'

The JCW group dissolved gradually over the next few minutes and Elijah made his way slowly to the back of the hall where Matthew was sitting with the two members of The Twelve. 'It's good to see you here, Father,' he said, barely acknowledging Catherine and Owen. 'To what do we owe this pleasure?'

Father Matthew stood and embraced the young American awkwardly. 'I needed to speak with our two friends, Elijah,' he explained. 'After what happened to poor Robert, we need to be a bit more security conscious in the church so Owen has suggested putting a couple of cameras in the church, probably at the weekend.'

Catherine and Owen shared a look of exasperation. Owen exhaled audibly.

'Great idea,' enthused Elijah. 'Let me know if I can help. As it says in Proverbs, chapter fifteen, "The eyes of the Lord are in every place, keeping watch on the evil".' He paused, looking with a smirk, first at Owen and then Catherine. '"And the good".'

31

Just under a week into his incarceration, Devante had understood the dynamics and the rough timetable of his new hell. Although his existence was spent mostly in complete darkness, there were occasions when distant light, as if from a fading star, meant that he could make out shadows within the cell he shared with Tyrone and Reece. It emanated, he surmised, probably from a room at the front of the property, maybe the kitchenette that he had passed when he entered the flat, at that point unable to imagine the terror ahead.

He and Tyrone had also managed to devise a way for their feet to touch if they twisted in a certain way and pulled their respective chains to their fullest extent. This occasional human physical connection was strangely comforting and reminded Devante, and probably Tyrone too, that there was a life outside of their current situation; a life to which one day they would both hopefully return. Whenever the room was flooded with light, for food or for toilet breaks, and when Elijah was otherwise occupied, the two young men stared into each other's eyes with unspoken camaraderie and defiance.

There was also routine. Elijah liked routine. In what

Devante supposed was the morning, he would visit the room, talk to his mother's broken skull to check she had had a restful night and then turn his attention to his captives and the morning toilet rituals of unchaining and re-chaining. This was followed by breakfast of plain porridge, eaten individually and in strict silence with Reece going first followed by Tyrone and finally Devante. After this was a long period of darkness during which Devante could sometimes hear music or the faint sounds of a television somewhere in an adjacent property. He had tried banging on the wall just in case but it was obviously too thick to alert anyone on the other side.

Devante would often sleep during the periods of darkness, awakened only by the sounds of Elijah arriving at some point in the early afternoon to provide water and dry bread and another toilet break if required. Sometimes he would hear Reece moaning forlornly in the corner or Tyrone doing what passed for exercise. After the second day, Devante had also begun to use the dark periods to stretch his limbs as far as possible and to engage in what amounted to one-armed press-ups in an attempt to keep his muscles active. He knew that at some point he may need to rely on as much strength as he could muster to escape this ungodly place, although the lack of nourishing food was already taking its toll on Devante's body.

The existence of the skull, silently keeping watch over them all in the darkness, was something which unnerved Devante for the first few days but eventually he grew familiar with it, even making up conversations with it in his head. He would ask about Elijah's childhood and invent replies. During these imaginary discourses, the skull would tell stories about visiting the beach with Elijah and him crying because a seagull stole his ice cream. Devante would quietly smile to himself as far as he was able with his mouth restricted. Humanising the skull and her hideous offspring somehow made his predicament more manageable.

Yet the threat of terrible violence hung over Devante's existence constantly. At least once every couple of days, Elijah would arrive unexpectedly carrying a pair of pliers or garden secateurs which he would wave around, eyes blazing with anger owing to something in the outside world that had shaped his mood, while asking his mother's skull which of the three captives had been misbehaving. After the perceived response, he would pick on one of the young men, usually Reece, and prepare to crush or remove either a finger or a toe before backing down at the last minute. 'It's just a gentle reminder,' he would say calmly, 'as it says in Paul's letter to the Romans, "'Now that you have been set free from sin and become slaves of God, the fruit you get leads to sanctification and its end, eternal life". But only if you continue to repent for the evil deeds that you have committed.'

Whenever such visits occurred, Devante would think of Robert and the events leading up to his death and the moment of his death and its aftermath. Had he left evidence? Would the police be searching for him at that very moment? He would gladly take a prison sentence over Elijah's grotesque justice. And what of those friendly old people who had started hanging around the JCW before Christmas? Maybe they were trying to locate him. Difficult though it was to do so, Devante clung onto the desperate belief that somebody somewhere was going to find them sooner or later.

32

Owen and Terry managed to fit the new cameras over the course of an hour and a half on Saturday afternoon and additionally organised a transmitter so that Owen could monitor all the goings on in the church from the comfort of his laptop. Catherine joined them, less in terms of a practical help but more as a conduit between the workmen and Father Matthew who still harboured doubts on the need for such technology, albeit temporary.

As they had suspected he might, Elijah arrived at the church just as they were completing the task to, in his words, 'check that there were no splinters from the drilling which might harm the parishioners at mass the following day. 'With Robert no longer here,' he said plaintively, 'I feel that it is my duty to protect Matthew's flock from peril. As it is written in John's gospel, "I am the good shepherd. The good shepherd lays down his life for the sheep".'

Father Matthew gasped and commented that he didn't think it necessary for Elijah to lay down his life for anyone. Besides, there had been rather too much death in the recent past and vicinity, as far as the priest was concerned. Terry allayed his fears, partially by demonstrating his portable vacuum cleaner with which he had rendered the floor of the church cleaner than it had been for many months.

Once satisfied that there were no small wood-based hazards remaining, Elijah gave everyone his customary hug, the dark mood of Wednesday having apparently dissipated, and said that he needed to get back to his mother. 'Before you go,' said Catherine, 'how would you feel if I invited you for a cup of green tea in the village next week? Just the two of us.' Elijah's face went through a number of contortions over the subsequent seconds as his mind weighed up the possible consequences of either accepting or refusing.

Finally, he decided that on balance, accepting held fewer pitfalls. 'That sounds great,' he said, enthusiastically. 'How's Monday at 3pm? I can meet you there. The one on the high street next to the pottery place, right?' Catherine confirmed that that was exactly the venue she had in mind. 'Great. See you Monday.' He bestowed a second, tighter hug and strode purposefully out of the church.

'That went better than I expected,' the ex-journalist muttered mostly to herself.

'You've clearly still got the gift,' whispered Owen, giving her bottom a playful squeeze.

Two days later, just before three in the afternoon, Catherine entered the small friendly café, half-expecting Elijah not to turn up but instead found the American already settled at a corner table with a cup of green tea. He seemed engrossed in a book on theology. 'Any good?' she asked, unbuttoning her coat before hanging it on the back of the chair opposite Elijah who immediately stood and enveloped her in his usual fashion.

'It's not bad,' he replied, placing a bookmark with a picture of Jesus into the relevant page. 'It's about how we can apply the teachings of the Old Testament to life in the twenty-first century. Now, I'm generally more of a New Testament kinda guy, but there are some interesting teachings here. What are you currently reading, Catherine?'

The former journalist had to think on her feet and blurted out the name of a popular cosy crime novel which she'd enjoyed before Christmas. Her actual current book, an anthology entitled *Coming Soon: One Hundred Women on How They Reach Orgasm* would need to remain securely in her handbag. The afternoon's conversation would require delicate handling and Catherine was aware that anything which might adversely affect Elijah's opinion of her could prove unduly problematic.

'I'll grab a coffee. Can I get you a refill? Maybe something to eat too? My treat.' Elijah gratefully accepted and a few minutes later Catherine returned to the table with a tray filled with a variety of sweet treats as well as a latte and a green tea.

'I didn't know whether you were vegan,' she said, 'so I bought an array of cakes of both varieties. You can always take away any leftovers in a goodie bag. Maybe your mother would like some. How is she, by the way?'

Elijah studied the sweet offerings carefully, finally plumping for a slice of plum tart. 'May I?' he asked before reaching over and transferring the sticky treat onto a small plate and tucking in with a fork. 'She's good. Thank you for asking. The move to the UK has really helped, I think. I mean...' He popped another mouthful and swallowed before continuing. 'Sorry. This is yummy. Um, I mean the US medical system is great but it's expensive, even with Medicare, and we know that mother is unlikely to be cured completely. The change of scene and the change of care has certainly been beneficial.'

'What's wrong with her, if I may ask? And if it's too personal then just tell me to back off.'

Elijah looked downcast momentarily. 'Not at all,' he said. 'She has a number of comorbidities, some of which go back a long way. I don't really want to go into the gory details but there's a lot of mental stuff going on, you know, and that impacts negatively on the physical.' Another forkful of tart found its way mouthwards. 'But she has me and I have her and we both have the good Lord to guide and keep us through difficult times.'

'I understand,' replied Catherine, eggshell-tiptoeing around the edges of their polite chat. Glancing at Elijah's book, she decided to shift the conversation more towards him. 'Did you study theology?'

The American picked up the book with his forkless hand. 'Oh,' he laughed, 'yes actually. I wanted to become a minister or a priest as you call them here. I might still try for the ministry at some point but right now I'm happy just to be helping these young people at the JCW and learning from good folks like Matthew. You have so many street gangs here in London. If we can turn some of these teenagers away from that world of danger and bloodshed, then we're doing good work. Right? Save a few lives as well as souls.'

'And Robert? Was he one of the good folk you were learning from?' asked Catherine, watching for any flicker of unusual reaction. There was none. Elijah's face took on a veneer of sadness and he placed his fork gently on the plate, a third of the tart still uneaten.

'Robert,' he began before pausing seemingly to wrestle control in a torrent of swirling emotions. A good twenty seconds passed. Catherine reached over and placed a sympathetic hand on his. Elijah grasped it like a buoyancy aid. 'Robert *was* a good man...' He faltered. 'But he was also a flawed man. His relationship with God was... fractured. Yes, that's the word. Not broken completely but fractured.'

'In what way?'

Elijah looked deep into the ex-journalist's eyes and smiled. 'He was a sinner, Catherine. And he knew that his place in the kingdom of heaven was far from certain. He and I spoke about it many times. The gospel according to Matthew teaches us that "When the Son of Man comes in His glory, and all the angels with Him, then He will sit on His glorious throne. Before Him will be gathered all the nations and He will separate people one from another as a shepherd separates the sheep from the goats".

'I loved Robert dearly,' the American unclasped his hand from the journalist's and helped himself to another piece of tart, 'just as I love you, Catherine. But let me be clear. Robert was not one of our Lord's sheep like us.' Catherine's heart seemed to pause momentarily as Elijah's eyes seared into hers and she recognised something both familiar and disturbing. 'Robert was a goat.'

33

'I don't suppose you managed to ask whether he knew anything about Devante and Tyrone?' Monica had taken Catherine's post-coffee call at the Baker Street house.

'I did,' said Catherine, 'but he says he hasn't heard from either of them since they moved away.'

Monica had been researching Twelve cases from the prolific Ian Bamford era of the 1970s. She had needed to move from the archive room into the main living area to get a clearer signal than just two uncertain bars, leaving Thomas to continue his own explorations into some of the darker recesses of The Twelve's history trove.

On finding out that the retired pharmacist, Bamford, had been involved in a remarkable fourteen assassinations in seven years, Monica's primary thought had been one of admiration for such productivity. Monica being Monica, her second thought was to wonder if the record of fourteen assassinations could perhaps be broken.

She had done a quick calculation in her head. The Burrows case would need to be discounted even though she had played a major role in incapacitating that particular serial killer. That was irritating. However, if she could reasonably include the McMullan business the previous summer – and after all, she had come up with the plan and lit the fuse, metaphorically speaking – then that would take her total to eight. Fourteen was definitely within range but she would need to get a shift on.

And then a third thought had occurred. *Monica, you should not be treating this as a competition to be won. What would Mrs Mendoza say?* The ex-chemist now assassin had then given herself a little shake and returned, chastened, to her research before her phone had rung.

Down the line, Catherine continued her update. 'He says they got moved by social services to different parts of the country and although he's tried to call them, they don't pick up. Just voicemails apparently. He worries that they might be in prison or worse. We can check with social services if you like but they aren't the most organised folk if prior experience is anything to go by. Understaffed, underpaid and generally worn out as far as I know.

'There wasn't really an opportunity to get his address either,' continued Catherine, 'which I know we need. However, we did get on extremely well and Elijah said that he would love to meet up again so I'll see if Owen can get a tracker or something that I can slip into his pocket while we're hugging. He likes a hug.'

'So I've heard,' said Monica wearily. 'Anyway, I'm just at Baker Street with Thomas going through some business so I guess I'll see you at yoga on Thursday. Lots of love.' She returned to the archive where Thomas was holding a dusty green folder.

'Everything all right?' he asked. Monica outlined the basics of her phone conversation with Catherine and the moderate success of her meeting with Elijah. 'Progress,' replied Thomas, ever the optimist, 'albeit of the slow kind. But still progress.

Talking of which...' He waved the green folder in her direction creating a small cloud. 'I believe you've been searching for Ian Bamford's chemistry notebook.'

The typed case notes from the seventies Bamford golden era had been meticulously detailed, as usual, but Monica had been mildly exasperated by the fact that whenever it came to the actual formulae for the bespoke poisons used in certain cases, someone, probably Bamford himself, had written *Refer to Green Recipe Book*. Monica had searched the seventies section of the archive time and again without finding this culinary grail. Now it appeared to be in Thomas's hands. It even had the words *Bamford Recipe Book* in faded biro written on the front. And it was green.

'Oh my goodness,' squeaked Monica, 'where was it?'

A look of pride mixed with mischief bloomed across Thomas's wide-eyed face. 'Found a secret drawer,' he said with a grin. 'Come see.' He led her to the furthest corner of the archive where there was a small writing desk set against a distressed brick wall with two drawers on either side.

'I went through those,' said Monica, bemused. 'They were empty.'

Thomas smiled. 'There's a third drawer.' He gripped one end of the desk and lifted it at an angle away from the wall. At the back, in the middle, was a drawer which Monica had never seen. It appeared to be lined with a few millimetres of lead.

She skipped over to Thomas, wrapped her arms around his neck and kissed him proudly. 'Clever boy,' she purred. 'What else is in there?'

Together they opened the drawer which was about three inches deep so there wasn't enough space for too many documents. Monica reached in and pulled out three additional folders. One very old document was entitled, *Eric Shillingford, 1885 Diary*. On the second much more modern folder was written, *Lexington Smith – A Life* (*draft*) in familiar handwriting.

The third document, again reasonably old, was a sealed envelope on which was written in urgent capital letters: *DO NOT OPEN UNLESS THE TWELVE IS IN MORTAL DANGER.*

'Good to know that's there, I suppose,' mused Thomas casually.

At that moment, both phones pinged with a WhatsApp message. 'It's Lexington,' said Monica. 'He's confirmed the lunch invitation to everyone over at his place on Sunday. He must truly be on the mend. We can ask him about all this stuff when we see him.'

34

Just under thirteen months since the majority of them had gathered at Lexington's Pimlico apartment for a spontaneous New Year Eve party, the full Twelve contingent plus Bobby City congregated around his huge wooden table for Sunday lunch. Martin was on particularly good form after an energetic gym session the previous day, "Sondheim Saturday", during which the entire 2004 Broadway cast recording of the maestro's little-known musical *Assassins* was played just for him. The cabbie was keen to stress that he hadn't let slip any secrets but merely had expressed a passing enthusiasm for the show at an earlier visit.

The meal was mostly prepared by Terry with help from Bobby and Chris who were acting as his sous chefs for the day, the surgeon mostly peeling, tearing and chopping in homage to his former career.

Resisting the temptation to cook a traditional Sunday roast, Terry had curated a menu which started with a butternut and sage soup. To accompany this, the locksmith had baked fresh bread 'using artisan flour from dark, satanic mills on account of our current case.' Martin enquired whether he had also churned the butter and Terry replied that no, he'd simply bought some from Tesco. For a main course, there was a choice of meat lasagne or vegetarian with aubergine and courgette. A sticky toffee pudding with vanilla custard brought up the rear for those with sweet teeth. Chris scoffed two portions.

Predictably, Lexington's extensive wine collection provided a variety of options to complement each course including a particularly fine sherry which perfectly accompanied dessert.

'"One cannot think well, love well, sleep well, if one has not dined well", according to Virginia Woolf and I tend to agree,' pronounced Lexington halfway through the main course. 'Luckily we have Terry and his kitchen battalion to ensure we receive the full benefit of the bounty available to us.'

'Did you know her?' asked Thomas, resisting the offer of more wine from a circling Bobby. 'Virginia Woolf. You seem to have met pretty much everyone.'

Lexington emitted a chuckle which oozed into a cough. 'I'm afraid not,' he said. 'I was only tiny when she died and still living in New York. I could be wrong but I don't believe Virginia ever crossed the Atlantic but even if she had, I would have been entirely oblivious to her Bloomsbury charms. E M Forster I did meet, though. In the sixties. I think he took rather a shine to me but I was in a relationship with an actress at the time so I wasn't remotely interested. Not an especially famous actress, I should add, before your imaginations begin to run riot. Although she did have a bit part in an early Bond movie. Anyway, that's quite enough about me for a while. I can't tell you how delightful it is to be able to host you here again. Shall we spend some time nattering about the current case? For old times?'

Catherine and Owen took the lead in updating the old man on the situation in the Barnes church while Veronica brought everyone up to speed with Simone's woes at La Stella.

Lexington had been in regular contact with the Italian and had promised to visit the following month if his health allowed. 'I'm still taking things slowly,' he said in a slightly disconsolate tone. 'Doctor's orders. But with any luck I'll be tucking into a celebratory plate of pappardelle at my usual table before Easter. I also have a few projects I wish to complete. As Ingrid Bergman used to say, "Getting old is like climbing a mountain. You get a little out of breath but the view is much better".'

'Did you know *her*?' asked Thomas hopefully and with a growing certainty that he was going to get one right eventually.

'Ingrid? Oh yes, absolutely.' Thomas treated himself to a mini fist pump under the table. 'We became firm friends when she moved to London at the tail end of the seventies. I was distraught when she died. Such a delight to be in her exquisite company.' Graham suggested that one of the projects Lexington had mentioned should be an autobiography, a proposal to which everyone around the table nodded approvingly. 'I've started one,' revealed the old man. 'Well, I've written the driest bones of a draft anyway. I did it a couple of years back when there was a bit of a lull in cases. I popped it in a drawer and forgot about it but I'll dig it out again before the year is out.

'I am not sure that anyone would be particularly interested in the ramblings of an old codger like me but then again I have been fortunate to have lived a long, eventful and happy life and, if you'll indulge me for just a second, the most important advice I can offer to you younger folk is that you must all endeavour to live and to love the way that I have done. Passionately, fearlessly and completely. There is no better way. You'll experience bumps and scrapes along the way, of course. That's only natural. But they'll be worth it in the end. Better a life lived to the full than a life resigned to mere adequacy. Better to look back and think *I'm glad I did that* than to rue *I wish I'd done that*.' He glanced towards Bobby. 'Vanilla was never my favourite flavour,' he added with a wink. 'Except when it comes to this delicious custard, of course, Terry.'

Monica took this opportunity to mention that she, or Thomas to be precise, had found the drawer and its contents, although naturally she had to take great care not to reveal the location as the majority of The Twelve were unaware of the archive room at Baker Street. 'I knew you'd find it eventually,' Lexington said, smiling, 'particularly if you watch the jolly TV programme *Taskmaster*. Remind me, what else is in the drawer? I've not opened it in a while.'

Monica listed the contents. 'Ah yes,' said Lexington with a chuckle. 'The Bamford folder is completely beyond my limited understanding but someone with your extensive scientific knowledge may find it of value. The Shillingford stuff is interesting. He was the original owner of the Baker Street house and a member of The Twelve in the 1880s as you'll know. I should warn you that it does contain some state secrets which could have disastrous consequences for our increasingly fragile monarchy if they ever became wide knowledge.' He tapped his nose conspiratorially. 'Best kept securely in the drawer in my opinion.'

'What about the other envelope?' asked Monica, choosing to avoid causing alarm by going into any detail.

Lexington looked bemused for a moment until Monica's wide brown eyes helped him to register the envelope to which she was referring. 'Oh that!' he said. 'No idea. Never had any need or desire to open it. But I do have my suspicions.' Monica leaned in. 'In the late 1960s, one of The Twelve was an actor and comedian named Larry Farnes. He wasn't particularly good, either as an actor or a comedian although he did once star in panto at the Wimbledon Theatre alongside Bruce Forsyth and Tommy Trinder. I digress. He was, however, a rather good assassin. The writing on the envelope looks like his so I surmise that it is simply a joke. It probably says something inside like "Call the police" or "Don't panic, Mr Mainwaring".'

After dessert and coffee, Lexington said he felt a little tired and, if it wasn't too much of an imposition, he would go and have a quick nap just to refresh himself. 'But do please stay and enjoy more wine,' he implored. 'If someone could please rouse me in an hour or so then we can continue our lively conversation into the evening unless anyone has any pressing engagements.'

35

While Thomas, Martin and Owen washed up the lunch dishes, the other members of The Twelve separated into smaller groups dotted like atolls around Lexington's apartment. Veronica, Terry and Monica stood looking out towards Battersea as they nursed glasses of Chilean Pinot Noir and chatted about their current and recent favourite books, both fiction and non-fiction. Catherine, Chris, Graham and David huddled in a corner to discuss religion once more. Bobby, Belinda and Anna settled on a sofa and began planning trips to the theatre.

After an hour and ten minutes, Anna volunteered to go and wake Lexington, returning a couple of moments later with a look of grave concern. 'Chris, can I borrow you for just a second,' she murmured, her voice remaining level but her eyes signalling something approaching panic. The ex-surgeon accompanied her down the short corridor to Lexington's bedroom where the former leader sat motionless in a high-backed armchair, his head lolling back and to his right side. 'He is, isn't he?' Anna stammered. 'I mean, I'm pretty sure but I thought I'd seek a second medical opinion.'

Chris searched for a pulse, then a heartbeat without luck. 'He is,' he said flatly.

'I thought so. Probably about forty minutes ago by my professional assessment.'

'Right. Too late to realistically do anything.'

'Hm.' Anna's lower lip began to wobble as her composure crumpled. She sat on the bed and started rocking gently back and forth. Chris sat next to her and placed his consoling arm around her shoulder into which she folded gratefully. 'We should tell the others. Perhaps Monica first,' she said, sniffling. 'Scientists' unemotional club and all that.'

'I'll go,' said Chris, wiping a tear from his lover's cheek. 'You're a bit smudged.' He returned moments later with Monica. 'Lexington is dead. Died in his sleep. Too late to do anything. Even if we started chest compressions, which at his age could be fatal anyway.'

Monica put her hands to her mouth and began weeping softly. 'But he was... He was... just here,' she said. 'We just had lunch.' Anna stood and the two women hugged the tightest hug known only to people who never wish to let go.

'His heart wasn't in the best shape,' said Chris. 'He knew that. It literally could have happened at any time.'

The three friends stood together in silence for a moment, the sounds of animated laughter and chatter emanating from the front of the apartment. Monica spoke first. 'You're quite sure he's...'

'Luckily or unluckily depending on how you view it,' said Chris, 'you have both a doctor and a forensic pathologist in the house. Together, we cover most of the bases when it comes to this sort of thing. There's no element of uncertainty.'

'Right.'

At that moment, the bedroom door was pushed open slightly and Thomas poked his head in. 'Everything okay?' he asked brightly. 'Catherine was just wondering when she might crack open the gin.' He glanced towards Lexington, slumped back in the chair. 'Is he still napping?'

'He's dead, my darling,' said Monica, holding back more tears. 'He died in his sleep.' Thomas stared at Lexington silently as if he were an ancient and valuable artefact that had just been unearthed. Monica wrapped her arms around him although his arms did not seem prepared to reciprocate, glued as they were to his sides in shock.

'But we were just...'

'I know, darling.'

'He can't be.'

'He is.'

Monica led Thomas, dazed, towards the bed where he sat quietly for a moment in contemplation of the unthinkable.

'I'll tell the others,' said Chris and left the room to venture in the direction of the noisy conversation knowing that he would be the one to extinguish it in the most brutal and catastrophic manner.

Sure enough, within seconds Monica, Anna and Thomas could hear silence followed by gasps, shouts and crying. At once, the bedroom was filled with bodies. Bobby walked over to Lexington and embraced him as if he were living, whispering in his ear until Monica gently prised her away. Belinda ran from the room in tears closely followed by Veronica. Owen and Graham hugged each other and started crying.

Martin was one of the most distraught, initially angry that an ambulance hadn't been called and then adamant that he could take the old man to hospital in his taxi. 'What's the closest hospital? St Thomas's I reckon. I could take a short cut through St George's Square, be on Millbank in three minutes. Over Lambeth. We could be in A&E in, what, fifteen tops?'

Chris placed his hands on the cabbie's broad, muscular

shoulders. 'It's too late, old friend,' he said gently. 'He's gone, Martin. I'm sorry.' The surgeon watched the tears brim in Martin's eyes before he too was overcome with grief and collapsed sobbing into Chris's arms. Over the next few minutes, everyone embraced in various permutations, muttering hasty, difficult condolences while individually coming to terms with the situation. Finally, Chris suggested they call an ambulance, explaining that there would be no need to accompany him and Lexington on this penultimate journey but that, if anyone wanted to come, then they could.

Bobby replied that Lexington, somewhat predictably, had already engaged a funeral director many years previously and that she would instead call them to ask for the body to be collected. She would also go with them so that Lexington had a second friendly voice to accompany him. 'Also, there's probably paperwork,' she said softly. 'And that's my area really, isn't it?' She smiled weakly. Chris confirmed that he could sign the death certificate.

'I'll wait for you here until you get back,' said Monica with a consoling cuddle for both of them.

The following hour at Lexington's apartment was a furious period of comfort and distress; of cacophony and silence; of activity and inertia; of faith and disbelief; of denial and acceptance; of quiet and intensity; of businesslike composure and passionate desolation; of comings and goings; of time passing and time stopping.

By seven that evening, Lexington's body had been removed to the nearby undertakers. Chris had returned while Bobby had stayed with Lexington to make some initial arrangements. Like refugees returning to a familiar place that has changed utterly, The Twelve felt their way in dribs and drabs back to the dining table, now empty apart from some flowers which Veronica had brought as a gift. Their joyful Sunday lunch which had been consumed only a few hours earlier seemed a lifetime away. They sat silently for a moment, some head in hands, others staring solemnly into space.

Finally, David spoke. 'If you think about it,' he said, 'that was the perfect Lexington exit.' Martin looked up with bemusement. A few of the others nodded slowly, instantly understanding the plumber's train of thought. 'I mean, if you've had such an incredible life, you wouldn't want to die in a hospital bed, would you? Wired up to machines. Or in pain somewhere. Or, God forbid, alone.'

'What could be better,' agreed Terry, 'than to go quietly in your sleep after a wonderful meal with friends? I think I'd put my name down for that option.'

'Precisely what I was thinking,' said David, forcing a smile for the first time in what felt like many hours.

Around the table, one by one, The Twelve began to slowly retreat from their grief. 'An extraordinary life and then a beautiful, gentle death,' said Monica. 'We should have a toast. Terry, could you bear to go and choose something suitable please?'

The locksmith scuttled off to Lexington's wine rack while Thomas and Owen located some clean glasses. 'Here we go,' said Terry, '1959 Nuit-St-Georges Bouchard Père. Great vintage and it'll taste fantastic. Lexington would have been about twenty when these grapes were picked.' He uncorked the wine after a brief struggle and poured twelve glasses. 'I should really decant it and wait for a bit but bugger that, eh? Under the circumstances.'

Monica thought for a moment. There was so much she wanted to say but she decided that now was the time for brevity, not least because she couldn't be entirely certain that her own emotions were fully under control. She recalled the words that Lexington himself had used before going for his final nap and raised her glass. 'To Lexington Smith. As he told us himself only a matter of hours ago, he lived his incredible life fearlessly, passionately and completely. May we always strive to do the same. Farewell, old friend. Safe travels until we all meet again. We love you. In all three ways. In every way.'

36

By the time Bobby returned just after ten, only Monica and Thomas remained at Lexington's apartment, the other members of The Twelve having drifted off in small groups during the evening, Martin still so upset that Terry had decided to accompany him home and stay with him in the cabbie's spare room. Monica had imagined that Bobby might want a quiet cup of tea and a sit down but instead the organiser was in the mood to do what she did best. Organise.

She quickly located a file in Lexington's desk which included documents outlining in detail all of his post-death wishes, his will and a list of emails and phone numbers of around six hundred people whom he felt might be remotely interested to hear of his passing.

His desire was for a quick and eco-friendly cremation, for which he had prepaid, attended by a small number of family and friends, followed by a larger memorial to be held at a sixteenth-century hall in the City of London with capacity for five hundred. Lexington's note in the margin, handwritten with typical humility, read, *Feel free to find a smaller venue as required.* Monica strongly suspected that they might in actuality need to source a larger one.

His ashes should be split with one half going into the Thames near Tower Bridge and the other half to be taken to New York where he had been born and dispersed fanfareless into the East River.

A cursory look at his will, meanwhile, left a life-changing sum to his niece and great niece, the Pimlico flat and various pieces of fine art to The Twelve to sell or otherwise use as they wish, and eight small but significant sums of money to a couple of riding stables for the disabled and miscellaneous struggling charities across London including an LGBTQ+ theatre group and an organisation helping displaced families in Syria of whom Lexington had grown fond following the murder of Nabil Shahid on a Victoria Line Underground train many months earlier.

'Shall we split the list of people to contact?' suggested Monica, realising the daunting nature of the task even for someone of Bobby's unnatural abilities. Bobby agreed and divided the relevant pages so that they could both make a start in the morning. 'What will you do now, Bobby? Do you need a lift home?'

The organiser frowned. 'I think I'll stay here tonight,' she said softly. 'I have some overnight stuff in the flat. I probably won't sleep but if that's the case then at least I can make a start on these emails.' Monica asked whether she would like company but Bobby felt it best that she was alone. 'There's a lot to process,' she said with tranquillity and strength. 'You should get back to St John's Wood. Let's do a call in the morning.'

'Before we go,' murmured Monica, 'and this may sound strange, but could I please take a quick look at where he kept his jackets?' Understanding Monica completely, Bobby took her hand and led her back to Lexington's bedroom where, on the furthest wall, stood a couple of old wooden wardrobes side by side.

'The one on the left,' whispered Bobby.

Monica walked slowly across the room and opened the wardrobe door. She pulled out a dark grey woollen jacket, which she recognised as one of Lexington's favourites, breathed out and then filled her lungs with him for the last time.

'What a day,' said Thomas as the two of them prepared for bed just under an hour later, the taxi journey home completed in silent hand-holding. 'Do you think Bobby will be okay?'

Monica had just finished brushing her teeth. 'From what I know of Bobby, she'll be fine. She doesn't have a problem with being alone. She's used to it. Like you and I got used to it.' She kissed Thomas mintily. 'You know, I used to be the sort of person who craved solitude, but these days I'd much prefer to be with you than to be on my own. Even when we're not doing anything, just your presence is enough.'

They got into bed and snuggled close. 'Do you think you'll be able to sleep?' asked Thomas, his mind overwhelmed with emotions and memories.

'We should try,' replied Monica. 'Let's just close our eyes and see what happens. I can always put the radio on low if that helps.'

Thomas closed his eyes and did his best to empty his mind using some yoga techniques learnt from Anna over the months. 'I'll miss him so much,' he said after a few moments, holding back a tear.

'We all will, my love,' whispered Monica. 'We all will.'

After a fitful sleep, Monica woke late and checked her phone for messages and emails. It quickly became obvious that Bobby had spent much of the night emailing people on her half of the list and copying Monica in so that she could read any replies. As a result, there were an impressive three hundred and sixty-four unopened messages massing like infantry in her inbox.

Monica opened one, to a previous American ambassador to London who had recently moved to Tokyo. The ambassador had expressed heartfelt condolences and asked to be alerted regarding the date of the memorial so that she could drop everything to be there. Monica opened a second one, to a famous actor whose return message from a film set in California was much the same. 'If everyone wants to come to the memorial,' she murmured quietly to herself, 'then we're definitely going to need a bigger boat.'

Beside her, Thomas stirred and glanced at the clock on his bedside table. 'It's late,' he mumbled. 'Although I don't think I really got to sleep properly until about two.' Monica waved her phone in front of his bleary face and suggested that Bobby probably hadn't had any sleep at all.

'We'll all need naps later,' she suggested. 'Although right now I'll need a coffee or six to get through all these emails before making a start on my own list.' Around midday, after three coffees and an oatmeal bar, Monica had finally managed to catch up with the influx of Bobby's missives, helped by the fact that the organiser had called at eleven to say that she was finally going to sleep for a while. She had also begun a spreadsheet of people contacted, their preferred method of contact and whether they had expressed an interest in attending the memorial. All but two had confirmed that they would definitely be there and, of those two, one was unable to travel on health grounds and the other was themselves recently deceased, an apologetic reply coming from the unfortunate recipient's daughter.

Monica began her emails with the intention of writing personalised notes to everyone. However, by half past one and only twenty-four emails in, she had decided to resort to cutting and pasting the salient points. Many people responded within minutes and Monica dutifully filled in the spreadsheet with an efficiency of which she felt Bobby would be proud when the organiser woke up.

The fifty-somethingth name on the list was Clare Lashone-Brown, the new Twelve leader in New York and Monica realised with acute embarrassment that she hadn't organised a video call with the woman as had been promised before Christmas. She sat gazing at her computer for a few moments in a state of inertia. *Pull yourself together, Miss Lodhia*, she internalised, *although I probably shouldn't cut and paste with this particular message.*

Monica constructed what she thought was a suitably apologetic and reverent email, reread it, changed a couple of words, reread it again and finally pressed send. Ten minutes later, Clare's reply sprang into Monica's inbox. Monica opened it. The email was long.

'I'm going to need another coffee,' Monica mumbled to herself with a sigh.

37

The bulk of Clare's email was an emotional stream of early morning consciousness about Lexington and how much of a good friend he was to The Twelve in New York. Towards the end of her message was a firm but friendly ticking off for Monica's failure to organise a call. The last line of the email filled Monica with a combination of excitement and terror.

I'll come over for the memorial, it read. *We can catch up properly.*

Oh crap, thought Monica before she noticed the postscript. *Don't worry, I won't forget you're married.* This was accompanied by a winking face emoji.

Monica frowned. *I'm not married*, she thought, mildly irritated for reasons she couldn't fully comprehend. Yet, at the same time, she had no desire for a repeat performance of her solitary night with Clare six years earlier. Or did she? Monica's eyes settled on Thomas who was reclining on her sofa attempting to dilute his grief by reading a biography of an Olympic heptathlete whose path he had crossed briefly during the nineties. This wonderful man had made her happier than she could remember. She would never do anything to hurt him.

Thomas noticed her gaze and gave a little wave. 'Need another coffee?' he asked with puppyish enthusiasm.

Monica shook her head and smiled. 'I have everything I need,' she replied and consigned the memory of her night with Clare to a tiny cupboard in a recess of her mind where she hoped it would remain undisturbed.

By 6pm and after approximately nine hours almost solidly at her laptop typing emails, monitoring responses to Bobby's emails which had recommenced in the early afternoon, and logging data on the spreadsheet, Monica had finally cleared her section of the list. Around four fifths of the recipients had replied and, of those that hadn't, Monica surmised either that they were the sort of people who only checked their messages sporadically or were struggling to process the news. An artist based in Madrid, for example, had simply typed, *Too upset to respond fully. More in time. X.* A longer email appeared three days later outlining in slightly too much detail, even for Monica, a passionate summer that the artist had spent with Lexington in the early eighties and how she had never forgotten him and never would.

A non-Lexington email from Owen confirming that he was now able to monitor and record the altar at the Barnes church constantly came not only as sweet respite to Monica amidst the outpourings of grief but also a timely reminder that there remained an ongoing case.

'I had planned to go food shopping today,' she said, as Thomas hugged her from behind, inhaling her aroma from the nape of her neck where it was often strongest, 'but that's had to take a back seat. It'll have to be tomorrow.' She rolled her shoulders in an attempt to coax a smattering of muscles back to life after hours of disuse.

Thomas had already anticipated this and had booked La Stella for 7.30pm as a surprise. He would have gone shopping himself but it had been raining hard for most of the day, only clearing during the last hour or so.

———

They took a taxi to the restaurant and settled into the corner table where Lexington had recruited Thomas into The Twelve a brace of Octobers ago. The portrait of Marlon Brando seemed to Thomas to be a little more downbeat today than he had ever seen it before.

Likewise, Simone was very emotional and hugged them both tightly when they arrived, so much so that a couple of nearby customers asked their waitress whether the owner was okay. 'I cannot believe it,' he said and sniffed loudly. 'I thought… I hoped that somehow he would go on forever.'

'If you have time later,' said Monica, rubbing his back as a comfort, 'why don't you come and sit with us and we can remember some good times.' The Italian said that, as it was a Monday, and an unusually quiet one, he should be free at around nine to take up their kind offer. In the meantime, he had asked the chef to prepare some complimentary antipasti for them while they decided on main courses.

For Thomas, the choice was easy. The gnocchi with sage and butter on which he had feasted during his first meeting with Lexington at the same table fifteen months earlier. Monica plumped for risotto with black truffle and porcini mushrooms after which Simone insisted on another gifted dessert of Sicilian orange cheesecake. 'We'll leave a massive tip,' whispered Monica. 'We can't have Simone out of pocket especially with this Tansa nonsense going on.'

Just after nine, the Italian pulled up a chair and joined their table, transferring the responsibilities of waiting on the remaining four tables to his attentive staff, one of whom brought over three tulip-shaped grappa glasses into which was poured generous measures of Italian brandy. Simone's sadness hadn't abated but before they could talk about Lexington, there was something else on the Italian's mind.

'They have been trying to steal my staff,' he hissed. 'The bloody Tansa people. They wait outside at the beginning of the shift and tell them they will pay almost double what I am paying. Luckily, my staff are loyal and they love working with me. Is like a big family at La Stella. But I'm still angry.' He took a big sip of grappa. 'I'm sorry. We should be talking about more important matters. I just wanted to get it off my chest, you know?'

It was almost midnight by the time Monica decided that they should probably be going. The evening had involved more tears on every side but just as much laughter as the three of them reminisced about the times they had each experienced with Lexington as well as the stories he had told them about his earlier life. 'Of course I will be at the memorial,' said Simone. 'And if you need catering then you simply have to ask.'

They ended the meal as it had begun, with grief-blanketing embraces and tearful kisses. Thomas hailed a taxi and he and Monica collapsed gratefully into the back of it. She took a brief and grappa-hazy look at her phone. Seventy-eight new emails and a text from Bobby stating that the cremation had been organised for the second Tuesday in February.

And that Lexington had expressed the wish that Clare Lashone-Brown from New York be invited. *Oh crap*, Monica thought for the second time in twelve hours.

38

The following morning, aware that Clare wouldn't be awake until roughly eleven London time, Monica breakfasted with coffee and Nurofen and made an early start on the unopened emails which had overnight increased their number to ninety. On closer inspection, at least a dozen were marketing messages from various businesses alerting her that Valentine's Day was approaching at pace. This day always held a special place in her heart, not purely for romantic reasons but because it was also the day that Lexington had first telephoned her nine years earlier to entice her to join The Twelve.

She had been reading an Iain Banks novel on her sofa in St John's Wood when the mobile rang. The serene, elderly voice at the other end of the line had had an immediately calming effect and, as Monica recognised the Beethoven piano sonata which was playing in the background in Lexington's Pimlico flat, she was sufficiently intrigued and listened intently to the offer which he presented. Years later, Lexington had admitted his uncharacteristic nervousness at making that call, knowing even then that Monica had the abilities and the character to become one of The Twelve's most important members.

She urged back a tear and purposefully deleted the Valentine's marketing emails as Thomas emerged dazed from the bedroom. 'I can't really do two late nights in a row with alcohol anymore,' he mumbled. 'Actually, I'm not sure I ever could.' He sat on Monica's historic sofa and thought. 'No, wait. Sydney Olympics 2000. A group of high jumpers forced me to go out drinking two nights on the trot. After their event had finished, of course. There was a harbour-side bar. And tequila. Oh my goodness.' He shook his head at the memory and then stopped abruptly because the shaking was only making his hangover worse.

'There must be a better collective noun for high jumpers,' said Monica, joining him on the sofa and placing a curative arm around his shoulder. 'An elevation of high jumpers. That should do. Coffee and a painkiller?' Thomas nodded, less brutally this time, and lay down on the sofa as Monica prepared medicine before returning to email duties. A call from Bobby, now back at her own home, had explained that Lexington and Clare had remained in regular contact over the years and that he had assigned her to be the person to scatter the stateside portion of his ashes.

Monica cleared the email backlog quickly and steeled herself before drafting a short but friendly message to Clare outlining the situation and asking whether she might be able to get to London for the 8th. Clare's reply arrived just after 6am on America's East Coast which was shivering amidst what the local TV channels were calling an Arctic Blast.

Darling, it read, *I'll be booking tickets this morning. I'll let you know my flight details. Maybe the gorgeous Martin can pick me up from Heathrow. I'll stay at The Dorchester as usual. Can't wait to see you. So much frickin' love. CLBx.*

Monica permitted herself a wicked smirk as she recalled another night at The Dorchester six years earlier. The cupboard into which she had secreted that particular memory was clearly refusing to remain inaccessible.

———

The following days passed quickly. Clare was due to arrive on the Sunday before the cremation but before that both Monica and Bobby were engaged in an almost constant blizzard of paperwork, organisation and communications with Lexington's friends and contacts.

Additionally, Catherine and Owen were channelling their own grief by spending more time at the Church of the Immaculate Virgin with Owen simultaneously acquiring a minute tracking device which impersonated a small button to avoid suspicion. On the first Wednesday of February with a cold snap requiring Elijah to wear his most lavish coat, Catherine was able to drop the button undetected into the American's pocket. Later that evening, Owen traced it to an address in a secluded Hammersmith square between the flyover and the river where it curved south towards Fulham and Putney. 'At least we now know where he lives,' said the surveillance expert. 'Just in case.'

Catherine had also noticed that Elijah was spending more time at the church, he claimed, in order to be able to take up some of the work that Robert had been doing before his sudden and untimely death. The refreshments at the JCW meetings had become less alcohol-free over the weeks and the meetings themselves had become noticeably more unruly affairs with some of the older attendees obviously using the occasions to take advantage of the free drink on offer. When challenged, Elijah seemed unconcerned, although his discussions had become somewhat more apocalyptic during late January, as if he sensed that his own time at the JCW was drawing to a close.

'"Do not fear what you are about to suffer",' began his group talk on the day that Catherine had placed the tracker in his coat. '"Behold, the Devil is about to throw some of you into prison that you may be tested and for ten days you will have tribulation. Be faithful unto death and I will give you the crown of life".'

The following day, after checking with Chris that this passage was from the book of Revelation, Catherine gently enquired over green tea and coffee about his choice of text.

Elijah smiled and simply remarked that the cold winter days had drawn him back to the final book of the Bible. 'It's one of my personal favourites,' he said with a grin that mildly unnerved Catherine. 'The people of this old city have much to learn from Revelation.'

39

Clare had caught the red-eye from JFK, turning left for first class as usual upon boarding the aircraft in Queens in order to sleep during the flight. Martin was at Heathrow bright and early to collect her in his taxi. Monica had asked the visitor to text upon landing, despite the fact that it would be early on a Sunday, and this message arrived just after seven as she and Thomas were half-snoozing in semi-darkness having set a challenging alarm for 6.30am.

The New Yorker and Martin had taken a selfie at Arrivals and texted it to Monica before leaving for Central London. 'She looks well,' said Monica as Thomas returned sleepily to their bedroom with cappuccinos. 'She's had a haircut but it suits her.' Monica held out the photo on her phone and Thomas, who had envisaged someone sterner, saw a beautiful black woman with an enormous smile and cropped grey hair leaning across and kissing Martin playfully on the cheek as he pretended to pull away.

'She looks about fifty!' said Thomas, placing the mugs with care on the relevant tables. 'How old did you say she was?' Monica replied that Clare was seventy-one and used to wear her hair in a dyed black bob. At some point in the last few years, she had clearly decided to embrace the grey and ditch the bob. Both suited her. Clare somehow looked more distinguished than she had at their last encounter. But then she was now leader of The Twelve in New York so maybe that had had something to do with the image change.

From somewhere in the Chiswick area an hour later, and while Thomas was brushing his teeth, Clare texted again suggesting lunch at The Dorchester for the three of them. *It would be great to catch up as well as to meet the husband*, she had written, accompanied by a smiley face emoji. Monica had been slightly dreading this moment but figured that biting the bullet early might mean that the remainder of Clare's trip would maybe pass smoothly. 'Fancy lunch at The Dorchester?' she asked as Thomas emerged from the bathroom.

'Sure. It'll be a first for me.'

'Do you fancy a shower together first?' Monica's suggestion was laced with reassurance as well as intent.

Thomas smiled. 'Always,' he replied.

———

They arrived at the hotel restaurant just before 12.30pm to find Clare already seated and enjoying a glass of champagne. She was wearing a fuchsia dress with a red jacket and was taller than Thomas had imagined, approaching six feet tall even in flats. He still estimated her age at mid-fifties and couldn't quite fathom how she looked quite so youthful.

Clare scooped Monica into an enveloping hug which almost lifted the former chemistry professor from the ground, before turning her attention to Thomas and opening her arms to him too. 'I am so delighted to meet you,' she said with a molasses-rich voice, huge mouth beaming with seemingly the greater compliment of teeth than was strictly necessary. 'Lexington always used to sing your praises whenever we spoke, and now I can partly understand why.' She stood back and admired Thomas who felt momentarily like some sort of museum exhibit. 'You are a fine figure of a man. I would have snapped you up myself if men were my thing.' She glanced at Monica and grasped her hand in congratulation and affection. 'You did well, girl! Will you have some champagne? I'm buying. It's a Louis Roederer 2005 and it is divine.'

The guests took their seats and a sommelier brought two more glasses which she then filled with vintage bubbles. 'We'll get onto Lexington real soon,' said Clare, holding out her glass, 'but I just want to toast you guys first. It's so wonderful to be back in London after all this time and to see you again, Monica, and to meet you, Thomas. Cheers, as you say here.'

Thomas, who had briefly researched the menu including drinks while Monica was getting ready that morning, was careful not to spill a drop of the champagne for fear of wasting a small country's entire education budget-worth of pricey French fizz.

Over the course of the next two hours, Clare and Monica caught up with the various Twelve cases on both sides of the Atlantic, the American's interest piqued in particular by the Barnes church business, as well as gossip about their mutual acquaintances, especially Catherine. Clare also asked all about Thomas and his first career; it transpired that the two of them had both been at the 1996 Atlanta Olympics but that their paths hadn't obviously crossed as Clare had been imprisoned within the corporate offices engaged in some legal work with one of the sponsors while Thomas had spent all of his time either in the Olympic Village or at the stadium.

They naturally spoke at length about Lexington and Monica ran through the highlights of the extraordinary list of contacts he had left, focusing occasionally on the household names whom she had needed to email with the news of his death. 'He was one of the most well-connected people I know,' said Clare. 'And always willing to reach out to people he knew if it could help a friend. You know, a few years back, I was trying to get tickets for a Mariah Carey Christmas show at a little theatre on the Upper West Side and, even with my extensive contacts it was a challenge. Lexington made a couple of calls and within four hours I had a courier at my apartment with two stalls tickets and a signed T-shirt from Mimi.'

'I don't remember Mariah being on my list,' said Monica through a mouthful of seared trout.

'I don't think he knew Mariah herself but clearly he knew someone in her senior management well enough to get to the top. I tell you, I wasn't going to start asking questions but I thanked the man that Christmas with a case of the finest Californian wines I could find. Not that he ever asked for thanks, you understand? That man would quietly and humbly just do good things without any expectation of a reward. We've lost an angel with his passing, may God bless him.'

Around mid-afternoon, Clare announced that she was planning to take a nap for an hour as it would help her to recalibrate her body clock. 'I have dinner with Chris and Anna at her place at eight so I need to be fresh for that.' She settled the bill, bestowed hugs on Monica and Thomas and left them to finish their coffees in peace.

'She seems nice,' said Thomas. He was surprised that neither Clare nor Monica had brought up their shared history but then, he supposed, such a conversation might have proven embarrassing for one or two or even all three of the lunch companions, so perhaps it wasn't a surprise after all that the subject had been overlooked on this occasion.

Monica, however, was fully aware through what had been

left unsaid that hers and Clare's night together had never been far from the New Yorker's thoughts. Particularly judging by the inviting look Clare had given when she mentioned going to her room for a lie down.

That night, Monica dreamt about Clare for the first time in years. The furious and intense ballet of their lovemaking. The elegance and ferocity of it consuming her as she slept.

40

Something felt different. Devante woke drowsier than usual but he was aware that somehow the smell in the room had subtly changed. There was no way to know what time it was but, as Elijah hadn't arrived with breakfast, Devante assumed it was pre-dawn, although this in itself was open to considerable doubt. It might just as easily have been midnight or late evening. The young man's body clock was thoroughly out of sync and who was to say that Elijah wasn't bringing breakfast at all hours just to further distort the minds of his three captives.

With his free hand, Devante scratched an itch on his side and noted in doing so that his hip bone had become more prominent since his arrival in Elijah's flat. He was gradually wasting away and began to weep softly as a sudden wave of helplessness surged over him. In all his short and troubled life, Devante had never experienced a sense of despair quite as acute as this.

He attempted to stretch a leg to see whether he could reach Tyrone for a moment of comfort but it was impossible to see whether his neighbour was even in the right position. After a few attempts without success, Devante assumed that his cocaptive had moved and he drifted back into a troubled doze, as if drugged.

A few moments later, or it could have been hours, the distant dim light heralded a visit from Elijah. Devante hoped firstly that the American was in good spirits and secondly that he was bringing food. His stomach felt emptier than he could remember. The faint sound of footsteps was followed as usual by the blinding and concentrated light, the glare of which took a while to dilute into something more manageable for his abused retinae.

The first thing Devante noticed was that Elijah looked tired. Usually he would arrive refreshed but today's Elijah looked like he had barely slept. Today's Elijah was also less talkative than normal. He kissed the skull, muttered a few words of greeting before glancing around the cell and then announced that he would return with porridge. The American then left the room, closing the door behind him but leaving the light on.

This was most unusual.

Devante looked over at Tyrone, still blinking and dazed and, as expected, slightly out of reach. It was then that Devante registered what had changed during the hours they had been asleep.

There were now only two of them. Reece was gone.

41

Lexington's cremation was, as he had specified, fairly small and suitably brief and took place in the late morning of a bright but harsh February day. Apart from the members of The Twelve, the small chapel in south-west London hosted Clare; Mrs Mendoza; Bobby; Suzanne Green; Simone; Lexington's niece, a delightful woman named Harriet who toured the world as a clarinettist in a major orchestra, and grand-niece Milly, who was in her late teens and had taken the day off from university where she was studying geography and climate science.

It was possible that Milly's interest in the environment had rubbed off on Lexington in his final years; his coffin was made of willow which, the young lady had proudly told Chris and Anna prior to the short service, was one of the most eco-friendly options.

Clare had been one of the first to arrive and spent a few minutes chatting with Monica and Thomas before the arrival of David and Terry, both of whom she had met during her previous visit. She greeted them as old friends and the two men politely introduced her to the five members of The Twelve who had joined since that last occasion. Monica watched out of the corner of her eye as the American welcomed each new arrival with customary exuberance. 'I've heard so much about you,' she would say on a couple of occasions even though Monica had barely mentioned the various subjects of her attention in her sporadic emails. Lexington had clearly been much more informative in his communications with Clare.

'Americans,' she muttered to no one in particular. 'Always on stage.' She made particular note of a gathering that spontaneously formed once almost everyone had assembled with Clare engaged in a vibrant conversation with Catherine, Belinda and Veronica, all of whom had joined The Twelve in the years since Clare was last in London.

Martin arrived last, having collected Mrs Mendoza from her home just off Brick Lane, and spent much of the time before the ceremony complaining about a poorly signposted roadworks diversion in the Battersea area which had delayed their journey inordinately. Mrs Mendoza, meanwhile, was being treated like a minor celebrity herself, as it was a rarity for her to be seen in the wild outside of her consulting room. Virtually every member of The Twelve as well as Bobby and Clare, were visibly jockeying for position to be able to sit next to the ageing counsellor; each of them suspecting that the old woman might require more emotional support on this saddest of days. 'Just one of us left now,' she whispered to Chris as he gave her a cuddle, a reference to a piece of recent Twelve history that only the two of them now recognised.

In the end, Mrs Mendoza managed to squeeze herself between Martin and Clare who immediately and comfortingly grasped her hand for mutual support. 'We'll get through this together,' the American said quietly.

As a qualified celebrant, Terry was able to conduct the service which he did with both grace and professionalism. Monica read a poem by Frederick Seidel as per Lexington's wishes and Bobby gave a brief overview of Lexington's life, obscuring the darker parts of his later years for the sake of his relatives. Finally, a short piece of solo piano music which had been specially written by Herbie Hancock for the occasion and sent to Monica via email was played over a loudspeaker while the wicker coffin embarked on its final journey.

More tears than expected were shed, notably by Owen and Thomas, who was personally surprised at how this particular death had affected him. 'We have to vacate this space by one o'clock,' said Terry after a short silence to permit everyone to collect their thoughts, 'but that still gives us an hour or so to chat and reminisce if we so wish.'

Clare immediately made a beeline for the cluster containing Catherine, Belinda and Veronica, and the four of them recommenced talking animatedly.

'I can't stay,' whispered Suzanne, sidling up to Monica who was gently comforting Thomas with a loving arm around his shoulder, 'but I do need a quick word about this Barnes church situation.'

Monica gestured for Terry to come and be her substitute on comforting duties before accompanying the commissioner to the rear of the chapel. 'A young man's body has been found,' began Suzanne quietly. 'In the river close to Hammersmith Bridge. He hasn't been identified yet but the DNA matches that on the body of Liam Tucker back in August.'

'Do you know how long he was in the water?' asked Monica, trying to subtly glance over Suzanne's shoulder at Clare and Veronica who were now holding hands. The commissioner replied that it was too early to say but that she would be in touch once the post-mortem and forensics had been completed.

'From what I know so far, he wasn't especially decayed which suggests he wasn't in the river for long before he was found. However, he is quite emaciated and he had three missing fingers. I should know more by the end of the week.' The commissioner took a peek at her watch. 'Sorry, I have to dash. Between you and I, there's another problem brewing with some of the right wingers in parliament unhappy about the way their recent protest marches have been policed. The usual unjustified accusations of heavy-handed tactics and all that nonsense. It should blow over but you can never be sure in this challenging political climate.'

The two women hugged and Monica watched as the commissioner walked briskly towards the door of the chapel before disappearing.

'She's cool,' said a deep New York voice behind Monica as Clare's hand slipped around her waist. 'Nicer than the current police commissioner of the NYPD at any rate.'

Monica felt a frisson of energy at the woman's touch which caused her to move away slightly to avoid electrocution. 'I'll make sure you get half of the ashes to take back with you,' she said hurriedly. 'Remind me when is your return flight, Clare?'

'It's a first class open return,' Clare said with a smile. 'I could scoot on the weekend or...' She glanced over at Veronica who waved enthusiastically. 'Or I could stick around for a while. I think I'll see which way the wind takes me.'

42

With nothing planned for the following day, Clare accepted an invitation from Catherine and Owen to view how they were progressing on the current case, meet Father Matthew and attend that evening's JCW meeting. The mention of the case at her Dorchester lunch with Monica and Thomas had germinated a nagging feeling in the American's mind and there was only one way to scotch it.

The three of them met late on Wednesday afternoon for tea at Catherine's house – Clare rapidly became a fan of smoky Earl Grey which the ex-journalist had received as a part of a Fortnum's hamper Christmas gift from Monica and Thomas.

At six thirty they wandered over to the vestry where Father Matthew was waiting to greet them with yet more tea, this time less smoky and naturally less expensive although no less delicious. 'You British people are obsessed,' announced Clare as she downed her third cup of the afternoon. 'Although, I can't really blame you. And what are these cookies called? The ones for actually putting into the tea?'

'Rich Tea,' said Owen, extracting one of the said 'cookies'

from its packaging and snapping it in half for greater dunking convenience.

Clare stared at him, wide-eyed. 'Wait, Rich TEA? Just as I told y'all. Obsessed!'

After toilet breaks, Father Matthew suggested a quick tour of the church which Clare excitedly accepted. She was fascinated by the *Stations of the Cross*, the fourteen plaques depicting Christ's final journey to crucifixion and entombment, and even more so by the confessional box nestled in a discreet corner of the nave. 'So how does this work exactly?' the New Yorker asked.

Father Matthew explained that those of the Catholic faith believed that sins could be absolved through confession and repentance. 'My parishioners, like Catherine here, come to me privately and we make ourselves as comfortable as we can in this box and I hear their confession in strict secrecy. Only the two of us, along with the Almighty, are present inside the confessional. After that, I ask the Lord to take away their sins if they truly repent and I provide them with some prayers to say before they leave the church and that's pretty much that.'

Clare was amazed. 'And that works for any sin?' The priest agreed that it did. 'So what if I'd murdered someone? Could I get forgiveness for that shit? Sorry, excuse my language. I'm just stoked for this. Can I give it a go?' Father Matthew explained that although Clare wasn't a Catholic, she could nonetheless ask for a seal of confession which would permit her to receive absolution from her sins and these would remain secret between the two of them plus the omniscient deity.

'Wait a second.' Clare had closed her eyes and was waving her hand trying to make rational sense of what she was hearing. 'So you mean to tell me that I can kill muthafuckas – oh shit, sorry again. That I can kill people and then come to church and do the confession and I'll get forgiven by God? And nobody else needs to know?'

'That's it,' confirmed Catherine. 'I come for confession after every case, regardless of how big or small a role I've played. It just helps me to balance my mind. Mrs Mendoza fully approves although she, of course, is agnostic. I can't believe you didn't know this stuff.' Clare explained that she grew up in a Baptist community and more or less abandoned that when she was eighteen and discovered pleasures of the flesh. It was the dawn of the seventies in New York City and the place was awash with opportunities for misbehaviour.

'Can I?' the New Yorker added, still processing this exciting information. 'Can I try this out right now? Do we have time? Even though I gotta warn y'all that me and Matthew may be a little while in there unpacking all the sins I need to offload.' Father Matthew suggested that, as they needed to get to JCW before seven, maybe Clare could limit herself to just the very basic sins she wished to confess. 'Let's do it,' she said, bounding into the confessional box like a springtime lamb.

'Give me twenty minutes,' Matthew said with a sigh as he ambled with somewhat less enthusiasm into his side of the booth and pulled the curtain closed behind him. Owen and Catherine moved away from the confessional area for extra privacy and settled at the rear of the nave where they sat mostly in silence while the faint sound of giggling emanated sporadically from where Clare was listing her myriad indiscretions.

Sure enough, twenty minutes later, Clare and Matthew emerged, she exhilarated, he apparently slightly stunned. The priest shook his head in despair towards Catherine and Owen who, in turn, looked at each other with intrigue. Clare was carrying a piece of paper on which were the words to the Lord's

Prayer which she already knew and Hail Mary which she didn't.

'I just have to sit quietly for a while and say these prayers a few times,' she told the two Twelve members, 'and then we good to go. Bear with me, y'all.' She sat in a front pew and bowed her head while reciting the holy words. After five minutes, she stood up and looked towards the back of the church where Matthew had joined the small group. 'Father, I lost count,' she shouted. 'Am I okay to do a couple more just to make sure I'm all done?'

Matthew agreed that a couple more should do it. 'Although in truth,' he whispered, 'considering the things that woman has done, I don't even know if the Pope would be able to accurately calculate what might constitute complete absolution.'

When Clare was satisfied that she was forgiven, the four of them donned coats for the short walk to the JCW hall, the exuberant shouts of the young people getting louder as they approached. 'So what happens if you tell someone about what goes on in that confession box? If you spill the beans, as you people say,' asked Clare.

The priest replied that, depending on your beliefs, disclosing anything that is said during confession would result in excommunication from the church, or worse, damnation in the afterlife. Neither of these outcomes would be particularly ideal. 'You must keep a lot of secrets, Father,' said Owen as they reached the hall. Matthew nodded solemnly, shoulders fully burdened.

As they opened the door to the JCW, they were greeted by a wall of excited chatter. Shayna, Riley and Letitia were talking loudly just inside the entrance and a boy they'd never met before was trying to impress them with his breakdancing, without obvious success.

'Hey, girl,' said Shayna, giving Catherine and Owen a quick hug before introducing herself to Clare. 'What's happening?'

Clare explained that she was visiting from New York and wanted to come and see what all the fuss was about.

'I just had all my sins forgiven by Matthew,' she exclaimed with a huge grin, 'and I'm feeling cleansed, girlfriend.'

'Oh my God, I love your accent,' said Riley as the breakdancing boy wandered away in disappointment, his audience distracted by this elderly newcomer. 'I'd love to visit New York. Furthest I ever been is Balham.'

'That's not true,' said Letitia. 'I took you up West End for Christmas shopping, is it.'

'Oh yeah. Sorry. West End.'

At that moment, Elijah trotted over to give his trademark hugs to Catherine, Owen and Matthew before turning his attention to Clare who stared at him in disbelief. 'And who do we have here?' he asked brightly. 'Another new friend to draw into the welcoming arms of Jesus?'

'This is Clare,' said Catherine. 'She's a friend of mine from New York. Just over for a visit.'

Elijah looked towards the heavens, his hands together as if in prayer. 'A fellow countryman. I mean countrywoman, forgive me. I'm honoured.' He pulled Clare into the biggest of hugs and, after a moment of uncharacteristic reticence, Clare responded. It was as if she were an actor on stage who had momentarily forgotten her lines and then suddenly snapped back into the role. 'Are you here for the evening?' continued Elijah. 'If I get time, we could chat for a bit. I'd love that.'

Clare stuttered that she would love that too but that the duration of her presence at JCW was uncertain. 'As you can imagine, um, Elijah,' she said solemnly, 'there are a great many draws on my time.'

'Well, look,' said Elijah, 'I would just love to sit down with you at some point. If we can't talk this evening, then Catherine and I are now café buddies so maybe we can entice you to join us at some point.' He hugged her again and ambled off to talk to Nathan and Harrison who were drinking beer in a corner. Clare stared after him as if she had just witnessed a shooting.

'You okay?' asked Catherine, conscious that the post-confession euphoria seemed to have dissipated rapidly.

Clare breathed in deeply, her eyes focused on the American. 'What did you say that man's name was?'

'Elijah Timothy. Why?'

Clare lowered her voice which assumed a steely resolve. 'That ain't no Elijah Timothy. That man's name is Carson Tresk and, unless he's had a major character change, he's as far from being a Christian as anyone you ever met.'

43

Catherine asked Father Matthew if the three of them could return briefly to the vestry where Owen thought he might have left a glove and the priest rummaged in his pocket to retrieve a key saying that he would stay in the hall just to make sure the behaviour of the young people didn't get out of hand. 'The mere presence of a man of the cloth appears to have a positive and somewhat restraining effect, even upon the more excitable youngsters,' he said with a smile. This was followed almost immediately by a slight grimace as two young men drinking from bottles of beer strode past with a cheery, 'All right, Father Christmas? Ain't you supposed to be in the north pole or summat?'

Once inside the vestry, Clare breathed out, seemingly for the first time in minutes. 'I thought he'd gone to Canada,' she began slowly. 'In fact, I even briefly considered dispatching a couple of members of The Twelve in New York across the border but then we had no idea where exactly he'd gone and we had no way of tracking him. I can't believe I hugged that muthafucka. God, I need a shower. I may need two showers to wash that man's bad energy from my bones.'

Catherine asked whether Clare had met Elijah/Carson before and the American explained that she hadn't but that a member of her team named Anthony Schillaci had been working on an assassination plan which was nearing completion the previous spring when their target left home and disappeared, leaving behind two young men imprisoned in his basement apartment in the Red Hook area of Brooklyn. The Twelve in New York managed to rescue the men just days before one of them would have died from malnutrition and the other one, a twenty-year-old named Travis Dale, told them that Carson had grown suspicious that he was being followed and decided to bail. Clare had been troubled by the similarities between the two cases during her lunch at the Dorchester but had partially dismissed the idea that Carson could have somehow found his way to London.

'He is one of the most charismatic but manipulative people you will ever meet in your life,' warned Clare, 'as well as being pure evil and a psychopath. He hates organised religion but uses it to his advantage which is to kill people who don't fit in to his warped mindset of what's "normal". Gays, prostitutes, immigrants, trans people, they're all targets but he doesn't kill them himself. He's cleverer than that.

'Carson has a first-class degree in psychology from Yale and a masters in theology from Berkeley. He uses his intimate knowledge of the scriptures and his deep understanding of human frailty, particularly in young men, to control an individual to carry out his will. He chooses them with meticulous care. It's always between the ages of seventeen and twenty-three and it's always men with damaged pasts, care-home kids, foster kids, people who lack a powerful father figure and can be easily influenced. Also, they have to be the sort of kids who won't be missed and they can't have criminal records.

'He takes his time to worm his way into their lives and

separates them from their friends, much like a wild cat picks on the weakest in a group of antelope. He buys them gifts and becomes their only friend until they're in a position to basically do whatever he wants.'

'Which is kill,' said Owen. 'Should I put the kettle on, by the way?' Catherine agreed that coffee might be a good idea, both for refreshment purposes as well as a way to keep warm in the draughty vestry. Owen went and filled the kettle from the small kitchen and shouted over the running water. 'But what happens after these boys or men have committed murder? Don't the police arrest them?'

Clare was texting Anthony in New York to tell him that Carson Tresk was not in Canada but in London and that she'd just bumped into him in a church hall in Barnes, naturally needing to explain what and where Barnes was. 'They disappear,' she said, multitasking. Catherine recovered the half-empty packet of biscuits. 'And for a while we had no idea what was happening. They weren't at their foster homes or refuges. They didn't turn up dead in the river. They just vanished. After Carson fled to Canada, we broke into his apartment and found the two guys chained to a wall in a basement. It smelt real bad down there. They both admitted to homicide and both are due to stand trial later this year but I suspect it'll be on a charge of third-degree murder considering the shit they've been through.'

Owen returned with three coffees which he placed on a small table near where his two companions were standing. Catherine was taking her time to fully comprehend this new information. 'So Elijah, sorry, Carson killed Robert. Well, no, he didn't but he got someone to do it for him.'

'Devante,' said Owen. 'He disappeared around the time of Robert's death.'

'There ya go,' said Clare, reaching for a mug and raising it in a grim salute to the pieces slotting into place. 'Same evil pattern right there.' Her phone rang. 'It's Anthony. One second. Yo, Anthony. Can you believe this shit?' She wandered into a corner of the vestry and began an animated conversation with her colleague three thousand miles away.

'Just pulling all these threads together,' said Owen. 'I guess that the prostitute in November...'

'Kathy,' confirmed Catherine.

'Right, Kathy. I guess she was killed by Tyrone and then the librarian chap, what's his name...?'

'Liam.'

'Exactly. Liam. He was killed by Reece. Which means that Elijah, Carson, whatever, is holding the three of them prisoner somewhere. Probably that basement flat where we know he lives.' Owen's initial thought was that they could simply go and rescue the young men but then he suspected that Clare, and for that matter Monica, wouldn't want Carson to slip through the net a second time and that a degree of patience may be required if they were going to assassinate Carson and save the young men.

'Okay, bye. See you soon. Bye.' Clare strode back to where the two Brits were sipping their coffees. 'So what Anthony thinks has happened is that Carson went to Canada and got a new passport forged somewhere like Toronto. It's not hard if you have the knowledge and the money, which he does. He's the heir to a very successful real estate business worth a fortune so he's not short of dollars. Then Anthony thinks he headed to New Brunswick and found a container ship in Saint John to take him to London for a cash payment, no questions asked, and that's how he found himself here. He picked out a church that would let him do some volunteering as a youth worker; he probably impressed Father Matthew with his Bible knowledge. And so his horror show starts all over again in a new city. With new victims.'

'We can't tell Matthew,' said Catherine.

'Oh, absolutely not,' agreed Clare. 'Anthony's on his way over. He'll be here Friday morning. I suggest we have one of your kick-ass meetings with everyone on Friday afternoon after he's had a nap and we can brief you on everything we know and maybe together we can pull together a plan to deal with this evil piece of shit once and for all.'

Catherine remained in a state of partial shock and disbelief. She had befriended this monster. She had even been strangely attracted to him. 'But he lives with his sick mother,' she stuttered. 'He's her carer.'

'I hate to break this to you, girl,' said Clare as Owen took the mugs to be washed up. 'Carson's mother is dead. It's highly likely that he killed her.'

44

The venue for the Friday afternoon meeting was Clarges Mews just off Piccadilly. It had been chosen by Monica for a number of reasons. Firstly, it was easily walkable from The Dorchester where the two Americans were temporarily and decadently resident. Secondly, it was one of the more impressive of The Twelve's London properties with its fine selection of Dutch and British nineteenth-century art; Anthony had not visited London since becoming a member of the New York group and although Clare had experienced Clarges Mews on her previous visit, nonetheless Monica felt that it would show the original Twelve in a positive light. Americans like impressive, she surmised. Some of the other Twelve meeting places, delightful though they might be, were basically normal homes with the odd structural adaptation to accommodate large groups.

The final reason was simply that Monica had another Fortnum's craving, this time for those smoky Earl Grey teabags which she acquired prior to the meeting and stashed in her spacious shoulder bag for safekeeping. She had also stocked up on marmalade for good measure.

It was Clare's suggestion that Mrs Mendoza also attend this meeting to help everyone to better understand the psychology behind the killings. When Monica proposed this idea, explaining that Martin would be able to transport her to and from home to avoid the indignity of the Tube, Mrs Mendoza was enthralled. 'It'll be my first official appearance at a meeting since 2007,' she said with an excited flourish before enquiring whether Terry would be baking biscuits. 'How wonderful!'

Earlier that morning, Martin had also returned to Heathrow to collect Anthony – 'I prefer it if you pronounce the "h" please' – a dapper, besuited and scrupulously polite man in his late sixties who had been a nightclub owner before selling up and joining The Twelve New York five years earlier. Despite being slightly younger than Martin, Anthony's face had more lines than the subway map, imprints of a life well lived, and during their journey the two men bonded easily over a mutual love of musical theatre. As a child growing up in The Bronx, Anthony had snuck into the original 1959 Broadway production of *Gypsy* with Ethel Merman and Martin grilled the New Yorker on every detail that could be recalled, envious that he himself had only managed to witness the 2015 West End revival.

The fifteen of them slotted easily into the huge space with its wooden table centrepiece. Anthony was refreshed after a deep and restorative two-hour snooze after lunch with Clare at a sushi place in Shepherd Market. The fact that the Clarges Mews drinks cabinet stocked his favourite Bourbon was an added bonus. 'This reminds me to get a new bottle for our Washington Street location down in the Financial District,' he said, sipping a glass of the liquor neat with one rock of ice. 'We ran out last time we were there. I remember pouring the last drop into your glass, Clare.'

'But then we were celebrating the successful conclusion to a case,' Clare reminded him. She was seated between Catherine and Veronica at the end of the table nearest the door and the three of them were sharing a bottle of Californian Merlot. 'Maybe celebrating a little too hard in some instances but we'll gloss over that right now.'

Terry had made an abundance of NYC chocolate chip cookies in honour of the two visitors and Monica called the meeting to order as Mrs Mendoza nibbled her way delicately through her second one. 'Sadly, Suzanne, the Metropolitan Police Commissioner, cannot attend but I will send her a full update afterwards. Now, if I may ask Anthony to please kick us off with an overview of what happened when our American friends were planning to assassinate Carson Tresk and then we can see where we are currently and begin to pull together a plan of action to bring this whole thing to a satisfactory conclusion. Anthony?'

'Do I stand up?' asked the American. Monica said that it was entirely optional. Belinda reached for a cookie. Anthony elected to remain seated.

'The case first came to us through a pastor friend of The Twelve who resides in a place called Flatbush. That's in Brooklyn. You know Brooklyn?' There was a mixture of nodding and shaking heads with Mrs Mendoza amongst the nodders and Martin amongst the shakers as his festive trip with Joanne had focused purely on the tourist haunts of New York. 'Okay, so Brooklyn is one of the five boroughs and it's just over the East River from Manhattan which I'm sure most of you know.' Martin crossed over to the nodding contingent.

'Anyway, this pastor was working with young people in the Latino and Italian communities and he had got suspicious of this young guy, Carson, who was befriending individuals who would then disappear. Carson said they had moved out of town to long-lost relatives in the Midwest but we started doing some monitoring and some subtle investigations and we began to reveal the full story which, as we know, is not a pretty picture. I'm gonna try a cookie at this point before Chris and Mrs Mendoza eat them all. One second please.' The psychologist and the ex-surgeon smiled guiltily at each other. Terry ambled to the kitchen and emerged with extra supplies.

'Once we knew what was happening, our plan was to overdose the guy with fentanyl, the opioid of choice where we are right now because it's so easy to access, and then take him out to Jamaica Bay where we have a boat, and just drop him overboard. It's one of our preferred ways of doing things currently. It's eco-friendly and we're all about saving the environment as well as getting shot of the lowlifes, you understand me? We weight the body with bags of dead fish so everything eventually gets eaten. The bags are made from a compostable material which dissolves over the course of a week and we make sure we dump the bodies somewhere where the tide is going to take them out into the Atlantic and not back to shore. We don't wanna be flooding the good people of Martha's Vineyard with rotting corpses, right? That would really mess up the view from the pretty beachfront condos. We have a friend in the local coastguard who helps us to keep everything hush-hush.'

Anthony chuckled at this point and Thomas muttered a 'Right' in response, even though he'd never been to Martha's Vineyard and had neither the intention nor the desire to do so.

'Why does he choose young men of roughly the same age?' asked David, nursing a white rum. Anthony replied that Mrs Mendoza might be the best person to answer this question and opened the floor to the octogenarian who quickly gulped down the remnants of a fourth cookie with a swig of weak tea and a momentary cough to dislodge any stubborn crumbs.

'Is anyone familiar with the California Caverns?' she asked brightly.

Only Clare raised her hand and even then with a comment of 'Vaguely.'

'Jolly good,' continued Mrs Mendoza. 'It's a cave system located around one hundred kilometres east of San Francisco and quite challenging to access owing to its narrow entrance which twists and turns until you reach the main cave area.

'The interesting thing about it from our current viewpoint is that the people who look after the caves have found various skeletons over the years, some of which are very old and some of which are more recent. These skeletons, regardless of how long they've been down there, always belong to young men in late teenage or early twenties. It is this particular age group for whom the thrill of risk vastly outweighs the assessment of danger. From a clinical point of view, the prefrontal cortex of these young men, the part of their brains which calculates risk, is not yet fully formed. As a result, they are far more susceptible to manipulation and misfortune. This also explains why young men who have recently passed their driving test have a statistically far greater chance of being involved in a fatal accident, particularly when they are in groups where peer pressure adds to the potentially lethal mix.

'Carson, with his knowledge of human behaviour, would know this and hunts his unfortunate disciples accordingly. He's methodical as many psychopaths are. This makes him very dangerous indeed.'

Both Clare and Anthony applauded as neither of them had fully experienced Mrs Mendoza's knowledge and expertise at close hand. 'We could,' proposed Anna, 'just hand this one over to Suzanne and let the police deal with it. I appreciate that's not generally The Twelve way but...'

The ringtone of Monica's phone cut short Anna's line of thinking. 'It's Simone,' she said. 'I told him he could call anytime. Please accept my apologies.'

From the muffled sounds coming from Monica's phone, the Italian restaurateur was again in something of a state of forlorn exasperation. After listening and comforting for around five minutes, Monica assured him that she would think of something and would visit over the weekend to set his mind at rest in person. With Simone finally calmer, she hung up with a sigh. 'He's not in a good way, poor man. He's found out that the Pasta Tansa place is opening a week on Monday and already his bookings are taking a hammering. He's had three cancellations for tables that week just in the last hour. Anyway, sorry, where were we?'

'Anna was suggesting that maybe we let the Met deal with this one,' said Graham, 'which might actually be a decent idea if Carson is as dangerous as we believe.'

Monica thought for a moment. 'I think we'll keep it,' she said decisively. 'For now, at least. We'll all need to work together on this one and we'll need Suzanne's help eventually, but I have an idea which could potentially kill more than one bird with a particularly well-directed stone. That's if Clare and Anthony are happy to stick around for a couple of weeks.'

'Girlfriend,' said Clare with a dramatic wave of the hand. 'Working as a team to assassinate muthafuckas is my jam!'

45

'Veronica, didn't you say that you vaguely knew Jeremy Tansa?' The TV presenter confirmed to Monica and the group that they had briefly rubbed shoulders at an awards event a couple of years ago and then, of course, she had endured a longer conversation at La Stella the previous month when she lunched spontaneously with Belinda. They had also met Tansa's executive head chef, Jason, who, according to Simone, was now a regular fixture in the new restaurant as they prepared for the launch party. 'Do you think you could use your exquisite blagging talents to wangle a quick tour of Pasta Tansa as soon as possible please, and also a couple of invites to the launch party?' Veronica said that shouldn't be a problem and that she would wander over there at the weekend. 'Maybe take Terry with you so he can make an educated assessment of the security situation.' The locksmith nodded and said that he would liaise with Veronica after the meeting to finalise arrangements.

'Depending on when you're going, I would offer to give you a lift,' said Martin, 'but bear in mind that it's "Sondheim Saturday" at the gym and you know how much Joanne and I love to keep in shape. It's *A Little Night Music* this week.'

'Will you be making your entrance again with your usual flair, dear?' quipped Graham. Martin stood and theatrically pretended to take a bow.

Monica then asked Owen whether he could use the infrared camera that he had acquired in the summer to monitor Paul and Tiffany Storey to see how many people were living in Carson Tresk's basement flat. 'I'll do that on Sunday, Monica. No problem.'

'Catherine,' Monica said next, 'how easy would it be to get Carson to come to dinner at La Stella? I know you've had friendly coffees...'

'And green tea. He only drinks green tea.'

'Right. Coffee and green tea. I know you've had a handful of those meetings. Do you think he might be tempted by some lovely pasta?' Catherine said that only that week, at the JCW on the previous Wednesday, Elijah, or Carson, had expressed how much he would love to meet up with Clare before she flew back to the States. 'Excellent,' said Monica. 'See if you can arrange this for Monday. Tell him it's the only date that Clare can do before she leaves and that she's always wanted to dine there. We'll pay, obviously.'

Monica then asked everyone to keep that Monday free as they would all have an important role to play. 'Apart from Terry, is anyone else confident cooking in a restaurant kitchen?'

Anthony raised his hand. 'You don't grow up in an Italian household in The Bronx without learning how to cook,' he drawled. 'In fact, for a while back in the early eighties, the guys used to call me Chopper Schillaci on account of the way I cut herbs. Just the woody herbs, you understand. Rosemary, mostly, and thyme and sage. You don't ever chop the delicate herbs like basil. You tear them.' It was Terry's turn to give a sitting ovation.

'Hey,' interjected Chris with excitement, 'my nickname used to be The Cutter. We should team up. We'd be great. The

Cutter and the Chopper!' Anthony leant across the table and high-fived the ex-surgeon.

At that moment, Monica's phone rang again. 'Suzanne,' she said to the assembled group. 'One moment please. Again.' The commissioner's call was a brief one as she was in her car between meetings. The identity of the body pulled from the river earlier in the month had been confirmed as that of Reece Mayhew, twenty years old and last seen in August of the previous year. According to Suzanne, Reece had been staying in a hostel for young people since leaving his foster care a couple of years before. Her team were following up with people who knew him but so far there wasn't much information available. One of the residents in the hostel had recalled him talking about moving to a different part of London and so they'd simply assumed that was what he'd done. His room had been emptied of Reece's few belongings either shortly before or shortly after his disappearance.

Monica asked whether Reece had been designated as a missing person and the commissioner replied that he hadn't. 'The chap at the hostel apparently said that in his final weeks there, he became more isolated and so, when they stopped seeing him around, they didn't really give it a second thought. Monica, I've just arrived at my meeting so I'd better go but can we meet early next week, please? I sense that this one could have more to it.' The leader of The Twelve explained that they were already planning to meet on Monday and that she would extend the invitation. 'Great. Thank you. One more thing. There was no water in Reece's lungs so he didn't drown. He was dead before he entered the water. It looks like starvation.'

'California Caverns,' muttered Mrs Mendoza solemnly after Monica had relayed this grim information to the group.

'I appreciate,' began Clare in what was, for her, a more considered tone, 'that the passing of this young man might suggest the need to move quickly but I would still advise patience. Carson is dangerous and methodical and he will already have an escape strategy for what to do if he gets even the slightest sniff that shit is going down. He must not suspect a thing. You hear me?' Monica agreed but if the plan taking form in her mind solidified then they wouldn't have too long to wait.

'Um...' Thomas had raised a tentative hand, even though Monica was seated right next to him. 'Is there anything you'd like me to do at this stage?' Monica reached up and clasped the elevated hand in hers before bringing it gently down to her chest and placing it over her heart.

'Absolutely,' she said, remembering that her lover had wanted to play a more direct role in the next assassination. 'You and I have to go and talk to Simone. He needs to teach you how to wait tables.'

'If you're planning what I think you're planning,' mused Clare, 'then you're some special kind of psychopath.'

Martin inhaled sharply as if readying himself for an important pronouncement. 'You can compliment her all you like,' he said, 'but it won't butter no parsnips.' Many years in the future, Monica and Thomas, long retired from The Twelve, would still giggle to themselves at the memory of the Americans' bemused faces in response to Martin's outburst.

Monica smiled and accepted Clare's comment gratefully. 'That may be so, but I'm a psychopath with a heart of gold and that makes all the difference.'

Mrs Mendoza reached for one of the last four remaining cookies and glanced with appreciation first towards Monica and then towards Clare. 'It takes one to know one.' She glowed with obvious, almost maternal pride.

46

The branded window boards which for weeks had diligently shielded the building work taking place within Pasta Tansa had overnight been removed. Presumably this was so that potential customers could now peer inside at the beautiful banquette tables, industrial-style pipes criss-crossing the ceiling, huge graffiti wall to the left of the diners and, further back, the open-plan kitchen where Jason and his team of eager chefs finessed the menu. Veronica and Terry had met at La Stella at noon on the Saturday for coffees and toilet breaks before their reconnaissance mission two doors down. Monica and Thomas had joined them for the coffees and so that Monica could outline her plan to Simone and in order that Thomas could begin his somewhat late apprenticeship into the hospitality industry.

Squinting through the window at Jason, who was impatiently instructing a pair of junior chefs on knife technique, Veronica finally managed to catch his eye and waved frantically, bordering on psychotically. With weary reluctance, he excused himself from his tutoring and strode over to the door of the restaurant to unlock. 'Virginia, isn't it? We open to the public on Tuesday after the Monday launch.'

Veronica politely corrected her name, reminding Jason that she was a former television presenter, and asked whether she and her friend might be able to have a quick look around. 'Terry is only in town for a short time,' she said, 'and he's one of the world's most sought-after architects.' The locksmith nodded despite the slight alarm at this off-the-cuff subterfuge. 'He just loves seeing how new trends are working in different spaces and I noticed you're using graffiti in a dynamic and very twenty-first century style. Could we come in for just a minute please, Jason? We promise not to be in the way.'

The chef huffed. He knew Jeremy was exhaustingly proud of the graffitied walls which had been created by two of the most in-demand street artists of the moment, the secretive Sisters of Tag whom nobody had ever seen. Maybe this TV presenter could use a few of her contacts to get some publicity for the interior design. 'All right, just a couple of minutes.'

Veronica covertly held out a hand behind her back which Terry low-fived.

'What are you guys chopping?' the locksmith asked as the group wandered over to where Jason had been demonstrating his knife skills. 'Looks like basil.' One of the young chefs, a woman in her twenties with blue hair, confirmed that it was. 'I was always taught to tear basil and never chop it because then you get more flavour from the rougher edges of the torn leaf.'

Jason scowled. 'The old ways are not always the best ways,' he grumbled. Terry's eyebrow elevated. 'Chopping is more efficient. Less waste. Plus, we can ensure that every dish is exactly the same in terms of taste and quality. Jeremy's customers prefer uniformity.'

Terry wondered what Anthony would make of this

explanation but chose not to dwell on it. Veronica, meanwhile, was carefully studying the graffiti, the distressed walls upon which the designs were spray-painted, and the open kitchen, covertly taking photos with her mobile phone while Jason was distracted.

'Something smells good,' said Terry. 'If my senses don't deceive me, it smells a bit like a beef giouvetsi but why would you be cooking up a Greek dish in an Italian restaurant?' Jason's face adjusted from its usual glower into something marginally more amicable. Clearly this 'architect' knew a bit about food which is more than could be said for some of the so-called chefs that Jeremy Tansa's recruitment team had sent him to knock into shape. Luckily, most of the dishes at Pasta Tansa had been pre-prepared in a dark kitchen in Southall so the majority of what was required on site was merely reheating and plating up with the odd garnish to give everything a veneer of freshness and authenticity.

'It's my, sorry, it's Jeremy's Italianised version of a classic giouvetsi,' he explained. 'You want to try it? It's one of my personal favourites and it's been flying off the menu at all the restaurants during the winter months. We use beef shin to save money and add flavour and we cook it on the hob instead of baking it in the oven.' Jason led the locksmith to the rear of the kitchen where a couple of young chefs were keeping an eye on the bubbling, meaty stew. Jason grabbed a couple of spoons from a rack and handed one to Terry before dipping his own spoon into the pot, extracting a few millilitres of beefy, oniony liquid with a couple of tiny pasta shapes which Terry recognised as stelline, and, after blowing lightly, placing the spoon in his mouth. 'Amazing,' he proclaimed. 'You want to try, Terry?'

The locksmith tasted the stew, making sure to rummage for a piece of slow-cooked, fragmenting muscle to get the full mouth-feel experience. He rolled the rich, unctuous sweetness around his tastebuds for a few seconds. It was slightly overseasoned but Terry elected not to mention this. 'It's good,' he said. 'Have you tried adding two or three spoons of good red wine vinegar? It might lift some of the more subtle flavours like the cinnamon.'

Jason's face shifted again, this time into a picture of mild disbelief. 'You and your old ways again, Terry,' he muttered.

'Just try it,' said Terry, kindly. 'Have you got any good red wine vinegar knocking about?' One of the young chefs replied that they definitely had red wine vinegar although whether it constituted 'good' was anyone's guess. She trotted off to the storage cupboard and returned with a bottle of supermarket own-brand vinegar which caused Terry's nose to crinkle slightly and not in the good way. 'Oh well,' he said, 'it's worth a try, even with this old plonk.'

He reached for a ladle and poured a bowl of stew before adding a few drops of vinegar and giving it a languid stir. Then the locksmith tasted his adaptation and nodded appreciatively before offering the bowl to Jason to test. Again, the look on the senior chef's face was transformed. 'That's delicious,' he said. 'My palate is beaming. That's brought it all together beautifully. Don't fancy a job, do you, Terry?'

The locksmith grinned. 'Already have one,' he said as the two younger chefs each tried the enriched stew while making satisfied noises to each other. 'But thank you.'

'Everyone making friends here?' asked Veronica as she leant over the pass where plates and dishes would, in a few days' time, be shuttling back and forth between busy kitchen and expectant customers with military precision. The chefs and Terry all nodded. 'So, Jason, how would I go about trying to get an invite to the launch party on Monday week?'

47

A pertinent text from Jason to the Pasta Tansa PR lady whose name, somewhat predictably, was Pandora, and both Veronica and Terry were on the guest list, the latter having decided to change his non-existent flight out of London and rearrange some meetings in order to attend. 'It should be fun,' said Jason, 'certainly for the guests. Hard work for those of us in the kitchen but I have to admit that one of the nice things that Jeremy does is that halfway through the evening, when everyone's a bit tipsy, he gets all the kitchen staff, even the KPs, to all come and stand at the pass so that the guests can applaud them. He gives a little speech too. It's a lovely moment and it'll be even more special here in London because we've got a few friendly critics coming down and some influencers and a smattering of celebrities. Pandora's hoping for some TV news too, although apparently they don't confirm until the day itself.'

'Anyone I know? In the celebrity world?' asked Veronica, intrigued. Jason rattled off half a dozen names of minor personalities who used to be in soap operas or reality TV shows.

'If I'm honest,' said the chef, 'Jeremy isn't really the sort to make close friends with other celebrities.' Terry and Veronica glanced at each other with the unspoken suggestion that they weren't entirely surprised. 'So it's mostly the sort of people who would happily come to the opening of a bag of crisps. You'll probably end up being the most famous person in the room, Veronica. Except for Jeremy, of course.'

The former TV presenter smiled at the inference. 'You've been very kind,' she said, 'but we mustn't take up any more of your time. We'll just use your bathroom, if that's okay, and then we'll be going.'

'I'm assuming it's all plumbed in?' said Terry. Jason confirmed that the toilets were fully functional and pointed them both in the appropriate direction. 'That Pandora's opened a can of worms if she gets TV news to come along,' muttered the locksmith, causing Veronica to suffer a fit of giggles.

Two doors away, Simone was teaching Thomas the rudiments of waiting tables while Monica watched with amusement. 'Is a good job that you're not relying on this as a career, Signor Thomas,' said the Italian with a smile as the former sports coach spilled some latte onto a table while delivering it to an imaginary customer. 'But we can get you to a satisfactory point, I'm sure. Certo.'

'Do you recall, Simone,' began Monica as she nursed an unspilt latte at a corner table, 'about nine years ago when Lexington and I assassinated a chap called Heath here in the restaurant?'

The Italian scratched his grey stubble with a pensive frown. 'Heath,' he repeated, sifting his memory like pasta flour. 'The one with the properties in South America that fell down. Ah, si, of course. I think I helped drag him out of the back door. Why you ask, Signora Monica?' The leader of The Twelve beckoned Simone over to her table and began to outline her plan.

'It depends on a whole bunch of variables,' she said, 'and, of course, there will be a plan B, but in principle, would you be agreeable to us doing something similar again? You'd need to make sure the place was empty of regular customers of course.' Simone said that although he didn't especially want The Twelve to make a habit of killing people on his business premises, twice in nine years was hardly prolific. When was Monica thinking? 'Monday week,' she replied. 'The evening of the Pasta Tansa launch.'

Simone went to his back room, retrieved his laptop and navigated his way to the bookings page. 'Monday week,' he muttered, 'allora. Ah, si. We have a couple of tables booked but I know them both so I can ask if they can move to later in the week. I'm sure they won't mind. They are regulars. Neither of them are birthdays or anniversaries or anything like that.' He confirmed that he would take no further bookings for the Monday evening and Monica in turn stated that The Twelve would ensure that he was fully compensated for the loss of income. Staff would not be required but Monica confirmed that she would also provide a full day's pay for all employees who would normally be working that night.

'Furthermore,' she said, 'I think we can help solve your Pasta Tansa problem.'

A knock on the window behind Monica signalled the return of Veronica and Terry, full of excitement following their visit to Simone's imminent competition. 'It's all good news from Simone's point of view,' announced Terry, stretching an arm around the Italian's broad shoulders. 'For a start, they can't cook. Not like you guys can anyway, Simone. They cook by numbers as opposed to instinctively and it's mostly reheating anyway. Any critic worth their salt is going to taste right through it. Secondly, V's got us into the party. Apparently it'll be full of critics and food bloggers and that. Swanky. I'll have to dig out me posh drawers.'

The most interesting news, however, was that there would

be a moment during the evening when everyone would be distracted during Jeremy Tansa's speech. 'Apparently,' explained Veronica, 'he does all this "aren't I humble" stuff and sometimes introduces all the staff, although according to Jason he forgets most of their names so he just makes stuff up. Anyway, there will be a good five minutes when everyone's attention will be on him.'

'And not on the back entrance to the kitchen,' Terry added. 'If I could just borrow everyone for a moment.' He led the group to the rear of La Stella where Simone's door opened out onto a small courtyard with various bins and a pile of boxes awaiting recycling. The five of them stepped out into the chilly February sunshine and looked across to where one of Jeremy's KPs was having a crafty cigarette on a set of three metal steps behind Pasta Tansa.

'That back entrance,' whispered Terry, barely nodding towards the smoker.

48

Following a quick lunch of leek, walnut and goat's cheese casarecce which Simone conjured spontaneously even though it wasn't on the menu and served by Thomas with an obvious increase in agility, Veronica said that she had to leave because she was meeting Clare for tea at The Dorchester. Monica's wary eyebrow did not go unnoticed. 'Since the funeral, we've been getting along famously, so Clare thought it might be fun to have tea. Just the two of us.'

'At her hotel,' added Monica. 'Probably in her suite.' Terry was too busy tucking into a plate of winter greens and wild garlic lasagne to register her tone of suspicious caution.

'Precisely,' said Veronica excitedly, choosing either to miss or ignore the inference. 'I think I've only had tea at The Dorchester once before and that was with Angela Rippon when I was a bit more in the public eye. It'll be fun.' Monica stifled an ironic mumble as she watched Veronica stroll out onto a chilly Moscow Road to hail a taxi.

Thomas took the opportunity to use the seat that Veronica had vacated. 'I'm getting better,' he enthused. 'At the waiting stuff. I didn't spill anything this time.' Monica reached over to stroke his face and said how impressed she was at the speed with which he was picking up the necessary skills, reasonably basic though they were.

'There is one more skill that I will need you to acquire,' she said, 'but I'm waiting for a piece of equipment to arrive. When it does, we can practise at home.' Thomas expressed the hope that this 'equipment' wasn't a cigar following his experience of the previous summer and Monica confirmed that he was correct. 'No smoke will be required for the assassination of Carson Tresk. Not if my plan works out.'

For much of the following day, Sunday, Monica was engrossed in the Bamford cookery book of poisons. Thomas spent the day reading his own book, a crime novel which Terry had passed on after enjoying it himself, and watching sport while sporadically practising his new skills by furnishing his lover with teas, coffees and snacks with a clean tea towel draped over his lower arm for effect. 'He was quite secretive, this Bamford fellow,' said Monica during the half-time advertisement break in the football match in which Thomas was semi-engaged, 'but also ingenious in his combinations of toxins. They didn't always work, and he's helpfully noted the failures here, but when they did work, he could pretty much calculate the exact moment when the effects would kick in.'

Thomas asked whether she was actually researching the best way to conclude the Tresk case and not simply immersing herself in her admiration for a deceased fellow chemist. 'I'm working on it. I think I'm getting very close. One slight issue is that after Bamford left The Twelve, there wasn't really anyone qualified to take over his work. Until me, that is. So I'm dealing with fifty-year-old research notes. There's no reason to suspect they won't still be effective but we'll need a backup just in case.'

It was mid-afternoon when Owen texted to say that he and Graham had been monitoring for a couple of hours from a hired van outside Carson's basement flat and the infrared could detect three individuals inside. One was clearly Carson as they had watched him leave and then return with a carrier bag of shopping. The other two were more or less static, suggesting that their movement was restricted. 'Devante and Tyrone,' he concluded. 'At least they're alive.'

An hour later, having heard from Suzanne regarding her availability, Monica scheduled a Monday meeting for 11am at the former Bamford house in Shepherd's Bush and texted the group as usual. Most of The Twelve, along with Clare, responded within ten minutes. Veronica's reply came two hours later while Thomas was serving up a spicy pork stew which he'd been gently simmering for much of the afternoon, filling the flat with the aroma of paprika. Monica frowned and started fiddling anxiously with her beryl ring.

'You know,' she said casually, dipping an introductory chunk of sourdough into the stew and trying to distract herself from what might be happening at The Dorchester, 'a third marriage wouldn't be such a bad idea.'

Much like an L-plated delivery driver on a second-hand scooter, Thomas felt that this statement had appeared out of nowhere and yet somehow it wasn't something which shocked him. He'd tumbled the thought around his mind so many times, particularly in the early mornings when he had woken before Monica and adoringly watched her doze peacefully. 'Is this what a day reading about deadly poisons does to you?' he asked casually, topping up her glass of Trebbiano. 'Your thoughts drift automatically from toxins toward matrimony? Oh, and incidentally,' he gazed nostalgically at the sofa where they had had their first kiss, 'aren't we in slightly the wrong place for moments of impetuousness and romantic whim?'

Monica giggled and reached for a piece of kitchen roll having carelessly dribbled stew down her chin. 'Maybe. I don't know, I guess the Lexington business focused my mind and then being on the home straight towards the end of a case always make me think of my own mortality, especially after nearly losing Chris last year.'

Since joining The Twelve, Thomas's own concerns about the perils of what they were doing had abated somewhat since that first assassination. He had barely given the risks a second thought during this case, probably because his proximity to the action had been limited up to this point.

'Are you worried that we'll be in danger on this one?'

Its temperature now perfect, Monica tucked into the stew as if she had been separated from food for some days. 'Not especially. I think there are enough of us, what with our American friends, to mitigate the dangers but there's always an element of risk. You know that. Weren't we talking about marriage, by the way or are you trying to subtly deflect the conversation? How would you feel? After this case. Just a small group of us. Close friends and family. Forty or so. Fifty tops. Might that be vaguely of interest?' Monica's eyes seemed to have acquired an added sparkle.

'Let's do it,' Thomas replied, taking her hand and kissing it softly. 'Straight after this case we can start planning. I love you. So much.'

'I love you so much too,' Monica replied. 'And that was surprisingly easy.'

49

As Monica suspected they might, Clare, Anthony and Veronica arrived for the Monday meeting together, the TV presenter looking as if she hadn't slept for several days. 'Everything okay?' Anna asked as Veronica crumpled onto a sofa beside her and rested her head on the pathologist's lap.

'Strong coffee,' she croaked, eyes drifting shut. 'And maybe a pillow. Please.'

'Your doing?' asked Monica, a stern eye focused on Clare who, in contrast to Veronica, was as spritely as a kitten with a new toy.

Clare grinned devilishly and wandered over to give Monica a friendly hug. 'Since Saturday evening,' she whispered with obvious pride. 'With a couple of short breaks to fetch clean clothes and to get room service.' She glanced at the lightly dozing Veronica before lowering her voice further as she closed in on Monica's ear, giving it a light kiss. 'I guess some people have less stamina. If you know what I mean. I don't recall *you* falling asleep.'

Monica sighed wearily, her eyes scanning the room before they settled on Anthony who was returning from the kitchen with two espressos. 'Hey, don't look at me,' he pleaded. 'I went to see the Tina Turner musical with Martin and Joanne. Such a nice lady, that Joanne.'

'Simply the best,' muttered Martin who had already flopped into a comfortable leather armchair. Terry, who had baked chocolate Florentine biscuits, said that he could cover for Veronica in terms of reporting back on the situation at Pasta Tansa. The TV presenter, from her roughly horizontal position, raised an exhausted hand of gratitude. Anna was now stroking her hair sympathetically.

Last to arrive was Suzanne, owing to the slight overrun of her previous meeting in addition to traffic issues on the Shepherd's Bush roundabout. 'Is Veronica okay?' she asked, gratefully accepting a latte and a Florentine from Chris. 'Or are you practising poisons on Twelve members now, Monica?'

'V has spent the weekend being...' Monica paused while she filtered out some of the less appropriate verbs from the indecorous list in her head, 'entertained by Clare. And, as I know from experience, such a weekend, pleasurable though it may be, can also take its toll. Rest assured, Veronica will be back to full working order in the fullness of time.' The TV presenter grunted affirmatively, raised herself sufficiently to take a sip of espresso and progressed with caution from Anna's lap to Anna's shoulder.

Once Suzanne and Anthony had been formally introduced, Owen gave an account of his observation of Carson's basement flat. 'Unusually for The Twelve,' said Monica, 'we may need the Met's help, not to deal with Carson, we can do that, but to rescue Devante and Tyrone while we're otherwise occupied.' Suzanne agreed that she would allocate the requisite officers to carry out this duty as necessary.

'If Carson's place in Brooklyn is anything to go by,' added Anthony, 'you'll need a highly trained locksmith to get to where the guys are locked up. Or a Terry.' Monica reminded everyone that Terry would be required to accompany Veronica to the launch party but that, if everything went to plan, he could be made available around the middle of the evening to assist. Suzanne, in turn, suggested that Terry would probably not be required as the Met had specialists who dealt with locks all the time. Terry mumbled something unintelligible before announcing that it sounded like he'd be earning his Twelve annual bonus during this one night alone. 'If you'd like me to pop back and forth to help with the cooking at La Stella, I could probably do that too if you like,' he said, not entirely unseriously.

Monica's plan was developing satisfactorily but was not yet fully complete. The jigsaw still required a handful of additional pieces to fall into place. It was likely that Catherine's invitation to buy Carson dinner at La Stella would be accepted, particularly with the attraction of Clare added to the mix. Thomas's apprenticeship at becoming a waiter was progressing smoothly. The piece of extra equipment necessary for the success of the case would be arriving later that day according to an email from the delivery company. So far, so robust.

Furthermore, the final section of the plan, following Terry and Veronica's valuable Saturday trip to Pasta Tansa, was moulding into reasonable shape. In Monica's mind, the difficulties came with the middle part. The poisoning bit.

She could always keep it simple and use a cyanide compound like sodium or potassium and yet it somehow felt appropriate, especially as they had been using his former home for most of their meetings, to channel the work of Ian Bamford into this particular assassination. Monica had marvelled at his ingenious combinations of poisons during the 1970s, specifically designing unique toxic substances for different circumstances.

A cold breeze suddenly blew in from the direction of the

back door followed by the guttural noises of a man struggling to remove wellington boots. 'Nippy out there,' said a surprise voice arriving from the kitchen. 'Oh sorry, folks. Didn't know you were having a party. Charlie Turkington, gardener.' Charlie was a short, muscular man in his late fifties wearing jeans, a warm sheepskin jacket and black socks adorned with blue flowers. His green eyes darted around the room and settled on Monica, one of four faces he recognised, although two of these, Suzanne's and Veronica's, he only knew from the television. 'Don't mind me, Monica. Just having a slash then it's back to cutting back the wisteria otherwise you'll get no flowers in the spring. Nice to see you.'

The gardener ambled to the downstairs toilet from where urination sounds could be heard followed by the noise of vigorous hand-washing. 'I couldn't help noticing,' said Charlie on his return through the meeting, 'that there's a pot of fresh coffee in the kitchen. Do you think you could spare a couple of mugs please? It's not getting much above freezing today.' Terry shook the gardener's chilly hand and said that he'd make a fresh pot for the Turkingtons as well as wrapping two Florentines in a piece of kitchen roll for them to snack on when they felt the urge. 'You're always so kind to me and my boy,' Charlie added. 'Not like some clients.'

Before he left the house, Monica asked how long Charlie would be working in the garden. He replied that once the wisteria was done, they'd need to make a start on the ornamental grasses halfway down the garden and also trim back the ivy on one of the far walls. They should have completed their tasks by early afternoon.

'Perhaps Thomas and I could have a little tour before we go?' asked the former chemist, thoughtfully. 'I'm not sure I've ever ventured all the way down to the bottom.'

50

The February garden of the former Bamford house was, as with most British gardens in midwinter, a landscape of decay but equally a topography of hope and expectation. To the casual observer, it was a battlefield of horticultural austerity, a frozen terrain of plant carcasses, mud and mulch, the damp and dust of what were once petals and stems, sepals and stamen, the decomposition of leaf blades and midribs.

Yet amidst this carnage, nature was, as always, re-emerging, recognising as it annually does that warmer days were slouching closer and that, in just over a month, the planet's familiar tilt would again shift northwards and herald the perennial explosion of activity. The unseen breakdown of cell walls had created a winter energy store, preparing nourishment for embryonic buds swollen with expectation and already just visible on myriad branches and twigs. Puddles of snowdrops already blanched the cold ground, pale harbingers of days ahead, while daffodils and primroses threatened to imminently cluster-bomb the borders with vibrant yellow.

Springtime was encroaching by the hour, sporadic apricity

gently warming the soil. Life, as always in this season of death, was finding a way.

Having liberated some wellingtons, albeit slightly too large in size, from an outhouse on the sheltered east side of the garden, Monica and Thomas wandered coat-wrapped in the still winter light towards Charlie Turkington who was wielding a pair of secateurs menacingly towards the side shoots of a wisteria not far from the house. In the distance, Monica could make out the taller and more muscular figure of Jonty Turkington aggressively pulling away ivy from a high wall at the bottom of the garden. 'Much to do this time of year?' asked Thomas whose own garden in Notting Hill consisted of a small, paved, west-facing yard containing a handful of easily satisfied shrubs in pots.

Charlie explained that although winter appeared, on the face of it, to be a quiet time in the garden, it was nonetheless vital to prepare for spring and summer if one wanted to enjoy the abundance of colour that those glorious seasons promised. 'Lovely Florentine, by the way. Terry knows his baking, doesn't he?'

Monica's eyes were drawn to the ivy-pocked wall which occupied Jonty. 'Is that wall new?' she asked. 'It doesn't look like it's been here for ages. I always assumed it was the end of the garden but I wonder whether I'm wrong.'

The older gardener's mouth curled into a grin. 'I built that,' he said with obvious pride. 'With me dad. He was Charlie as well. Charlie senior. We had to build a wall in the eighties on account of the dogs.'

Monica had to explain to Thomas about the fake dog charity that The Twelve had needed to rapidly create after Ian Bamford's death to shield the group from inconvenient questions surrounding his will. 'You had to keep the dogs away from what's behind the wall?' she asked. Charlie nodded.

'You know what dogs are like. Scavengers. They'll eat anything. Could have been very messy.'

'What's behind there?'

The gardener placed his secateurs with care on a wooden bench. 'Come and see,' he said. 'But don't touch anything if you've not got gloves on.' Monica was already wearing a pair of black leather gloves; Thomas rooted around in the pockets of his coat and discovered a grey, woollen variation with irregular holes at the end of two fingers, possibly mouse-created.

Around the side of the wall where Jonty had been working was a robust wooden door, padlocked from the outside. Jonty, after formally introducing himself to the visitors, trotted over to a second, larger garden shed to retrieve the key hanging from a hook inside the door. Behind the wall was a much more compact section of the garden but with a small greenhouse in one corner and an even smaller, swampy pond in another. A two-person teak bench which backed onto the wall by the door completed the furnishings. 'Welcome to Mr Bamford's poison garden,' Charlie announced. 'We don't tend to advertise its existence as I'm sure you can understand.'

Despite the time of year, this venomous portion of the estate appeared ironically full of life. Monica noted a medium-sized rhododendron, a dwarf bay tree and a tall plant which she suspected might be monkshood, a suspicion which Charlie was delighted to confirm. 'The boy and I come here from time to time and just sit and wonder at the destructive power of the plant world. And to maintain it of course.' Thomas asked whether he had ever met Ian Bamford and the gardener paused for a moment before responding. 'A couple of times towards the end of his life. He'd retired by then, of course. He was a quiet man but very kind. I was only a teenager when I started here with my dad but he was the sort of man who would always look after us when we were here. He used to bake cakes, a bit like

Terry. I was quite anxious about eating them, to be honest, what with his reputation, but they were delicious and, of course, I understood the work he had been doing as part of The Twelve, even back then.'

The gardener eased himself down onto the bench and patted the wood next to him as a signal for Monica to join him. 'I remember this part of the garden used to be larger but when he died it was decided to minimise it just in case The Twelve needed to sell the property. The dog business meant we closed it off but we've been looking after it with care of course. Lexington used to come and sit here once or twice a year when he was younger. Said it inspired him. He always revelled in the history of The Twelve.'

Monica felt a tear begin to form at the thought of sitting where Lexington had been many times over the years. 'Did you ever see the results of Ian's work?' she asked. Charlie replied that he hadn't. He'd been too young; although in his more fanciful moments, he would imagine being part of The Twelve and helping to assassinate criminals. Monica commented that it wasn't beyond the realms of possibility that the organisation would recruit someone with his green-fingered expertise, causing the gardener to blush. 'There is, perhaps, one way that you might be able to help with our current case,' she added, thoughtfully. 'There's a job coming up and I've been trying to work out how best to complete it. I remember in one of Ian's cases from 1977 he used water hemlock tea combined with cyanide to cause a fairly swift demise. You wouldn't know where we could find water hemlock, would you?'

'It's over there,' said Jonty, peeking round the door with a handful of cut ivy in a gloved hand and pointing towards the pond. 'Nasty little bugger.' Monica smiled as more puzzle pieces slotted into position.

'One more question,' she said tentatively, 'to you both this time. Are you busy at all next Monday evening?'

51

'We'll need La Stella to look busy,' explained Monica in the taxi back to St John's Wood, 'and at the moment we've got Terry and V going to the party down the road, and you're doing table service. Catherine and Clare are sitting with Carson. We can't have Owen, Chris or Anna in the restaurant because Carson knows them already so he would immediately be suspicious. That also cuts out Anthony and Terry for that matter. So in terms of other customers we've just got me, Belinda, Martin, David and Graham to pretend to be casual diners. Even if we change the seating it's going to look distinctly odd and Carson's alarm bells will start ringing so we need to fill out the room a bit with people who know what's going to happen and don't particularly mind being a minor part of it. Another six should probably cover it if we remove some tables and spread the others out a bit. Any ideas?'

Thomas's initial thought was that in Monica's reimagined version of La Stella, he would be looking after seven or eight tables when he was barely confident tending to one. 'You'll be fine,' Monica reassured him. 'We'll get Terry to help prep everything in the kitchen as far as possible before he has to go to the party with V. Simone can help too. It's just the customer numbers really. The Turkingtons can be a table of two. Who else can we rope in?'

Their taxi arrived at Monica's flat moments before the delivery of a small package marked *Fragile* which the former chemist gratefully accepted on the steps of her building. 'More pieces coming together,' she said with a smile, carrying the box up the stairs to her home while Thomas followed with a combination of anticipation and dread for what may be inside.

Once inside and with the coffee machine going about its spluttering business, Monica found a notebook, climbed onto a high stool at her kitchen island and started to create a plan for Monday's dinner, scribbling small squares representing tables containing names to represent each guest. 'I could add Mrs Mendoza,' she said. 'I'm sure she'd love to be a part of an assassination again, albeit a very minor role. If I can just fill one more table.' She stared at her makeshift diagram, willing it to provide inspiration.

Suzanne was out of the question because she would almost certainly be recognised. The possibility of DI Ted Black crossed Monica's mind but then she couldn't be sure that he wouldn't take matters into his own hands and besides, he would probably be required at Carson's basement flat for the rescue element of the evening. 'I'm a bit peckish,' said Thomas as he placed an espresso in front of his lover. 'Nothing too substantial though; I couldn't manage a big lunch. I had three Florentines. I think there's some sourdough left over. Can I tempt you to some toast with that marmalade you like?'

'Toast,' Monica mumbled to herself. 'That's an idea.'

'I'll take that as a yes.' Thomas smiled and began rummaging in Monica's bread bin for treasure.

'No,' blurted Monica, making Thomas jump, 'I mean yes. To toast. Yes, please. With the marmalade. But also Toast. As in

James Wheeler and Bobby of course. James knows what The Twelve does. And I bet he and Bobby would be up for a free dinner even though it's going to have a bit of a grisly ending. I'll email them both.'

She typed a quick and semi-cryptic message to both the accountant and the organiser, suggesting, at least in James's case that the full details of her proposition might be better delivered in a phone call. This duly came a few minutes later just as Monica was reading a text from Veronica apologising for her morning lethargy and saying that she would be having a nap at home for the foreseeable future.

Over in the City, James Wheeler listened with interest to Monica's unusual proposal and, after barely a moment's thought, agreed that he would be happy to make up the numbers at La Stella provided he didn't have to take any active part in proceedings and also that there wouldn't be any blood because he was on the squeamish side. Monica replied that blood would be unlikely but made an adjustment to her table plan just in case; James and Bobby, whose response via text was suitably brief but helpfully enthusiastic, would now be seated closer to the door, meaning that Monica's and Belinda's table would shield James from the worst of any potential unpleasantness. 'There might be coughing and vomiting,' she confided in Thomas, 'but it shouldn't last long. I'll tweak the recipe accordingly.'

The mystery package, meanwhile, remained unopened and seemed to be waiting patiently for its moment. After she was finally satisfied that the thirteen diners were in the right positions for Carson's final meal, Monica extracted some scissors from her top drawer and carefully freed the tightly bubble-wrapped contents.

To Thomas's eyes, it looked like a standard teapot, albeit one in a colour, bright green, which didn't really match anything in

Monica's kitchen, and with a small hole in the handle. He watched as she assembled two clear beakers, a bottle of still water and second bottle of water into which she mixed a teaspoon of coffee, giving it a shake for good measure. 'Cold coffee or water?' she asked before magically pouring first a glass of one and then the other from the same container.

'What strange witchcraft is this?' asked Thomas, wide-eyed.

'It's an assassin's teapot. I had it made specially. Carson is extremely suspicious so we can't easily poison the food. However, if we pour green tea for him and Clare and Catherine from this teapot, taking care to position our fingers over the correct holes so that only Carson gets the poison, then we're in business. Basic chemistry involving surface tension and air pressure. We're going to use an adaptation of a Bamford recipe involving a small amount of cyanide with some water hemlock to ensure it's as quick and relatively painless as possible.'

Thomas gazed at the teapot in awe. 'When you say "we" pour the green tea...'

'I mean you, my darling,' replied Monica calmly. 'Assuming you're okay with that?'

52

Ever since the October meal with Lexington almost a year and a half before, the pivotal late-afternoon lunch at which the older man had, in his inimitable way persuaded him to join The Twelve, Thomas had been anticipating this moment with a combination of both excitement and trepidation. He had experienced numerous doubts about whether he was in fact capable of taking someone's life, even an individual as evil and deranged as Carson Tresk. That first case a year ago, during which Thomas had performed a key role and impressed his new colleagues, had helped to assuage any fears, but then his gnawing sense of a slight lack of purpose during the second case had had the converse effect. Thomas completely trusted that Monica knew what she was doing in allocating him *the* crucial element of this assassination, yet the doubts continued to rumble like distant thunder from an offshore storm.

Having learnt not to bottle things up since joining The Twelve, Thomas was not afraid to confide in both Monica and Chris whose advice was broadly the same. Focus on what needed to be done. Practise with the teapot and at La Stella until he could do what needed to be done blindfolded. Think about the victims of Carson Tresk, not about Tresk himself. Think about Robert and Liam and Kathy and Reece.

Clare had also been instrumental in settling his concerns. Over a lunch of ossobuco, leek and Gorgonzola pappardelle and risotto Milanese at La Stella on the Thursday, the New York Twelve leader shared new information regarding Carson's mother which she had gleaned from her contact at the NYPD. The previous evening at the Junior Christian Walkers meeting, Clare had successfully invited Carson to the fateful dinner or, as she was now calling it, his last supper.

'His mother's grave was desecrated a few days before Carson skipped town,' she revealed. 'We knew Carson had a difficult relationship with both parents, possibly as a result of abuse, we don't know. His mother was a bit of a religious fanatic and his father was very controlling, by all accounts. Either way, the father died a few years back in a traffic accident. It was in the days straight after one of our crazy winter storms that we have on the East Coast and the roads were still icy. The poor guy had a brakes failure and came off the road and went down a ravine. There were suspicions that someone had tampered with the brakes but nothing came to court. Carson inherited a fortune. He constructed a story whereby his father died in a Midwest church hit by a tornado because he felt this narrative worked better when approaching the organisations who would become his unwitting victims. Like Father Matthew.

'The mother, meanwhile, became addicted to painkillers. We suspect that was encouraged by Carson who then supplied the fatal dose and made it look like an accidental OD. About a year after that, he showed up in Brooklyn. You know the rest.'

'You mentioned her grave being desecrated,' nudged Thomas, eager to hear more, however gruesome the details.

'Right. Someone had entered the family vault – these are seriously rich people, y'all understand; they have a family vault

– and removed the mother's head. I mean, it would be just a skull at this point, right? Just a quick tug and it's off. Snap! But I can't think of anyone who would have a reason or indeed a desire to do something like that, apart from Carson. What he did with it, I have no idea. He's a deeply twisted individual. I still can't believe I hugged the muthafucka. I'll raise a glass when we watch him die.'

'After you've felt the usual sadness,' prompted Monica.

'Oh, totally,' replied Clare only half convincingly. 'I'm all about the usual sadness.'

Monica had also arranged for Thomas to attend an emergency session with Mrs Mendoza on the Friday, knowing that her words of wisdom would further settle any nerves. The elderly psychologist was in excellent spirits when Thomas arrived mid-morning just as the aromas of lunch prep at the Indian restaurant next door were filtering with mouth-watering efficiency through the building. The thought of being even slightly involved in an assassination had given Mrs Mendoza an injection of energy and chutzpah.

The nagging thought that Lexington's advice would have been beneficial chipped away methodically at Thomas's confidence. Mrs Mendoza was the next best option and typically her panacea of empathy, stories and fresh biscuits courtesy of a nearby locksmith was exactly what Thomas required. Her knowledge of his emotional and mental response to the previous cases allowed her to predict, with reference to his former career in the sporting world, that his adrenaline levels on Monday would help his mind and body to, as she put it, 'formally open your account. And these feelings of uncertainty are entirely normal for people like us. If we were actively looking forward to a death, then that would naturally be more of a concern.' Thomas left her East London flat with weight lifted, a spring in his step and a renewed confidence in his own ability to complete the task in hand.

Elsewhere, Anthony was bonding with Terry and Simone in the kitchen at La Stella as they familiarised themselves with the complexities of the restaurant's small but dynamic kitchen. 'We go to the market at five in the morning,' said Simone, 'to get the freshest ingredients and we can build the day's menu around what is available and what we have in storage. At the moment, for example, we have some truffles which are delicious and also citrus fruits from southern Italy. We can use some English rhubarb for a dessert, maybe. We got some beautiful leeks coming through so we can make a lovely caramelised leek orecchiette. We'll probably keep it simple with just three or four main courses. You don't have to come to the market though. Is best that you rest. Maybe get here about four in the afternoon, si?'

Thomas reminded the chef during a Saturday visit that the key ingredient would be green tea and Simone confirmed that he had already stocked up with a couple of options, one flavoured subtly with jasmine just in case that variation appealed to the victim.

In St John's Wood, Monica had constructed a temporary laboratory to recreate the Bamford poison recipe using water hemlock tea and a small but effective quantity of sodium cyanide. 'Assuming I have the measurements right,' she explained to Thomas over dinner on Saturday evening, 'there will be a bit of coughing, maybe a bit of vomiting and then that's it. Ten seconds tops. Minimal suffering despite the temptation to be more flexible with that irksome little rule on this occasion. I'll talk to Suzanne about the inevitable toxicology report but if Bamford is correct, the water hemlock masks the cyanide as well as contributing to the rapid death. It's quite brilliant.'

Thomas deflected the conversation onto the topic of Chris's

imminent grandfatherhood. The ex-surgeon was grateful not to be taking a major role in this particular assassination so that he and Anna could spend more time helping his daughter, Freya and her husband to prepare for the new arrival. Apparently Chris's middle child had enjoyed the second and third trimesters after the early nausea had passed, but now just wanted the baby to arrive so that she could get on with the sublime exhaustion of being a new mum.

The fourteen members of the extended Twelve spent Sunday in quiet contemplation wherever they found themselves. Even Clare stayed away from the group chat for much of day, preferring instead to take Anthony outside of the City for a tour of Oxford as he'd never visited. The two of them returned to The Dorchester in the early evening and regaled the group with photos and historical facts via text. *Calm before the storm*, thought Thomas as he attempted to sleep that night, finally dropping into an uneasy and restless doze around one o'clock.

53

The Monday of Pasta Tansa's London launch party was overcast but rainless; the city, and indeed most of the country, was bound within a slow-moving high-pressure system anchored precariously over Scandinavia which meant London felt entombed in permutations of grey with no respite. Suzanne had organised a small team of officers and a police psychologist, led by Ted Black, to access Carson's basement flat once Monica had texted to confirm that the American was no longer a threat. Although Carson would never return to that Hammersmith basement, nobody could be completely sure what they would find behind the flat's front door.

While Terry and Anthony had been in the La Stella restaurant kitchen since 3pm helping Simone to prep for evening service, the rest of The Twelve, plus Clare but minus Martin, had assembled in the restaurant's dining room by five, Owen with his laptop for the purposes of monitoring Carson remotely. Even Chris and Anna joined to give moral support to Thomas, warming his soul, in addition to helping to configure the tables to Monica's specifications.

The group chatted casually as if the forthcoming evening's

activities were the least unusual, the most humdrum. For some of the group, theorised Thomas in a familiar, introspective moment, this would be their tenth or eleventh assassination so maybe it would eventually feel "normal" for him too. 'It never feels normal,' reassured Chris. 'Nor should it. The taking of a life should never be mundane. It's a moment of reverence. Even those of us with a few of these under our belts feel it deeply.' The former surgeon pulled Thomas into a close embrace. 'You'll be great, old friend. I have complete faith.'

Charlie and Jonty Turkington poked their heads round the door just before six, as requested, followed by Martin who had collected a mildly euphoric Mrs Mendoza, and finally Bobby City and James Wheeler who had dyed his hair a more sedate brown over the weekend. 'I didn't want to stand out,' he explained. 'For a change.'

Monica outlined where everyone would be sitting, positioning each diner meticulously like aircraft in a holding pattern, and briefly ran through the strategy for the evening. 'The actual assassination is likely to happen towards the end of the meal,' she explained, 'as it might look suspicious if Thomas offered the green tea at the beginning. Of course, if Carson specifically asks for a green tea earlier then so be it.'

Simone had created an A-board sign reading *Closed for a Private Party* which Owen would place outside and then guard once Carson was securely in the restaurant. The former surveillance expert had recently acquired a new app from a friend within the security service which allowed him to temporarily jam the local CCTV from his phone.

Monica's seating plan had placed Carson, Catherine and Clare at a corner table nearest the kitchen and underneath a signed black-and-white photograph of the actor Robert Powell whom Simone recalled as a regular diner in the late seventies and early eighties. She instructed the two women to sit looking doorwards so that Carson would be facing the wall and therefore couldn't easily observe what was happening behind him.

David and Graham's table would be the closest to them, both men armed with syringes full of plan B morphine in case these were required. Monica and Belinda's table would be next closest with the three tables containing the Turkingtons, Martin and Mrs Mendoza, and Bobby and James furthest from the action and nearest the window. 'At this point,' Monica announced, 'the best thing you can all do is to study the menu and perhaps order some starters. And if anyone would like a drink, Thomas will take your orders. It needs to look like just a normal Monday evening in the restaurant.'

Just before seven, Owen announced that Carson had left his house and would probably be with them by 7.30pm as expected. Anna and Chris retired to a quiet, nearby bar to wait in case they were needed. Terry changed into clean clothes after his afternoon shift in the kitchen and he and Veronica ambled the short distance to the Pasta Tansa launch party which was slowly filling up. 'Stay in touch,' said Monica, giving them both a hug.

The occupants of the five tables away from the corner began to order starters and drinks and Thomas realised that Monica had made her earlier intervention so that he could spend the time before Carson's arrival relaxing into the roles of both waiter and assassin for the evening. The Turkingtons ordered a bottle of chianti, some bruschetta and some bagna càuda with winter vegetables which Simone had bought from the market that morning. Mrs Mendoza plumped for scallops with garlic and parsley while Martin decided on tomato and chilli soup. Thomas took each order with composed professionalism, trying to ignore admiring glances from Monica along with expectant looks towards the door from Clare and Catherine.

'He's here,' hissed Clare loudly as Carson's curious face appeared in the window of the door. He hesitated before entering, peering as if surveying the place for traps, but then spotted Catherine's friendly wave from the furthest corner of the restaurant. Thomas headed over to the door just as Carson gently pushed it open.

'Good evening, sir,' he began, his voice as strong and authoritative as he felt was necessary for the evening's performance. 'Welcome to La Stella. May I take your coat?' The American stalled momentarily before saying that he would hang it on the back of his chair if that was agreeable.

'I'm with the ladies over there.' He gestured towards the far table.

'Very good,' said Thomas and led him over to Clare and Catherine who created a three-way hug, Clare fighting the sudden and violent urge to abandon the agreed plan and instead hurl Carson through the nearest window with a fork in his throat.

'This is so nice,' the new arrival said, gazing around at the array of photographs which decorated the dining room. 'I guess it's been here a while judging by all the celebrity endorsements.'

Catherine briefly ran through the history of La Stella as far as she knew it, while Thomas shuttled back and forth from the kitchen to satisfy orders from James and Bobby's and David and Graham's tables before returning to their corner.

'Have you had a chance to look at the menu yet?' he asked, now very much in the hospitality zone. 'Perhaps some more water for the table and maybe some focaccia and some Carta di Musica while you decide? Maybe I can also tempt you to a cocktail or some wine?'

'Water and bread would be awesome, thank you,' replied Carson. 'What a great little place. I don't drink alcohol, as you know,' he turned his attention towards his dining guests, 'but please don't let that stop you.'

Clare smiled. 'You're so kind, Elijah,' she said. 'Maybe a couple of glasses of the 2012 Montepulciano if that's okay. To go with the bread.'

'The body and blood of our Lord,' murmured Carson with an angelic grin. 'If Jesus were Italian.'

54

Once inside Pasta Tansa, and after a moment of confusion with one of Pandora's PR juniors who had Veronica on the guest list as 'Virginia Madison plus one', the TV presenter and the locksmith stepped into a vortex of chatter with Jeremy Tansa holding court at its gravitational centre. The famous chef was in the middle of a cluster of minor celebrities while a London TV crew filmed from a discreet distance.

Veronica noted that a couple of well-known newspaper showbiz reporters were loitering within earshot, desperate to snag a morsel of juicy gossip. Meanwhile, another group of eight younger people, whom Terry surmised were food influencers, were taking photographs of each other posing theatrically with various canapés in front of the graffiti wall.

In the kitchen, Jason could just about be seen marshalling a small army of chefs who were preparing the easy-to-eat morsels, and front-of-house staff whose job was to deliver them promptly to the Tansa guests. *We're in*, Veronica texted to the group, although all but four phones were off to avoid suspicion in La Stella. Two doors away, only Monica's vibrated quietly within the dining room.

'Do you know anyone?' Veronica asked Terry as she scanned the room for friendly faces.

Terry stared at her in bemusement. 'I'm a fame-averse locksmith from Whitechapel,' he said, kindly. 'What are the chances of my knowing anyone? Apart from you.' A smiling waitress arrived with glasses of Prosecco although the fame-averse locksmith from Whitechapel opted for orange juice, suspecting that the evening ahead might require sobriety on his part.

A tabloid showbiz reporter, clearly bored of listening to Jeremy, sidled over and introduced herself to Veronica before asking whether she and Terry were dating, a question which provoked a fit of locksmith giggles. 'Terry is a dear friend,' replied Veronica, 'but as he possesses a penis, he is of no interest to me either sexually or romantically. You can quote me.'

'I very much doubt the news editor will be able to splash on that, Veronica,' said the reporter, stifling a giggle herself, 'but thank you anyway. Always good to see you. We don't see enough of you these days. It's almost like you've got something secret going on. Can I get a photo for the desk, please? They might not use it but you never know.'

'I'm a sixty-year-old former TV presenter, mostly daytime. What secret things could I possibly be up to at my age?' Veronica posed for both a solo shot and a selfie with the reporter who thanked her before oozing back into the mêlée surrounding Jeremy Tansa.

'Are we dating?' Veronica muttered under her breath. 'Honestly. Anything passes for news these days.'

In La Stella, Thomas's first official service was going as well as could be expected with no mishaps, all tables supplied with the right dishes at the right time, and conversations flowing. Carson had been drinking water but as the group was just finishing their main courses, veal Milanese for Clare, spaghetti with white truffles for Catherine and risotto with porcini mushrooms for Carson, Thomas felt his heart rate increase knowing that the climax of the evening was approaching. Monica, meanwhile, had observed that Carson had insisted that his dining companions try his risotto before him, suggesting a paranoid fear or suspicion of poisoning.

'Is everyone finished here?' asked Thomas as he approached the corner table. Catherine smiled and said that everything had been delicious. 'Can I tempt you with the dessert menu?'

Clare leant forwards and placed her elbows on the table. 'Not for me, thank you, but do you have any green tea at all?' Thomas replied that they had plain and jasmine. 'Just a plain please.'

'May I have one too, please?' asked Catherine. 'It'll help with the digestion.' There was a pause as everyone waited for Carson who seemed to be in a world of his own.

'Sorry,' he said, 'I was miles away. We've been talking about the scriptures and that always puts me in a thoughtful state of mind. Are you both having green tea? That would be great, thank you.'

A fleeting glance between Thomas, Clare and Catherine registered overwhelming relief.

'I'll make a pot,' said Thomas before retreating with the dirty plates and cutlery. He returned a few moments later with cups and saucers which he placed carefully in front of the three diners. Returning to the kitchen, he and Anthony filled the two chambers of the assassin's teapot with, respectively, pure green tea and Monica's adapted recipe with cyanide and water hemlock. 'I'll serve the women first,' said Thomas, 'so thumb over the hole for Clare and Catherine and then move the thumb for Carson.'

'You got this, man,' growled Anthony, gripping him firmly by the shoulder. 'You got this.'

Thomas returned to the table and poured first for Clare, then for Catherine and finally for Carson. 'Green tea,' he said without a hint that his heart was racing. 'It shouldn't be too hot but maybe just give it a minute.'

Clare thanked him and picked up her cup, raising it to her lips and blowing gently before taking a sip as Thomas moved back towards the kitchen, aware that the volume of conversation had dipped noticeably and that every eye in the room was now on him. He had just passed David's table when he heard a sound that made him freeze.

Clare was coughing.

55

After a quick pat on the back from Catherine, Clare returned to normality. 'Went down the wrong way,' she explained nonchalantly to David and Graham who were staring at her from the neighbouring table with extreme concern. 'Sorry to alarm y'all. It's nice though. I recommend the green tea.' Thomas meanwhile, just beginning to thaw, staggered back into the kitchen to regain some composure.

'Fuck,' he said, elongating the vowel as Anthony hastily found him a chair, 'I thought I'd killed Clare.' Anthony remarked that in his experience it would take more than that to bring about the demise of The Twelve's New York leader. She was constructed of sterner stuff than most humans. In the dining room, Monica was observing Carson's untouched cup of tea, silently willing him to drink. Carson, meanwhile, was deep in a conversation about good versus evil, a topic about which Clare apparently knew chapter and verse.

'On the face of it, Elijah,' she was saying, somehow maintaining a sense of restraint, 'you're a good soul, selflessly helping other people without seeking any sort of reward, just as it says in Matthew chapter six.'

'I'm simply doing my best to carry out the work of the Lord Jesus,' Carson replied, a faint element of sarcasm in his tone.

'But what happens when Elijah gets angry? I can't imagine there's nothing that upsets you. Maybe the inequalities in society or maybe when you see sinners walking the streets with impunity?' Carson's hand hovered over the rim of his cup, tempted briefly to indulge in a mouthful before reconsidering. Instead, he began stroking his chin. Catherine, who had been holding her breath for a moment, exhaled as slowly and inconspicuously as possible.

Carson pondered her question for a few seconds. 'I don't honestly know,' he began. 'I guess I trust in the good Lord to exact his own retribution when the time comes. As Paul said in his letter to the Romans, "The righteous shall live by faith for the wrath of God is revealed from heaven against all ungodliness and unrighteousness of men who, by their unrighteousness suppress the truth".'

The American's hand returned to the cup and this time, considering the temperature to have dropped sufficiently, he lifted the tea to his mouth and took first a sip followed by a bigger mouthful. The low-level chatter which had permeated the dining room suddenly ceased completely as if someone had flicked a switch. Almost immediately Carson began to cough uncontrollably and then retch.

Clare and Catherine stared at him impassively as he mouthed the word 'Poison' while his gaze switched wildly between his own cup and those of his companions.

'You know,' said Clare calmly, as she watched the young man struggle desperately for breath, 'Romans ain't my favourite. Paul was being a bitch the day he wrote that shit. I prefer his second letter to those misbehaving Corinthians. I'm sure you remember it, Carson. Chapter eleven, verse fourteen. "Forever

Satan disguises himself as an angel of light". Enjoy hell, muthafucka.'

Carson began shaking violently until he finally slumped forwards onto the table, scattering cups and cutlery in the process. The shaking continued for a few seconds before all movement stopped. Catherine noticed a small patch of vomit emitting from Carson's mouth onto the tablecloth, his eyes remaining wide open in surprise and shock.

'Is he dead?' asked Monica soberly. Clare checked for a pulse and confirmed that he was. Thomas, Anthony and Simone, who had emerged from the kitchen, breathed a simultaneous sigh of relief. 'Is everybody else okay?' asked Monica, looking specifically at the tables nearest the door for whom this entire scenario was new and highly unusual. James Wheeler and Bobby City were both understandably in tears, although James managed to whisper that they were fine, perhaps a little in shock but equally a little in awe. 'It's normal to feel sadness,' assured Monica. 'It won't last. Nobody touch him or anything that's been on this table without gloves, please. At least until we've disinfected everything.'

Charlie Turkington stood up, walked over to Monica and shook her hand. 'I do feel sad,' he said quietly, 'but also I thought that was brilliant. Mr Bamford would have been so proud.' Monica pulled the gardener into a hug before noticing Thomas in her line of vision. He was standing alone in the kitchen doorway and looked simultaneously smaller in stature yet at the same time somehow more substantial. She extracted herself from the hug and navigated the short distance to La Stella's kitchen.

'It *was* brilliant,' she said, giving Thomas the tightest embrace. '*You* were brilliant. How do you feel?' She gazed deep into his eyes and stroked his face with both hands, knowing from experience that he would slowly be coming to terms with what had just happened. With what he had done.

'It's a strange feeling, isn't it?' he whispered, melting into Monica. In Thomas's mind, this unusual sensation was mostly a feeling of quiet satisfaction but with a hefty dollop of sorrow with an added element of euphoria just around the edges. 'I'm not sure I've ever felt quite this way before,' he muttered. 'It's so weird. Not entirely pleasant but then not unpleasant either.'

Recognising his emotional state, Monica guided the makeshift waiter over to the spare table next to the kitchen for a sit down, the short journey punctuated with congratulatory kisses and kind words from other diners. As Thomas rested his head on her left shoulder, Monica texted Suzanne the news that Carson was dead. The commissioner's return text of a thumbs up emoji was followed five minutes later with a slightly embarrassed emoji and the polite ask, *I wonder whether it would be possible to borrow Terry just briefly. I'm sending an unmarked car for him.*

The Twelve's leader then texted Veronica and Terry to let them know that the first part of the evening's work was complete but that the ex-TV presenter would need to fly solo for about forty minutes because Terry's expertise was required in Hammersmith. Veronica responded with a kiss; Terry responded with a bag full of dollars emoji.

Meanwhile, Anthony, Graham and David donned Marigolds and carefully moved Carson's body out of the dining room and propped him up by the back door in readiness for the next stage of the operation. The three men then retrieved the broken crockery from the floor around the corner table and fully disinfected the area, placing all of the rubbish into a doubled bin bag for Martin to dispose of safely.

'Good teamwork, girlfriends,' said Clare with a smile as she embraced Belinda and Catherine. 'I've been waiting for that

SECRETS OF THE DEADLY DOZEN

moment for some time. Didn't expect it to happen here in London but hey.'

At that moment, Mrs Mendoza stood up delicately, looked towards the still seated Thomas and began to clap. Martin followed her lead and soon everyone in the room including Terry and Owen, who had both recently stepped inside, was applauding. Thomas lifted his head from Monica's shoulder. Suddenly there were tears welling up in his eyes. He couldn't tell whether they were tears of relief or of satisfaction or something else entirely. In truth, the nature of the tears was irrelevant. They felt cleansing. That was the important thing.

When the noise had abated and Thomas had regained some composure thanks to another cuddle from Monica, the former sports coach knew that he should say something profound but his mind couldn't conceive what that might be. Instead, he uttered the first words that came to mind.

'Can I interest anyone in a coffee?'

56

The unmarked police car with a blue light collected Terry a couple of minutes later and returned him half an hour after that. 'Slightly tricky Abus lock but nothing outrageous,' he explained over a delayed espresso. Monica asked about the welfare of Devante and Tyrone and the locksmith confirmed that both were alive if underweight and chained to a wall. 'I didn't stay long because I needed to get back but they're in good hands now. Suzanne's organised some paramedics. The two of them look naturally shocked because of what's happened to them but hopefully they'll make a full recovery. Oh, and there's a manky old skull with long hair in the room where they've been imprisoned. Anyway,' he said, opening the door to La Stella and stepping back out into the night, 'I'd better return to Veronica and assess the chaos she may have created in my absence. See you in a bit.'

'Carson's mother, in all probability,' said Clare. 'He was a sick fuck.'

James Wheeler and Bobby City had already left La Stella, their roles in the evening complete. Mrs Mendoza was happy to wait for Martin to take her home whenever it was convenient, her ordeal made more bearable by the arrival of some freshly-made tiramisu from Simone's fridge which she was sharing with the Turkingtons while discussing late-flowering perennials. She had already spent a few moments alone with Thomas, checking on his immediate welfare in the aftermath and, in addition, had made her way to Monica for a hug and a smile. 'Thank you, Monica. That felt just like old times.'

'Waiting game now,' said The Twelve's leader, to herself more than anyone.

By the time Terry returned to Pasta Tansa having had to briefly re-navigate the guest-list shenanigans, Veronica was deep in a discussion about antiques with a woman from Jeremy Tansa's marketing team who introduced herself to the locksmith as Margot Hansen and who turned out to be both a minor expert in eighteenth-century art as well as being hilariously indiscreet about her celebrity employer. 'Apparently,' said Veronica as she watched Margot disappear into the crowd, 'Jeremy has a tendency towards paying for sex, especially when he goes overseas on business trips. He's always asking their finance department for thousands of notes' worth of cash in the relevant currencies before he travels and he never provides receipts. Obviously. Oh, and also, the bit where he does his speech is roughly five minutes away. Margot says it'll take about ten minutes tonight as he wants to make an impression for the media who are here. I'll message Monica to let her know.'

Terry liberated a passing orange juice from a tray. 'Oh, I have an inkling that he'll make an impression all right.'

Two doors away, Monica received Veronica's text and imparted the information to the assembled group that stage two of their plan was imminent. David, Martin and Anthony positioned themselves next to the body of Carson Tresk and awaited the signal to move. Jonty and Charlie Turkington offered their assistance but Monica advised that as they weren't members of The Twelve, they should probably avoid direct involvement and focus instead on keeping Mrs Mendoza entertained, a task for which they appeared highly qualified.

Jeremy Tansa was tapping a spoon on a wine glass first subtly and then more angrily as he attempted to quiet the chatter in his newest dining room. 'If I could...' he shouted. 'Could I please have your...' If anything, the volume increased until Jason took matters into his own hands and screamed, 'QUIET!' at the top of his voice from the front of the kitchen where his exhausted staff were already congregating.

'Thank you, Jason,' muttered Jeremy as all faces, phones and a TV camera shifted in his direction. 'I just wanted to say a few words on behalf of everyone at Jeremy Tansa Limited on the occasion of the first London opening of my own Pasta Tansa.' Veronica texted the group to say that the second key moment of the evening had arrived while Terry slipped unnoticed down the corridor, past the trendy unisex toilets and into the kitchen via its internal rear door, extracting a pair of Marigolds from his pocket as he did so and pulling them on. He positioned himself by the back entrance of the kitchen and waited for a knock which came just under a minute later.

'Pasta Tansa is a team effort,' continued the oblivious Jeremy, illuminated by both expensive yet subtle restaurant lighting as well as dozens of iPhone and Android beams, 'and if you'll indulge me for just a few moments, I wanted to single out some of the wonderful people behind the scenes without which this glorious place could never have happened. First of all...'

Stooping to avoid being detected, Terry eased open the door and helped his three colleagues drag Carson inside. 'Me and David can probably take it from here,' he said as Anthony and Graham vanished back into the darkness. The plumber and the locksmith gently bore the dead American out of the kitchen and into Pasta Tansa's toilet where Veronica was already standing guard.

'Next, I wanted to pay tribute to my incredible PR department, led by the majestic Pandora who has been by my side through thick and thin for almost two years now, which makes her one of the most long-suffering of the team.' Pandora blushed dutifully as a cohort of phones twisted in her direction soundtracked by a ripple of polite laughter.

Terry and David positioned Carson on one of the toilet seats and rested his head against the side of the cubicle. 'Time to get out of here,' said David and the two of them exited the bathroom, David slipping out of the restaurant the way he had entered while Terry, having removed his yellow rubber gloves, and Veronica filtered back into Jeremy Tansa's waning audience, many of whom were now yawning.

'So finally, I just want to raise a glass and ask for a big round of applause to the wonderful team I've put together here at the new Pasta Tansa.' He waved an arm at the kitchen staff who all grinned obediently. 'That's everyone from Jason, my executive head chef, all the way to the KPs, Mo and GG.'

'JJ,' shouted Jason.

'Right,' said Jeremy dismissively, 'JJ. Whatever.' He raised a glass and puffed out his chest as a listless wave of clapping lapped lethargically around the room despite Pandora's best efforts to whip up more enthusiasm. The phone lights were extinguished and around twenty guests headed gratefully for the exit. Veronica indicated to Terry that a couple of the influencers were meandering tipsily towards the bathroom.

'Any second now,' whispered Terry.

57

The sound of screaming had the immediate effect of halting the stampede for the door. If the evening's events at La Stella had passed with calm efficiency, in contrast the next few minutes at Pasta Tansa descended rapidly into disordered havoc.

The corridor leading to the toilets almost instantly transformed into a place of mayhem with news reporters and the TV crew jostling with influencers to record what was happening while various members of the Tansa PR team along with senior members of staff from other Tansa departments attempted futilely to maintain a semblance of order.

The rumour that there was a dead body spread exponentially through the restaurant and became even more concentrated when a couple of influencers began showing mobile phone photos of Carson's lifeless body to whomever was nearby. Within seconds another rumour began to circulate that the victim had been poisoned. 'Did you see the froth coming from his mouth?' 'Had he tried to vomit before he died?' 'Oh God, was it those oyster things that were going round? I had three of them. I need to get to A&E immediately!'

Jeremy Tansa was standing becalmed and bewildered in the centre of this rapidly deepening hurricane, uncertain of his role. A man was dead. In his restaurant. On launch night. The sheer injustice of it.

A couple of critics who had previously been less than generous in their assessment of his food, sauntered up to him, patted him on the back in faux consolation and then left as silently as they felt appropriate under the circumstances, like mourners at the funeral of an unloved acquaintance. The tabloid reporters, having first taken photos on their phones of the grisly bathroom scene, made a beeline for Jeremy to get a comment. 'We might just be able to splash on this for the late edition if we can get a good line,' muttered one. Pandora, her eyes criss-crossing the floor like a demented searchlight, managed to hurtle across the restaurant to head them off before they reached the celebrity chef.

'We'll put out a statement as soon as possible,' she squealed, arms outstretched as a makeshift human barrier between the media and her employer. 'Jeremy will be saying nothing more tonight.' The journalists protested that this was a great story and 'good publicity for the restaurant in the long run.' Pandora countered that 'A man has *died*,' which only resulted in the tabloid duo thanking her for giving an official spokesperson's quote despite her desperate wail that it was 'off the record'.

In the kitchen, Jason was attempting to control his team, many of whom were either in tears, panicking or, in three cases, chain-smoking outside the back door from where David had invisibly exited moments earlier. After ten minutes, three police cars and an ambulance arrived, Monica having tipped off Suzanne.

After a struggle to reach the toilet area, two paramedics, aware of the poison risk, set to work on Carson's body while two police officers cordoned off first the toilet area and then the entire restaurant. 'Where am I supposed to have a piss now?' asked one of the influencers. 'Luckily I'm not bursting but I do need to check my hair,' to which a sympathetic policewoman responded that she would need to survive without a grooming assessment until she had made a statement and left her contact information. 'All my information is in the link in my profile,' she hissed, waving her phone in the officer's face. 'I've got nearly forty thousand followers for fuck's sake.'

The policewoman patiently responded that she could have as many followers as she liked but that didn't alter the fact that she needed to give a statement and still wasn't allowed in the toilet.

Veronica and Terry had, by this time, already slipped quietly from Pasta Tansa and strolled the short distance to La Stella where Owen, Chris and Anna had already gathered. 'It's carnage back there,' said Veronica, giving Thomas a congratulatory hug. 'Everyone okay back here?'

Monica confirmed that once again, albeit 'this time with a bit of assistance from our trans-Atlantic friends,' The Twelve had completed a successful assassination. 'I feel we shouldn't celebrate Carson's death,' Monica continued, despite a glance from Clare which implied that she didn't entirely agree, 'but I *can* justify celebrating tonight's international collaboration between Britain, the USA and, of course, Italy.' She nodded towards Simone who saluted gratefully. 'So if we have enough glasses for seventeen and a few bottles of Prosecco, I don't see why we shouldn't enjoy some fizz.'

The group were just enjoying their second glasses when Martin, who wasn't drinking but who happened to be closest to the front of the restaurant, heard some knocking and tentatively the door opened. Veronica recognised the influencer from Pasta Tansa. 'I don't suppose I could borrow your toilet to check my hair, could I?' she asked. 'I've got forty thousand followers and I'll give you a mention in my stories.'

The Seventeen, including Mrs Mendoza and the Turkingtons all turned towards the door with the same thought.

'No!' they said in unison.

58

Two of the following day's newspapers had managed to squeeze in the story of the dead body found at Jeremy Tansa's new London restaurant and the other news outlets carried it prominently in their online editions. Wild speculation surrounded the cause of the death, fuelled in part by the vacuum created by Tansa HQ's incomprehensible insistence on a 'no comment' policy. The local television news also covered it and by mid-afternoon social media was awash with conspiracy theories about Russian agents, MI5 and even other celebrity chefs who were known to be envious of Jeremy Tansa's success. The rumour mill whirled at such a furious pace that one rival was forced to issue a formal statement denying any knowledge and offering the alibi that he was in Germany on a press trip that week and couldn't have been directly involved. All this without anyone even knowing the identity of the victim.

That identification, when it came from the police midweek, deflected attention from Father Matthew's church by using the name Carson Tresk and ignoring his assumed name of Elijah Timothy. The photograph issued to the media, an old one acquired by Clare and passed on to Suzanne, further separated

Carson from Elijah so much so that, according to Father Matthew later in the week, neither the young people at JCW nor the older parishioners, who might have bumped into him on occasion, had made the connection.

After Carson's body had been taken away, Suzanne ensured that the toxicology report made no mention of the small quantity of cyanide found in his bloodstream and instead focused on the *natural substance, probably vegetable in origin* which had caused the sudden death. With help from Clare and from the American ambassador in London whom Monica had met at Lexington's New Year party fourteen months earlier, Carson's body was repatriated and placed without ceremony in his family crypt along with his mother's well-travelled skull. 'He'd hate that,' mused Clare, 'which is why I love it.'

Pasta Tansa remained closed 'as a mark of respect' for two weeks after the ill-fated launch party. During this time, the senior management at Tansa Holdings Limited held numerous meetings with lawyers and specialist crisis PR consultants before finally deciding that that particular branch of the chain should be closed permanently and that a new London flagship restaurant, probably in a more central location, would be announced within weeks. The landlord of the Moscow Road branch was eventually compensated by Tansa Holdings Limited to the tune of £1.5m and, during the summer, the property was leased to an upmarket fashion brand which delighted Simone as it meant more footfall to La Stella.

Devante and Tyrone spent several weeks in hospital before being assigned dedicated mental health care to help them through the trauma of what had happened in the Hammersmith basement. The Twelve offered one of their properties, a Clapham house which hadn't been used for a meeting for over three years, as a place to live rent-free. By July, they were housemates along with a couple of nurses from St George's hospital who had cared for them, and by September both young men had found jobs in local supermarkets as their recovery continued.

Anthony stayed in London for a few days after the assassination and managed to squeeze in a couple more West End shows with Martin and Joanne. He also allowed Martin to take him in the taxi on a tour of London tourist spots. Clare departed at the end of February but not before another few nights with Veronica which left the former TV presenter exhausted but invigorated. 'This has given me the impetus to maybe jump into the dating pool again,' she stated excitedly, 'daunting though it may be at my age.'

Clare had responded that New York was only eight hours away if she ever needed a boost. 'And it's not like we're short of time or money, right?'

The day after Carson's death, Catherine visited the Church of the Immaculate Virgin and found Matthew praying quietly in a front pew. She walked up the aisle, bent her knee before the crucifix and eased slowly into the space beside him. The priest lowered his eyes from the cross and turned to face the former journalist. 'It was Elijah,' she said softly. Father Matthew nodded in solemn comprehension. 'Although his real name wasn't Elijah. His real name was Carson Tresk and he hated religion. He was as far away from a man of faith as you could imagine. He used you and your church and your belief to commit the most heinous crimes. I'm so sorry.'

Father Matthew let his head droop and closed his eyes as Catherine placed a comforting arm around his shoulder. 'I knew you'd work it out,' the priest whispered. 'That's why I asked you.'

If Catherine was shocked, she made a decent attempt at masking it. 'You knew,' she said. 'Why didn't you report him to the police? You could have saved Robert. And Reece.'

Outside, a light breeze whistling through the bare branches of the trees and gravestones filled the silence as Matthew began to rock backwards and forwards in hushed sobs.

'What is revealed in the confessional box is an inviolable secret,' he muttered. 'I could not tell anyone while he was alive, however much I wanted to. The Twelve was my last hope.'

'You could have fired him,' said Catherine, slightly raising her voice so that it echoed around the nave.

Matthew slumped back in the pew. 'I was afraid of what he might do,' he whimpered. 'In the confessional, he would often talk about setting fire to the vestry while I was inside or mass poisoning the young people at his club. I didn't know what he was capable of. May God forgive me.' He began crying again, this time louder and more pitifully, unknowing at that moment whether or not he would ever feel true redemption.

59

It was towards the end of July, just after Monica's seventy-first birthday, that she and Thomas finally found a moment to get married.

Their original intention to have a small ceremony vanished in a puff of smoke when the two of them began, early one bright Sunday morning in late March, to embark on a list of potential guests. Numbers rapidly soared past fifty and then, a couple of days later, a casual mention to Bobby City opened the door to another thirty guests at which point Monica decided to research venues.

After a couple of hours of scrolling through a panoply of websites, her eye was drawn to an old Hampstead pub recently renamed The Pipette and Medal. 'It's like destiny,' she excitedly told Thomas as she dragged him to her laptop to study the layout and the wedding menu. 'I was a chemist and you helped people win medals. This is perfect.'

The two of them visited the pub for a reconnaissance lunch on the following Thursday and immediately fell in love with its low beams and cosy atmosphere, booking a date on the spot.

Terry would be able to officiate and four months would be plenty of time for overseas guests like Clare and Anthony to book flights and accommodation. Monica also made the decision, agreed by the rest of The Twelve, to forgo any new cases until after Lexington's memorial in September which was shaping up to be something of an epic event requiring all of Monica's and Bobby's organisational know-how for the remainder of the summer. After that, Monica and Thomas would finally take their long-awaited trip to Capri as a belated honeymoon.

This decision to ease back from cases also delighted Chris as it allowed him to spend more time with his granddaughter, Maya Alison, who was born around dawn on March 18th. He and Anna spent most weekends and occasional Wednesdays at Freya's house just lifting some of the pressure of caring for a newborn and allowing the new mother and her husband to get some rest. Anna, despite having no children of her own, took to childcare like a natural.

Veronica, meanwhile, used the downtime to visit New York for a week in May. On her return, the former TV presenter intimated to Monica that she was considering moving to the USA permanently and would make a final decision by the end of the summer. 'Naturally, even if I did decide to go, I wouldn't actually leave until you'd found a replacement for me,' she said. Monica was thankful for her consideration and focused Belinda's and Catherine's monitoring on the two candidates who would be most appropriate for any vacancy; a bookshop owner and a home economist both approaching retirement.

On the day of the wedding, Thomas woke early in best man Chris's East London house and indulged in a healthy breakfast of yoghurt with summer fruits and seeds because, in the words of the surgeon, 'You don't want anything heavy sitting in your stomach by the time your wedding night comes round.' He texted Monica who called him in response to tell him that she loved him more than anything in the world and that she would see him in a matter of hours. She was just making a final alteration to the wording of the marriage service, a change with which Thomas fully agreed.

Separately, both of them had in quiet moments been thinking of Thomas's first wife, Alice, of Monica's second husband, Patrick, and of Lexington, naturally, who would have adored everything about this day.

Just before eleven, the two of them were finally standing together in front of Terry in readiness for the ceremony. Thomas had bought a new designer suit for the occasion and Monica was wearing a red cotton dress with a gold saree sash for prosperity and good fortune.

Terry, revelling in his role as registrar, performed the ceremony with style and humour, relaxing everyone with his off-the-cuff interjections.

Following the exchange of rings, Monica and Thomas looked round at the smiling faces who represented their lives together. Bobby and James; the Turkingtons along with their respective partners; Mehmet and Doreen; Nikola and Mirela along with Dimo and his brother Ivo and their new partners; Simone and his wife, Angela; Suzanne and her husband; Mrs Mendoza, resplendent in flowing aquamarine; Clare and Anthony; Thomas's son, Simon and his fiancé, Akiko; his daughter, Emily with her new partner, Harry along the twins, Flora and Lucy; Belinda; Veronica; Catherine; David; Graham; Owen; Martin; Anna; Chris.

Despite their advanced years, this was their world. This was their time. The couple turned to each other and beamed, knowing that everything important to them existed in that room at that moment.

'I now pronounce you, woman and husband,' said Terry, unable to suppress an impish grin himself. 'You may kiss the groom.'

THE END

ALSO BY PETER BERRY

Lunch with the Deadly Dozen

Revenge of the Deadly Dozen

ACKNOWLEDGEMENTS

First thanks on this one need to go to the real Matthew Christmas and Ian Bamford for allowing their names to be recycled for characters (in truth, they both asked/pleaded to be characters but hey). They are friends of mine, Matthew for over forty years and Ian for over ten. Hopefully they still will be after reading *Secrets...* Also, important thanks to Mary R whom I don't know but who is always one of the first people to review my scribbles on Amazon and who is always so kind and generous with her words.

A far cleverer person than I (Ernest Hemingway) wrote: *It's your object to convey everything to the reader so that he (she) remembers it not as a story he (she) had read but something that happened to himself (herself). That's the true test of writing.* Hopefully some of you have related to The Twelve, maybe with a view to joining yourselves one day. When there's a vacancy. And when you're old enough.

Next, thanks must go to all the lovely people who have posted kind reviews on social media, told their book clubs, bought a copy for a friend, etc. They include (and I'm sorry if I forgot anyone or if you're mentioned twice like last time!): Sophie Berrill, Victoria Bucknell, Meaghan Walsh, Emma Atton, Adrian Hobart & Rebecca Collins for kindly inviting me on their excellent Hobcast, Mark Carlyon, Sue Warwick, Kathleen Hinde, Wyndham James for kindly inviting me on HIS excellent Hands Up If You're Human podcast', Phillip Loades, Ellen Roseblade, Colin Moorc, Alec Pollendine, Emma

Adam, Flossie Shaw, Julia Watson, James Nelson, Arwa Haider, Anita & Paul (I don't know your surnames but you're lovely), Peter Halliday, Oliver Lange, Simon Ponsford, Fiona Dyson, Jane Turton, Jo Emson, Mark Potter, Patrick and June Carpmael, Lisa Marks, Laura Connelly, Lisa Agasee, Chantelle Sturt, Donna Sturt, Katie Greenop, Tara Donovan, Sonia Ferreira, Clare Parker, Holly Griffin, Caroline Reid, Kate Bush, Justin Somper, Rhianna Cairns, Alex Hollywood, John Berry, Sheralyn Bamford, Molly Bamford, Jonathan and Catherine Bailey, Cara Fryett, Alyson Read, Beth Young, Jill Todd, Snibs and Dave Brabham, Molly Brabham, Dave and Carol Crowder, Davinia Woodhouse, Eve Cottrell, Andy and Catherine Sutcliffe, Ben and Rachael Edwards, Kelly Whyte, Clair Atkins, Kelly Marsh, Laura Benjamin, Jade Nomura, Marian Keyes, Trina Williams, Helen Haythornthwaite, Simon and Mary Ann Collins, Val Collins, Owen Bywater, Chris Rowland, Chloe Jackson, Sonia Patel, Emma Hunt, Abby Graham, Esther Bultitude, Marie-Claire Giddings, Shellie Waldron, Christina Lankhorst, Lisa Carter, Doug and Heather Richards, Azeta Roberts, Luutske Powlesland, Pooja Sharma-Jones, Emma Davies, Emma Cook, Kirsty Lobley, Adrian Lee, Gill Lee, Anthony Barnes, Tean Mahoney, May Bywater, Rachael Parr, Amy Phillips, Nicola Murray, Jed Novick, Vanessa Holz, Alison Irving, Rebecca Rougeau, Nicola Winter, Sarah Scarr, Richard Farley, Susan Durnford, Ben Hubbard, Gemma Bright, Daniela Hutchinson, Katie Bosher, Craig Cunningham, Paul Garnham, Toni Severn, Hannah Norris, Hugh Richard Wright, Frances Cottrell-Duffield, Rebecca Ross, Fran Mancey, Debs Cornwall, Sharon Carlyon, Caroline Morrow, Liam Black, Matt Utber, Bob and June Clewley, Etta and John Lazarus, Anu Kumar, Olly Lazarus, Emma Spacey, Lara Spacey, Bethan Spacey, Doreen Harbour, Erin Poland, Georgina Hayden, Marston York, Kirstin Chaplin, Natalie Knauer, Katherine Black,

Natasha Sebuwufu, Nadine Sargent, Mike Gayle and Vicky Bell.

Also thanks to Betsy, Fred, Tara, Hannah and all the Bloodhound crew for their continuing amazing work and general awesomeness and especially to Ian Skewis who edited *Revenge...* and *Secrets...* with such skill and gentle nudging to force me to make them better.

Finally, thank you always to Debi, Caitlin and Ella plus Oatie the dog for the support and love and Monster Munch. xxx

A NOTE FROM THE PUBLISHER

Thank you for reading this book. If you enjoyed it please do consider leaving a review on Amazon to help others find it too.

We hate typos. All of our books have been rigorously edited and proofread, but sometimes mistakes do slip through. If you have spotted a typo, please do let us know and we can get it amended within hours.

info@bloodhoundbooks.com